7

Tsutomu Sato

Illustration **Kana Ishida**
Illustration assistants **Jimmy Stone, Yasuko Suenaga**
Design **BEE-PEE**

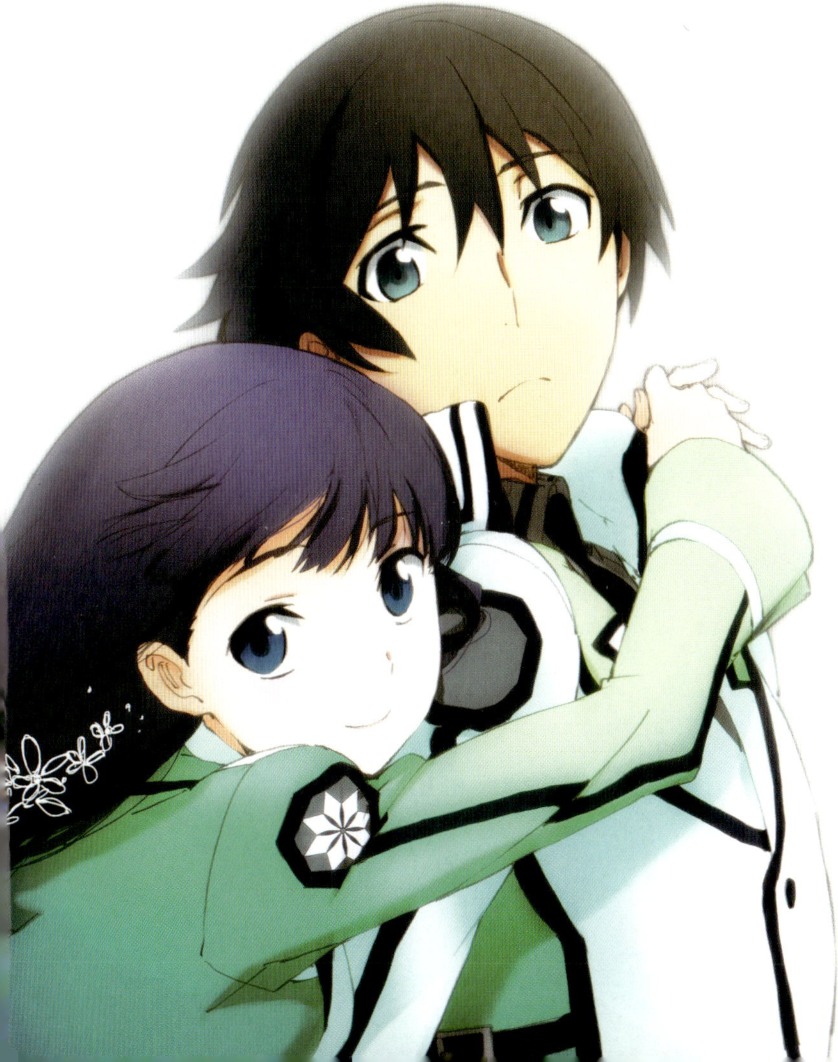

Kei Isori

A junior. Student council treasurer. A genius whose grades in magical theory are the best in his year. Engaged to Kanon Chiyoda, and they liven up their surroundings as a boisterous (?) couple.

"...Since last century, we've known the answer to the question of what's required to create a nuclear fusion power generator.

"The main problem preventing electricity generation from nuclear fusion lies in ensuring the atomic nuclei contact one another in time for them to cause the fusion reaction, acting against the electric repulsive force of the plasmatic nuclei.

"Though I'm sure this doesn't warrant an explanation, the electric repulsive force between two objects increases geometrically as their distance decreases. Objects with a strong homopolar Coulomb force will increase that force when drawing near, and so they will never collide.

Erika Chiba

Mikihiko Yoshida

Mizuki Shibata

Leonhard Saijou

"But we can decrease the electric repulsive force with magic. We have successfully developed a magic program to lower the apparent Coulomb force in this limited space to one-hundred-thousandth of what it should be."

Suzune Ichihara

Magic High School's student council treasurer. More suitable to be called a "beauty" than a "pretty girl." Has a composed appearance. Her nickname is Rin, but only Mayumi calls her that.

Shizuku Kitayama

Honoka Mitsui

Miyuki Shiba

"Hattori, Kirihara. Do either of you sense anything strange about this situation?"

Katsuto Juumonji

Senior at First High. Former chairman of the club committee, which oversees all club activities. A powerhouse, known as one of the three giants, along with Mayumi and Mari.

"...Even considering Yokohama's urban nature, it feels like there are a few too many foreigners around."

"The air in the city feels strangely excited, compared to inside the hall."

Takeaki Kirihara

A junior. Belongs to the *kenjutsu* club. Champion of the Kanto Junior High Kenjutsu Tournament.

Hanzou Gyoubu-Shoujou Hattori

A junior. Former student council vice president. Becomes chairman of the club committee after Katsuto.

Magic Swords

Aside from fighting techniques that use magic itself as a weapon, another method of magical combat involves using magic to strengthen and control weapons. The majority of these spells combine magic with projectile weapons such as guns and bows, but the art of the sword, known as *kenjutsu*, has developed in Japan as well as a way to link magic with sword techniques. This has led to magic technicians forming personal-use magic techniques known as magic swords, which are said to be both modern magic and old magic.

1. High-Frequency Blade
A spell that locally liquefies a solid body and cleaves it by causing a blade to vibrate at a high speed then propagate the vibration that exceeds the molecular cohesive force of matter it comes in contact with. Used as a set with a spell to prevent the blade from breaking.

2. Pressure Cut
A spell that generates left-right perpendicular repulsive force relative to the angle of a slashing blade edge, causing the blade to force apart any object it touches and thereby cleave it. The size of the repulsive field is less than a millimeter, but it has the strength to interfere with light, so when seen from the front, the blade edge becomes a black line.

3. Douji-Giri (Simultaneous Cut)
An old-magic spell passed down as a secret sword art of the Genji. It is a magic sword technique wherein the user remotely manipulates two blades through a third in their hands in order to have the swords surround an opponent and slash simultaneously. *Douji* is the Japanese pronunciation for both "simultaneous" and "child," so this ambiguity was used to keep the inherited nature of the technique a secret.

4. Zantetsu (Iron Cleaver)
A secret sword art of the Chiba clan. Rather than defining a katana as a hulk of steel and iron, this movement spell interprets it as a single concept, then the spell moves the katana along a slashing path set by the magic program. The result is that the katana is defined as a monomolecular blade, never breaking, bending, or chipping as it slices through any objects in its path.

5. Jinrai Zantetsu (Lightning Iron Cleaver)
An expanded version of Zantetsu that makes use of the Ikazuchi-Maru, a personal-armament device. By defining the katana and its wielder as one collective concept, the spell executes the entire series of actions, from enemy contact to slash, incredibly quickly and with faultless precision.

6. Mountain Tsunami
A secret sword art of the Chiba clan that makes use of the Orochi-Maru, a giant personal weapon six feet long. The user minimizes the inertia on themself and their katana while approaching an enemy at a high speed and, at the moment of impact, adds the neutralized inertia to the blade's inertia and slams the target with it. The longer the approach run, the greater the false inertial mass, reaching a maximum of ten tons.

7. Usuba Kagerou (Antlion)
A spell that uses hardening magic to anchor a five-nanometer-thick sheet of woven carbon nanotube to a perfect surface, thus making a blade. The blade that *Usaba Kagerou* creates is sharper than any sword or razor, but the spell contains no functions to support moving the blade, demanding technical sword skill and ability from the user.

The Irregular at Magic High School

YOKOHAMA DISTURBANCE ARC II

7

Tsutomu Sato

Illustration Kana Ishida

THE IRREGULAR AT MAGIC HIGH SCHOOL
TSUTOMU SATO

Translation by Andrew Prowse
Cover art by Kana Ishida

This book is a work of fiction. Names, characters, places, and incidents are the product of the author's imagination or are used fictitiously. Any resemblance to actual events, locales, or persons, living or dead, is coincidental.

MAHOUKA KOUKOU NO RETTOUSEI Vol.7
© TSUTOMU SATO 2012
Edited by ASCII MEDIA WORKS
First published in Japan in 2012 by KADOKAWA CORPORATION, Tokyo.
English translation rights arranged with KADOKAWA CORPORATION, Tokyo, through Tuttle-Mori Agency, Inc., Tokyo.

English translation © 2018 by Yen Press, LLC

Yen Press, LLC supports the right to free expression and the value of copyright. The purpose of copyright is to encourage writers and artists to produce the creative works that enrich our culture.

The scanning, uploading, and distribution of this book without permission is a theft of the author's intellectual property. If you would like permission to use material from the book (other than for review purposes), please contact the publisher. Thank you for your support of the author's rights.

Yen On
1290 Avenue of the Americas
New York, NY 10104

Visit us at yenpress.com
facebook.com/yenpress
twitter.com/yenpress
yenpress.tumblr.com
instagram.com/yenpress

First Yen On Edition: March 2018

Yen On is an imprint of Yen Press, LLC.
The Yen On name and logo are trademarks of Yen Press, LLC.

The publisher is not responsible for websites (or their content) that are not owned by the publisher.

Library of Congress Cataloging-in-Publication Data
Names: Satou, Tsutomu. | Ishida, Kana, illustrator.
Title: The irregular at Magic High School / Tsutomu Satou ; Illustrations by Kana Ishida.
Other titles: Mahōoka kōkō no rettosei. English
Description: First Yen On edition. | New York, NY : Yen On, 2016–
Identifiers: LCCN 2015042401 | ISBN 9780316348805 (v 1 : pbk.) | ISBN 9780316390293 (v. 2 : pbk.) |
    ISBN 9780316390309 (v. 3 : pbk.) | ISBN 9780316390316 (v. 4 : pbk.) |
    ISBN 9780316390323 (v. 5 : pbk.) | ISBN 9780316390330 (v. 6 : pbk.) |
    ISBN 9781975300074 (v. 7 : pbk.)
Subjects: | CYAC: Brothers and sisters—Fiction. | Magic—Fiction. | High schools—Fiction. |
    Schools—Fiction. | Japan—Fiction. | Science fiction.
Classification: LCC PZ7.1.S265 Ir 2016 | DDC [Fic]—dc23
LC record available at http://lccn.loc.gov/2015042401

ISBNs: 978-1-9753-0007-4 (paperback)
    978-1-9753-2711-8 (ebook)

10 9 8 7 6 5 4 3 2

LSC-C

Printed in the United States of America

The Irregular at Magic High School

YOKOHAMA DISTURBANCE ARC (II)

An irregular older brother with a certain flaw.
An honor roll younger sister who is perfectly flawless.

When the two siblings enrolled in Magic High School,
a dramatic life unfolded—

Character

Tatsuya Shiba

Class 1-E. One of the Course 2 (irregular) students, who are mockingly called Weeds. Sees right to the core of everything.

Miyuki Shiba

Class 1-A. Tatsuya's younger sister; enrolled as the top student. Specializes in freezing magic. Dotes on her older brother.

Leonhard Saijou

Class 1-E. Tatsuya's classmate. Specializes in hardening magic. Has a bright personality.

Erika Chiba

Class 1-E. Tatsuya's classmate. Specializes in *kenjutsu*. A charming troublemaker.

Mizuki Shibata

Class 1-E. Tatsuya's classmate. Has pushion radiation sensitivity. Serious and a bit of an airhead.

Mikihiko Yoshida

Class 1-E. Tatsuya's classmate. From a famous family that uses ancient magic. Has known Erika since they were children.

Honoka Mitsui

Class 1-A. Miyuki's classmate. Specializes in light-wave vibration magic. Impulsive when emotional.

Shizuku Kitayama

Class 1-A. Miyuki's classmate. Specializes in vibration and acceleration magic. Doesn't show emotional ups and downs very much.

Subaru Satomi

Class 1-D. Frequently mistaken for a pretty boy. Cheerful and easy to get along with.

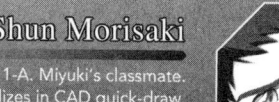
Shun Morisaki

Class 1-A. Miyuki's classmate. Specializes in CAD quick-draw. Takes great pride in being a Course 1 student.

Akaha Sakurakouji

Class 1-B. Friends with Subaru and Amy. Wears gothic Lolita clothes and loves theme parks.

Eimi Akechi

Class 1-B. A quarter-blood. Full name is Amelia Eimi Akechi Goldie.

Azusa Nakajou

A junior and is student council president after Mayumi stepped down. Shy and has trouble expressing herself.

Mayumi Saegusa

A senior and the former student council president. One of the strongest magicians ever to grace a magical high school.

Hanzou Gyoubu-Shoujou Hattori

A junior and the former student council vice president. Is the head of the club committee after Katsuto stepped down.

Suzune Ichihara

A senior and the former student council treasurer. Calm, collected, and book smart. Mayumi's right hand.

Koutarou Tatsumi

A senior and a former member of the disciplinary committee. Has a heroic personality.

Mari Watanabe

A senior and the former chairwoman of the disciplinary committee. Mayumi's good friend. Good all-around and likes a sporting fight.

Isao Sekimoto

A senior. Member of the disciplinary committee. Wasn't chosen for the Thesis Competition.

Midori Sawaki

A junior and a member of the disciplinary committee. Has a complex about his girlish name.

Kei Isori

A junior and the student council treasurer. Top grades in his class in magical theory. Engaged to Kanon Chiyoda.

Kanon Chiyoda

A junior and the chairwoman of the disciplinary committee after Mari stepped down. Engaged to Kei Isori.

Katsuto Juumonji

A senior and the former head of the club committee.

Masaki Ichijou

A freshman at Third High. Participates in the Nine School Competition. Direct heir to the Ichijou family, one of the Ten Master Clans.

Shinkurou Kichijouji

A freshman at Third High. Participates in the Nine School Competition. Also known as Cardinal George.

Midori Ichijou

Masaki's mother. Warm and good at cooking.

Takeaki Kirihara

A junior. Member of the *kenjutsu* club. Kanto Junior High Kenjutsu Tournament champion.

Sayaka Mibu

A junior. Member of the kendo club. Placed second in the nation at the girls' junior high kendo tournament.

Koharu Hirakawa

Senior. Engineer during the Nine School Competition. Withdrew from the Thesis Competition.

Chiaki Hirakawa

Class 1-G. Holds enmity toward Tatsuya.

Satomi Asuka

Nurse. Gentle, calm, and warm. Smile popular among male students.

Kazuo Tsuzura

Teacher. Main field is magic geometry. Manager of the Thesis Competition team.

Akane Ichijou

Eldest daughter of the Ichijou. Masaki's younger sister. Mature despite being in elementary school.

Ruri Ichijou

Second daughter of the Ichijou. Masaki's younger sister. Stable and does things her own way.

Haruka Ono
A general counselor of Class 1-E.

Harunobu Kazama
Commanding officer of the 101st Brigade of the Independent Magic Battalion. Ranked major.

Shigeru Sanada
Executive officer of the 101st Brigade of the Independent Magic Battalion. Ranked captain.

Muraji Yanagi
Executive officer of the 101st Brigade of the Independent Magic Battalion. Ranked captain.

Kousuke Yamanaka
Executive officer of the 101st Brigade of the Independent Magic Battalion. Medical major. First-rate healing magician.

Kyouko Fujibayashi
Female officer serving as Kazama's aide. Rank: Second lieutenant.

Retsu Kudou
Renowned as the strongest magician in the world. Given the honorary title of Sage.

Sayuri Shiba
Tatsuya and Miyuki's stepmother. Dislikes them.

Zhou
A handsome young man who brought Lu and Chen to Japan.

Yakumo Kokonoe
A user of an ancient magic called *ninjutsu*. Tatsuya's martial arts master.

Toshikazu Chiba
Erika Chiba's oldest brother. Has a career in the Ministry of Police. A playboy at first glance.

Naotsugu Chiba
Erika Chiba's second-oldest brother. Possesses full mastery of the Chiba (thousand blades) style of *kenjutsu*. Nicknamed "Kirin Child of the Chiba."

Ushiyama
Manager of Four Leaves Technology's CAD R & D Section 3. A person in whom Tatsuya places his trust.

Rin
A girl Morisaki saved. Her full name is Meiling Sun. The new leader of the Hong Kong–based international crime syndicate No-Head Dragon.

Xiangshan Chen
Leader of the Great Asian Alliance Army's Special Covert Forces. Has a heartless personality.

Ganghu Lu
The ace magician of the Great Asian Alliance Army's Special Covert Forces. Also known as the Man-Eating Tiger.

Glossary

Course 1 student emblem

Tatsuya Shiba's CAD

Miyuki Shiba's CAD

Magic High School
Nickname for high schools affiliated with the National Magic University. There are nine schools throughout the nation. Of them, First High through Third High each adopt a system of Course 1 and Course 2 students to split up its two hundred incoming freshmen.

Blooms, Weeds
Slang terms used at First High to display the gap between Course 1 and Course 2 students. Course 1 student uniforms feature an eight-petaled emblem embroidered on the left breast, but Course 2 student uniforms do not.

CAD (Casting Assistant Device)
A device that simplifies magic casting. Magical programming is recorded within. There are many types and forms, some specialized and others multipurpose.

Four Leaves Technology (FLT)
A domestic CAD manufacturer. Originally more famous for magical-product engineering than for developing finished products, the development of the Silver model has made them much more widely known as a maker of CADs.

Taurus Silver
A genius engineer said to have advanced specialized CAD software by a decade in just a single year.

Eidos (individual information bodies)
Originally a term from Greek philosophy. In modern magic, *eidos* refers to the information bodies that accompany events. They form a so-called record out in the world, and can be considered the footprints of an object's state of being in the universe, be that active or passive. The definition of *magic* in its modern form is that of a technology that alters events by altering the information bodies composing them.

Idea (information body dimension)
Originally a term from Greek philosophy; pronounced "ee-dee-ah." In modern magic, *Idea* refers to the *platform* upon which information bodies are recorded—a spell, object, or energy's *dimension*. Magic is primarily a technology that outputs a magic program (a spell sequence) to affect the Idea (the dimension), which then rewrites the eidos (the individual bodies) recorded there.

Activation Sequence
The blueprints of magic, and the programming that constructs it. Activation sequences are stored in a compressed format in CADs. The magician sends a psionic wave into the CAD, which then expands the data and uses it to convert the activation sequence into a signal. This signal returns to the magician with the unpacked magic program.

Psions (thought particles)
Massless particles belonging to the dimension of spirit phenomena. These information particles record awareness and thought results. Eidos are considered the theoretical basis for modern magic, while activation sequences and magic programs are the technology forming its practical basis. Yet, all of these are bodies of information made up of psions.

Pushions (spirit particles)
Massless particles belonging to the dimension of spirit phenomena. Their existence has been confirmed, but their true form and function have yet to be elucidated. In general, magicians are only able to sense energized pushions. The technical term for them is *psycheons*.

Magician
An abbreviation of *magic technician*. *Magic technician* is the term for those with the skills to use magic at a practical level.

Magic program
An information body for temporarily altering information attached to events. Constructed from psions possessed by the magician. Sometimes shortened to *magigram*.

Magic-calculation region

A mental region that constructs magic programs. The essential core of the talent of magic. Exists within the magician's unconscious regions, and though he or she can normally consciously use the magic-calculation region, they cannot perceive the processing happening within. The magic-calculation region may be called a black box, even for the magician performing the task.

Magic program output process

1. Transmit an activation sequence to a CAD. This is called "reading in an activation sequence."
2. Add variables to the activation sequence and send them to the magic-calculation region.
3. Construct a magic program from the activation sequence and its variables.
4. Send the constructed magic program along the "route"—the lowest part of the conscious mind to highest part of the unconscious mind—then send it out the "gate" between conscious and unconscious and output it onto the Idea.
5. The magic program outputted onto the Idea interferes with the eidos at a designated coordinate and overwrites them.

With a single-type, single-process spell, this five-stage process can be completed in under half a second. This is the bar for practical-level use with magicians.

Magic evaluation standards

The speed with which one constructs psionic information bodies is one's magical throughput, or processing speed. The scale and scope of the information bodies one can construct is one's magical capacity. The strength with which one can overwrite eidos with magic programs is one's influence. These three together are referred to as a person's magical power.

Cardinal Code hypothesis

A school of thought that claims, of the four families and eight types of magic, within which exists a natural foundation of "plus" and "minus" magic programs (sixteen in all), one can construct every possible typed spell by combining these sixteen.

Typed magic

Any magic belonging to the four families and eight types.

Exotyped magic

A term for spells that control mental phenomena rather than physical ones. Encompasses many fields, from divine magic and spirit magic—which employs spiritual presences—to mind reading, astral form separation, and consciousness control.

Ten Master Clans

The most powerful magician organization in Japan. The ten families are chosen every four years from among twenty-eight: Ichijou, Ichinokura, Isshiki, Futatsugi, Nikaidou, Nihei, Mitsuya, Mikazuki, Yotsuba, Itsuwa, Gotou, Itsumi, Mutsuzuka, Rokkaku, Rokugou, Roppongi, Saegusa, Shippou, Tanabata, Nanase, Yatsushiro, Hassaku, Hachiman, Kudou, Kuki, Kuzumi, Juumonji, and Tooyama.

Numbers

Just like the Ten Master Clans contain a number from one to ten in their surname, well-known families in the Hundred Families use numbers eleven or greater, such as Chiyoda (thousand), Isori (fifty), and Chiba (thousand). The value isn't an indicator of strength, but the fact that it is present in the surname is one measure to broadly judge the capacity of a magic family by their bloodline.

Non-numbers

Also called Extra Numbers, or simply Extras. Magician families who have been stripped of their number. Once, when magicians were weapons and experimental samples, this was a stigma between the success cases, who were given numbers, and the failure cases, who didn't display good enough results.

[8]

Saturday, October 29, AD 2095: All of today's classes were designated self-study.

For the most part, everything excluding practicums was basically self-study, and for Course 2 students, half of their practice was self-study, too, so today wasn't a day too different from normal... except that things weren't usually this rowdy.

"Practice" at First High often came with the noise of explosions thundering through the school, so saying that it was ordinarily quiet enough to hear a pin drop would be a slight overstatement. Still, the noise was usually a little more orderly; today's unruly commotion was the sound of final checks for the Thesis Competition, which was coming up tomorrow at last.

But amid all that, Tatsuya—directly related to this cacophony—was at his classroom terminal, hammering away at his schoolwork in silence.

Tatsuya was tackling work unrelated to tomorrow's event. But it wasn't because he was slacking off on his preparations or because he'd been dismissed from his representative spot—though perhaps, considering a high school student's modus operandi, "slacking off" would mean ignoring schoolwork for prep work rather than vice versa.

In terms of competition-related tasks he could do today, there was only the rehearsal of the presentation, in which he'd watch the spells and fix any bugs that came up (he'd done every other check besides that). Unfortunately, they couldn't do the rehearsal yet because the all-important Suzune hadn't come to school. She'd contacted him yesterday to say she'd come in the afternoon, so he wasn't panicked or bewildered, but Tatsuya found himself with nothing to do.

As first period ended and he was stretching lightly, a voice called to him from ahead. It wasn't Leo—who was turned around in the seat in front of him with his elbows over the back—but Erika, who stood next to him. Tatsuya turned to her.

"Tatsuya, what time do you get there tomorrow?"

She was careful to feign nonchalance, but next to her, Leo ruined her efforts by making it very clear that he was paying close attention.

Now what are these two conspiring…? Tatsuya thought dubiously, but he had no real reason to hide anything. "We arrive at eight, and it opens at nine. There will be a thirty-minute ceremony to start things off, and then presentations begin at nine thirty. Each team has thirty minutes, with a ten-minute interval between each presentation. After four teams go in the morning, we'll break for lunch from noon to one. The five other teams present in the afternoon, and they finish at 4:10. After that is judging and the awards ceremony, with everything planned to wrap up at six."

Erika looked bewildered at the mass of information she'd received—which was much more than she'd asked for—but she eventually seemed to piece it together in her head. "…Umm, and what time is our school presenting?"

His attempt to befuddle her failed, Tatsuya shifted to a more up-front answer. "First High goes second to last. We start at three."

"Doesn't that leave a lot of time left over?" she pressed.

"I suppose. That's why our main presenter, Ichihara, is getting there in the afternoon. Isori and I are going in early to keep an eye on the machinery and do emergency maintenance if there's trouble."

"I see…" she murmured. "Well, I guess that answers when everyone will be there. How are you getting the demo machines there?"

"The student council arranged a carrier. Hattori will be riding with them."

"Wait, wasn't Hattori supposed to be Ichihara's bodyguard?"

"Saegusa and Watanabe said they'd be going to get Ichihara the day of," he said with a casual shrug. "Anyway, why did you want to know?"

Erika faltered, hesitating.

Glancing at the flustered girl out of the corner of his eye, Leo, who had been silent until now, opened his mouth and asked, "Hey, could you let us help out with keeping watch?"

Erika frowned, unhappy, but didn't say anything. They seemed to have agreed ahead of time on what they were going to ask him.

"I don't mind, but…why would you want more work?" Tatsuya asked.

One might consider his question a natural one, but Leo gave him an awkward grin. "Well, I mean, uhh… We did all that training, so it would be a little frustrating if things ended before we got a chance to do anything…I guess."

Tatsuya looked at him, then at her, but Leo only returned his gaze with a self-deprecating smile, while Erika made no attempt to meet his eyes at all.

"I took off from school to put him through the wringer. If they settled this incident without giving us a turn, that would be stupid!" added Erika, voice sullen, still without looking at him. She seemed to know about the unpublicized incident at the special detention facility and was unhappy they weren't around for its resolution. Ganghu Lu was exactly the kind of opponent Erika had in mind when she'd trained Leo, so maybe her regret was inevitable.

"Whatever your motive, we could always use more hands," he said. "And there's nothing saying it's been fully resolved, either."

"Huh? Isn't that whole business done with?" Suddenly, Mikihiko barged into the conversation with timing that could only mean he'd been listening the entire time.

Without noting his eavesdropping—because there was another friend in the seat next to him who would panic and get bent out of shape if he did—Tatsuya answered, "There's no rule that says only one incident can happen at a time, you know."

Xiangshan Chen, the alleged mastermind, was still on the loose, but Tatsuya didn't tell his friends that. He didn't plan to, either. His answer was just a common-sense argument, which he decided was enough for the moment.

"Apparently," he continued, "people target the Thesis Competition every year. Including people on their way home afterward, too. Just because they resolved one thing before the event, it doesn't mean a different one won't happen the day of, right?"

"Right… I guess so." Mikihiko nodded, appearing to mull this over. Then, with an energetic expression, he asked, "But if that's the case, you think I could help keep an eye on things, too?"

"Sure. It'd be a big help."

They couldn't let their guard down just because one incident was resolved—Tatsuya's dedication was correct in that.

Speaking in hindsight, however, Tatsuya was wrong.

Suzune was visiting the hospital, having taken this day before the Thesis Competition off from school and postponing the group's rehearsal until this afternoon. She had only Hattori with her. She'd wanted to come alone, but with all the dangerous incidents happening, Mayumi and Mari and Azusa and Hattori and…well, *everyone* had strongly opposed that, so she compromised and let Hattori come with her alone.

She tapped twice on a room door.

"Come in," answered a calm alto voice from inside.

"Excuse me."

"Welcome, Ichihara. Could you sit over there?"

Suzune left Hattori in the hallway and entered the hospital room as Satomi Asuka, school nurse at National Magic University Affiliated First High School, welcomed her in. She had come to check on Chiaki.

On the bed was a girl, sitting still and upright, eyes downcast. Chiaki didn't react to Suzune's visitation.

"Ms. Asuka, has Chiaki Hirakawa been afflicted with a mental illness?" she asked, the question perhaps insensitive, since she didn't particularly lower her voice.

"No. We didn't find any emotional trauma, communication disorder, or any other symptoms of the sort. Of course, without directly examining her mind, I can't say for sure she's healthy."

"As long as she can hear my voice, that's enough."

Upon hearing Asuka's answer, Suzune rose. She went around the bed to the window and stood with her back to the bed. Then, without looking at Chiaki, she began to speak:

"Chiaki Hirakawa, with your methods, you can't get your hooks into Shiba."

Her voice was persistently cool and collected. It held no comfort or encouragement, nor was it sarcastic or scornful. She simply pointed out the truth.

"You can't draw goodwill out of him, of course, nor hostility, nor even malice. Right now, to him, you're just one more face in the crowd."

The way she spoke made it seem like an invariable truth.

"So what?!"

And that was probably the reason Suzune succeeded in drawing words and emotions from the stubbornly reticent Chiaki. Even if the emotion was 100 percent negative, it was still a first step.

"I know I'm no more than a face in the crowd to him. I really don't need you pointing that out to me!"

Chiaki had shown only rejection to Sayaka and Kanon, and now continued that stance with Suzune as well.

But Suzune didn't react like the other girls had.

"I believe your opinion of Shiba is, in a way, quite pertinent."

Suzune kept talking indifferently, her back still to Chiaki, as though she hadn't heard her cry out.

"He's certainly pompous. The crowd could wail and cry and scream, and he probably wouldn't care. He wouldn't show sympathy—he wouldn't even take the time to mock them. Even if someone pulled a prank on him, he'd just brush it off as a minor annoyance. The crowd is probably all just flies and mosquitoes to him."

Chiaki, still looking down, bit her lip in frustration. She could tell Suzune had given thought to the club-recruitment week in April. At the time, she'd thought he simply had no way to deal with the pranks people were pulling on him, but now she, as well as most of the students at First High, knew that was incorrect.

If he'd wanted to catch the people launching surprise magical attacks on him, he could have. The only reason he hadn't was because he wasn't interested. Anyone actually firing magic at him just felt like flies or mosquitoes to him. So wasn't she, who couldn't do anything at all, even *less* than an insect...?

Chiaki had to clench her fists tight enough to drive her nails into her palms to hold back the frustrated tears welling up.

Without looking at her—or maybe pretending not to notice—Suzune continued, her back still to her: "Do you know this, Chiaki? During the written portion of the first semester's examinations, Shiba scored so highly that second place and lower didn't even come close. He even scored perfectly in magical engineering."

"...Why does that matter?"

"Among the freshmen, the second-highest score on the magical engineering portion of the written exam was you."

Suzune turned around to face her. Her expression was cool and calm, not deriding, with her eyes and lips narrowed into a smile. "Ninety-two points out of a hundred. That score is so high that normally it would be on top."

"...So what?"

A tinge of surprise colored Chiaki's voice. She'd known her own score, but she probably hadn't thought it was enough to put her in second place in her grade.

"Unfortunately, you aren't able to threaten Shiba in anything other than magical engineering. But there, I think, it's possible for you to overtake him."

Chiaki's head shot up.

Her eyes were wide, speaking to both disbelief and a faint, dark hope.

"After working together with him for three weeks, I learned that Shiba isn't nearly as specialized in hardware as he is in software. Of course, his hardware-related skills are still far above normal high school standards, but they didn't seem out of this world. During freshman year, software is the focus of magical engineering, but come next year they'll weigh hardware more heavily. Of the two, you were better at the hardware side, weren't you?"

What Suzune was implying was this: If hardware became more important in class as a junior, there was a chance to turn it around—at least, that's how Chiaki understood it.

A voice briefly told her that was too convenient an idea, but she ignored it.

As Suzune watched the color of desperation fade from Chiaki's face and her earnest feelings begin to lighten her eyes, Suzune's expression softened. "If you can hold on to how frustrated you feel right now, I'm sure you'll be able to accomplish it one day."

She didn't say what *it* was.

And Chiaki didn't ask.

It didn't need to be something concrete.

She was fine with *it* being vague.

"Please come to the competition tomorrow. I'm sure you'll find something there."

As Suzune left the hospital room, Chiaki didn't watch her go.

Maybe, just maybe, she could accomplish that "something"—it was the drug called possibility.

She'd been injected with that drug, one that could, at times, resuscitate a mind on the verge of a breakdown, and it started a dramatic change in Chiaki's heart.

"Um…Ichihara? If you're not feeling well…"

As Suzune exited the room, Hattori's voice was clouded with concern over how terrible she looked.

"It's nothing that needs worry. Just a bit of self-loathing."

Suzune certainly wasn't the talkative sort. She was an excellent debater, but she didn't generally say things she didn't need to. She was relatively loquacious around Mayumi, but other than that, she was pretty much silent.

Hattori knew this, so even though the term *self-loathing* bothered him, he refrained from asking anything more and followed her quietly.

For Suzune, this trait of Hattori's to read the mood was why she'd allowed him to come. And as she'd expected, she didn't want to talk about her mental state right now.

I swear…I would be a great swindler.

Behind her cool poker face, she was mass-producing verbal abuse.

Her goal had been to get Chiaki back on her feet, but only because she valued her ability. And it wasn't for her sake, nor for Chiaki's sister's, who was in the same grade as Suzune.

It was for their school.

The Ichihara family was one of the Extra. Nobody shirked the Extra Numbers or held them in contempt these days (at least on the surface), but that had only happened within the last twenty years. Her parents' generation had grown up in the midst of deep-rooted prejudices. Her father had experienced harsh isolation from the magician community, so her family had hid the fact that they were Extras from her. They were formerly the Ichihana, with the *ichi* meaning *one* rather than *city*.

But Suzune had grown up feeling its shadow in her child's mind. And when she'd gone to middle school, she realized the truth her father had kept from her, and his reason for it. Perhaps that was why she'd never felt much camaraderie with the magician community.

The first time she'd felt like she belonged somewhere was when she came to her current school, the National Magic University Affiliated First High School.

Mayumi was the one who had given her that opportunity, which was why she felt indebted to her—and why she had such a firm, undying devotion to her school.

At the Nine School Competition, Suzune and the other First High officers had felt a sense of impending crisis about their underclassmen having few prospective magic engineers. They all agreed that the freshman boys' poor performance was partly due to that.

Sure, there was talent—Azusa, Isori, and Tatsuya were all outstanding. But talent was spread thin. After those three, the technical level plummeted.

They recognized that securing engineering talent among their underclassmen, especially the freshmen, was the most urgent mission they had in their half year before graduation. Digging out excellent Course 2 students was especially important; the Course 1 students had teachers personally instructing them, but they wouldn't see the Course 2 students. Discovering noteworthy talent from within their ranks was something only the student council and club committee could do.

And now, one among them had caught Suzune's attention: Chiaki Hirakawa.

She'd been a mere freshman caught loitering with an illegal tool, but when Suzune looked into her background, she'd found, other subjects aside, high marks in magical engineering and a high degree of proficiency in repairing and upgrading hardware.

Suzune had to get her to put her abilities to use for their school.

Eventually, she concluded that the most efficient way to do that was to plant the seeds of rivalry toward Tatsuya Shiba within her.

Well, I suppose nobody will be unhappy for it.

...And that was how Suzune wrapped up her inner conflict. The word *coolheaded* was definitely a fitting adjective for her.

As this year's venue was in Yokohama, the First High representative team would be assembling on-site the morning of the competition. But last year, when it was in Kyoto, they had gone the day before and stayed overnight.

For the same reason, the school teams far from the capital would be entering Yokohama the day or two before and staying overnight. It was the same for Third High, in the running for first place this year thanks to Shinkurou Kichijouji, aka Cardinal George, leading the team.

Third High's representatives would be presenting last. Given the speed and livability of modern public transportation, they would have plenty of time to travel to Yokohama from Kanazawa the day of, but they had no insurance that trouble would stay away on the way there. Therefore, the team and all the support members planned to leave school early in the afternoon the day before and stay the night in Yokohama.

"George, it's almost time," Masaki summoned.

"Already? Okay, I'll be right there," answered Kichijouji, absorbed in reading some unrelated materials.

I wonder if they'd let me take this along...

The three hours to Yokohama would be a little too long to spend doing nothing, and he gave the e-bookshelf, with its half-read literature, a baleful look. Unfortunately, the data it contained was for reference only, and its usage was restricted to National Magic University–affiliated facilities. Any request to borrow it would certainly be denied.

He sighed, cutting himself off from his lingering regrets (albeit not in such an exaggerated way as that might entail). Kichijouji returned the reader to the rack, then picked up the travel bag at his feet and stood up.

The plan was to use a jumbo bus with all their stage equipment onboard to move to the venue in Yokohama. More specifically, they would take the bus to the freight terminal, then load the entire bus into a long-distance, high-speed train (containers big enough to fit an entire bus were common these days), and finally head for Yokohama at a max speed of 370 miles per hour. Either way, it would be a straight shot to their destination, with no transfers (at least, the kind you had to get off the train for).

It was hard to call Kichijouji normal, but he was still a high school student in his midteens. No other passengers meant he and his friends could talk all they wanted, which probably wouldn't leave him with any time to be bored anyway, he decided.

And in Yokohama, he would probably meet that man again.

Or perhaps the term *confront* would have been more accurate.

As his thoughts lingered on his secret First High rival, he also figured it would be fun to spend the time using said man's little sister to tease his good friend Masaki, and he smiled mischievously.

Yokohama Bay Hills Tower: a skyscraper complex overlooking the Port of Yokohama. In a bar lounge close to its top floor, one couple was tilting glasses filled with ruby liquid, with the nightscape as their side dish.

"The new wine this year is quite good, isn't it?"

"You know, I don't really understand the tastes of wine. So I must apologize—as you're the one treating me to such a fine drink." Fujibayashi smiled elegantly, not in her usual business casual, but fully decked out, with makeup and clothing to the nines.

Chief Toshikazu Chiba waved an empty hand at her, seeming flustered. "No, they serve this wine to everyone whenever their private winery makes a new batch, regardless of the open date... It's not all that expensive..."

"Oh, but isn't it wonderful to drink something freshly made?" Fujibayashi brought the glass near to her nose, looked down, and swished the wine around a little, then turned her gaze back up to him.

Toshikazu gave a stiff, insincere smile. "...Well, I'm glad you're enjoying it. Our prospects for figuring this case out look brighter thanks to you, so I wanted to extend our gratitude."

"I should say the same to you, Chief. I wasn't about to leave them alone, either."

"Do you mean as a member of the Fujibayashi family? Or...no, I'm sorry," Toshikazu deferred, remembering his promise to her as she gave him a sobering stare.

The first term of their bargain for her to supply information and assist the investigation: not to investigate her lineage or goals. The former condition was a strange one, coming from her. He'd known from the start that Kyouko Fujibayashi was the daughter of the Fujibayashi family, renowned for its old magic, and granddaughter of the Old Master of the Ten Master Clans, Retsu Kudou. Her attaching that condition outright actually implied that she possessed some additional circumstance that shouldn't be readily revealed.

"By the way, Chief, was *thanking me* the only reason you invited me here tonight?"

"What?!"

The eldest Chiba nearly spilled the contents of his glass.

The daughter of the Fujibayashi, who had set up the surprise

attack, let out a giggle. "If it's all right with you, Chief, I'd like to stay with you tomorrow as well, not just tonight."

"Uh, I, um, right! If that's what you want, then gladly!"

It wasn't that Toshikazu had led a life of no relationships with the opposite sex. There were female students at the Chiba dojo, and he used to fool around enough in his student days that his younger sister called him frivolous and undisciplined.

It was less that he wasn't used to women, or bad with them, than it was that this one was special.

"Thank you," she said. "Would meeting in the morning at eight o'clock at the station in Sakuragi Town be acceptable?"

"...In the morning?" Toshikazu's face grew flustered before Fujibayashi's graceful smile.

"Tomorrow, the All-High Magic Thesis Competition will be held at the international assembly hall. Were you aware?"

"Well, I was, but..."

"A boy I'm acquainted with will be performing, and I'd like to go cheer him on."

"Oh..."

He couldn't exactly say it, but the words *that's not where I thought this was going* were written all over his face. He'd interpreted her invitation as a request to be with him tomorrow—night.

This was easy for Fujibayashi to read, but her smile never wavered. "Oh, yes. If you can, I'd like you to mention something to your subordinates. If they could prepare armament devices and live ammunition instead of just CADs, it would be a great help."

"Ms. Fujibayashi, you mean...?" He wheeled around, his timid expression pulling back as though someone had dumped ice water on it.

"It would be best if nothing happened, of course," she answered, quietly tilting her wineglass up again.

[9]

It was the day of the All-High Magic Thesis Competition.

Tatsuya and Miyuki arrived at the venue as planned, with no trouble to note. The trailer with their stage equipment had already fully unloaded as well, so roads must have been empty for everyone else, too. It appeared that Isori had already arrived, and Tatsuya could see Kirihara, too, with Sayaka in tow. In the end, the siblings were on time but nevertheless seemed to have been the last to arrive.

"...Tatsuya, should we not do something about that soon?"

Tatsuya had been caught up observing everything from the outside, pretending to be uninvolved, when Miyuki's voice brought him back to his position as someone indeed involved.

"Does it have to be me who does something...?"

While Tatsuya's face pinched together, his sister merely nodded. "Unfortunately."

Tatsuya's shoulders drooped as he looked back to where Erika and Kanon were glaring dangerously at one another.

"What's the matter, you two?"

Tatsuya wasn't the only one here who was on good terms with both Erika and Kanon. Level of familiarity aside, Miyuki was technically friends with both of them, while Isori was probably even more familiar with the two of them than Tatsuya was. Kanon would turn a deaf ear to any mediation on Miyuki's part, though, and despite his own feelings on the matter, Isori couldn't be neutral.

So it was up to Tatsuya to hold back a sigh and arbitrate between the glaring girls.

"Oh, Tatsuya! Morning!"

As soon as he'd said something, Erika came back with a light greeting, paying no attention to the one she was confronting.

Seeing that made Kanon's stare turn significantly more dangerous.

That was all Tatsuya needed to figure out the general situation. Nonetheless, it pained him not to be able to take either side.

"...Shiba. Would you mind saying something to this unreasonable young lady here?"

Good grief... he found himself thinking. *It sounds like she hasn't asked anyone else...*

It wasn't clear whether Kanon realized it herself, but her words made it obvious to everyone that she just wanted to foist the whole situation off on him.

"Haah..." He sighed. Still, he figured it didn't matter. Whatever Kanon's intentions were, it would clearly be faster for him to square everything away himself than to hear all their thoughts. Even if it meant being a little forceful.

"If you trust me with this, I'll gladly accept your request, but..."

His proposition didn't identify a "this," which gave him blank power of attorney.

Kanon realized that immediately and scowled. But after looking at Isori next to her and seeing that he wasn't objecting, she grudgingly nodded.

Tatsuya brought Erika and Leo to a sofa in the corner of the lobby and sat down. (Miyuki, meanwhile, sat down next to him as though it was where she belonged.)

"...So, if I understand what's going on," he began before the awkward twosome, "this is nothing for you to butt heads with her about, Erika."

"...I'm sorry. I didn't mean to make trouble for you..."

Erika's unusually deferential attitude gave Tatsuya pause. However, her general aptitude for causing others emotional trouble was a crime of willful disregard (and often a premeditated one, at that). But if she walked up to someone with the desire to help and ended up making more work for them, even she could recognize it was an awkward situation.

And in that realm, Tatsuya's own power of insight still had a way to go.

It seemed one couldn't measure another's feelings as simply as one could measure magic. So he was still surprised at her fluster, and that was probably why his voice softened more than he intended.

"...You don't need to be so enthusiastic about the security business—it would be perfectly fine if you cheered us on from the audience. If something does happen, nobody would complain if you *helped us* get things under control," said Tatsuya, leaving an unnatural accent on the words.

Erika's meek appearance gave way to something completely different—a meaningful grin that screamed of conspiracy. "Oh. 'Help,' huh?"

"If you have time before things start, you should come backstage to *hang out*. You're both *friends of mine*, so you don't need to be modest."

This time, he emphasized *hang out* and *friends* in his proposition. Erika and Leo exchanged glances, then smiled in silent amusement.

The waiting rooms for each of the schools grew livelier the closer they got to the curtains opening.

The schools near the end of the presentation order had hours to wait, but the type of student participating in the Thesis Competition—including those on the support staff who would do behind-the-scenes jobs rather than stand on the stage and speak—normally had a deep interest in the other schools' presentations. Many students could be seen in the lobby having friendly chats with students from other schools.

And students weren't the only ones reaching beyond their normal groups to exchange words.

Haruka had come to the Thesis Competition not as a counselor from First High but to do a job related to her position as a government agent.

Ever since the incident in April, Public Safety had displayed interest in Tatsuya. More specifically, Haruka's department *within* Public Safety had an interest in Tatsuya's identity. But apparently, whenever they tried to pry into his affairs, they received pressure from higher up the chain. She wasn't personally being pressured—she only learned of it when she had to sit through her boss complaining about it when giving her missions like this one.

The pressure had only served to deepen her manager's interest. Still, her boss couldn't officially send out any agents, which was how the investigation had ended up in Haruka's lap.

She'd opposed it, of course. She'd vehemently expressed an inability to handle this particular opponent—an inability starting back in April—but, naturally, she couldn't get anyone to listen. That was the context behind her not being able to keep up with Tatsuya yet also not being able to cut off involvement with him.

Investigating Tatsuya's identity was the assignment she'd been given, but experts had already pored through the digital data and came up with no clues.

She'd never had any skills in that field. Nevertheless, the work she was actually being relied on for—digging around for intel while counseling—had seen no developments, either. That was inevitable, since the subject under investigation never came around for counseling.

Right now, keeping an eye out for acquaintanceships, especially out-of-school ones, was the only method she could adopt. And it was inefficient and produced dubious results.

The subject of her investigation was currently keeping watch over the equipment in the waiting room allocated to First High. She did have pretexts to get all the way into the waiting room, but as explained before, Tatsuya was too difficult for her to deal with.

Caught between personal emotions and her sense of responsibility, Haruka ended up taking a more passive approach: keeping watch on the waiting room entrance with a coffee can in one hand. (As an aside, the pull-tab type of can had all but died out, replaced with reusable bottle-shaped cans.)

Thankfully, though, her efforts weren't for naught. Almost immediately after she'd begun keeping watch, a young woman visited the waiting room. She was clearly not of a high school age, nor did she look like a university student. She was probably the same age as Haruka.

Haruka searched through faces and memories. As far as people related to school went, she turned up no results.

But she remembered that face.

"...I knew it."

She used her terminal to read the video off her Public Safety contractor's hidden camera, had it do an image search, and confirmed that her memory was correct.

"The Electron Sorceress..."

Back when Haruka was a student, the woman, younger then, had been her hero. Or her heroine, perhaps, considering her gender, but the word *hero* stuck with Haruka better.

The central figure who'd driven Second High to a Nine School Competition championship—the Electron Sorceress.

Haruka, whose dreams of magicianhood had been dashed immediately upon taking high school exams, had looked up to the young woman with a mix of envy and aspiration.

She'd heard rumors of the woman advancing to the Magic University and entering the Ministry of Defense afterward. Why would she be visiting the First High waiting room rather than Second High's, her alma mater?

It wasn't *overly* unnatural. It was Sunday, so it wasn't strange for her to be in plain clothes. Maybe she was doing some early recruitment. She might not have known the Shiba siblings were the only ones in the room right now, and she might have been after Miyuki in the first place.

But Haruka's gut told her this was a clue to unraveling Tatsuya's true identity.

Unaware of the overanxious sentry outside the room—or maybe actually in full knowledge of her—the siblings welcomed their visitor, Fujibayashi, with genial smiles.

"It's been a while, Miyuki. Has it really been half a year since we saw each other in person?"

"Yes, ever since we met in February. It's been a long time since I've seen you."

"I went to see the Nines. I invited Tatsuya to a tea party in a hotel room—you should have come with him," said Fujibayashi, glaring at Tatsuya as if to ask him why he didn't bring her.

Of course, Tatsuya wasn't one to let that unsettle him. "I believe it would have been conspicuous to have Miyuki with me." With his eyes, he added, *I didn't want to attract attention.*

Miyuki offered a somewhat awkward look, and Fujibayashi smiled, her face saying *it couldn't be helped.*

...It seemed like she couldn't get him to answer the question unless she spelled it out for him.

"By the way, Ms. Fujibayashi," said Tatsuya. He didn't call her "lieutenant," since this was a normal, public(ish) facility. They'd swept for bugs and cameras, but that didn't mean he didn't have to worry at all. "Was it all right for you to come here—to First High's waiting room?"

That question wouldn't have made any sense to someone who didn't know their circumstances, and for those who knew a little bit, it would lead them to a misunderstanding. Someone who knew only of her student life would understand it as *Is it all right for a Second High alumnus to be hanging around a rival school's waiting room?*

"It's okay." Of course, Fujibayashi had no way of misunderstanding. "It's convenient to have an official title at times like these. Nothing wrong with an engineering officer from Ministry of Defense Technology Headquarters Weapon Research Division visiting someone who unveiled advanced technology at the Nines."

"Not to mention as someone of the Fujibayashi family?"

"Exactly. So you can call me whatever you want—Lieutenant Fujibayashi, Miss Fujibayashi, Big Sister Fujibayashi… Anything goes."

"I don't recall ever calling you Big Sister," said Tatsuya, actually half smiling at her surprisingly mischievous joke—though it was still in the "dry grin" category.

"Well, that's enough pleasantries… I've got good news and bad news. Which do you want first?"

I feel like I've heard that before, too, thought Tatsuya, but then figured staples were staples because of how often they were used. "The good news, then."

"…Aren't you supposed to ask for the bad news first?"

"Then I'll take the bad news first," he said, changing his stance out of hand.

Fujibayashi gave him an appalled look, then sighed, as it garnered no response. "…No, it's fine. I'll start with the good news. The MOVAL suits are finished. Captain Sanada says he'll be here tonight with them."

"I see… Fast work as always," Tatsuya stated. "But it could have waited until tomorrow, when we were back in Tokyo…"

"We'll be demonstrating them here tomorrow. The captain was the one who devised that plan, of course, so he probably just wanted to brag about them to you as soon as he got the chance. Their key components ended up being completely dependent on you, so he at least wanted to do a good job on the finished product. Yesterday he was going on about how it would preserve his dignity, or something pitiful like that."

"It's not pitiful at all. When you get right down to it, I'm the one who couldn't make something that could hold up in real combat."

"Could you tell that to the captain? I'm sure it'll be a load off his mind," said Fujibayashi with a wink.

Tatsuya answered with another pained smile.

"Now for the bad news," she continued. "It looks like things aren't over yet."

"Has there been a problem?" Tatsuya's look did more than tighten—it hardened. Miyuki gazed up at him, worried.

Fujibayashi couldn't brush this one off with a smile, either. "See this for the details," she said, handing him a data card. It was apparently important enough not to transmit over a wireless broadcast. "I've put some insurance measures in place myself…but things might get pretty shady."

"Understood. We'll make preparations on our end as well."

Tatsuya turned to Miyuki and the two nodded to each other. Fujibayashi's face clouded at that, but she didn't tell them not to prepare. "It would be best if nothing happened, but…should things get to that point, we'll be relying on you for help."

However painful it was, the siblings were precious and powerful parts of their forces. In her position, she couldn't tell them not to get involved.

◇ ◇ ◇

The time was 8:45 AM. The seats in the audience were just starting to fill up.

As Tatsuya was looking over the data Fujibayashi had brought, Isori entered with Kanon in tow. "Shiba, do you want to switch?"

They would change lookouts between every presentation. They'd decided the order during a meeting beforehand. Isori in particular had been interested in Fourth High's presentation, "The Creation of Magic Support Tools via Molecular Rearrangement," which would be second, so he'd offered to watch their things during the first presentation.

Tatsuya figured the order didn't matter much, since the waiting rooms all had screens, so he'd agreed to Isori's timetable and had been standing guard until now.

"Sure. Thank you."

After a brief reply to the young man, Tatsuya and Miyuki headed for the audience seating.

…However.

They found themselves stopped in the lobby.

"Shiba!"

The one called was Miyuki.

The one doing the calling was a young man—no, a boy. The voice felt stiff; was its owner feeling nervous? The person turned out to be someone the siblings hadn't seen in two months.

"Oh, Ichijou."

The one to address Miyuki had been Masaki Ichijou. He wore a band on his left arm that said "security." He seemed to be participating in the Thesis Competition as a member of the combined nine-school security team headed up by Katsuto rather than as a support member for Third High's presentation team. He'd probably been on patrol, looking around the venue, when he'd spotted Miyuki and called out to her.

"It's been a while, Shiba. Since the dance at the after-party."

"…Yes, it has been a while, hasn't it?"

There was a pause there, just short enough not to seem unnatural, most likely due to the discrepancy in how they saw each other; Masaki saw Miyuki as a dance partner from the party, and Miyuki saw Masaki as her brother's rival whom he'd fought at the Nine School Competition.

In order to hide that, or perhaps to sidestep it, Miyuki had responded with a deliberately polite answer and a bow.

"Oh, yes, well…" stammered Masaki. Unlike Tatsuya, Masaki was used to being with rather important celebrities, but he stood bolt upright. Even the boy next to him (probably part of the same self-protection team) looked like he'd seen a ghost and stiffened up. It was amusing, but Miyuki's ploy seemed to have worked.

"Were you patrolling the building?" she asked with a smile, as though anyone couldn't tell from looking at him.

"Y-yes, I was."

A little pathetic to fumble about just from that, isn't it? thought Tatsuya, but then reversed his thinking—maybe, when faced with Miyuki, there was nothing he could do about it.

Even Tatsuya, who was closest to her and also possessed a modified mind, sometimes found himself charmed by her. For this boy, who was both a complete stranger and in a position to possibly acquire the unattainable prize if he reached for it, perhaps it was actually only natural that he find himself overly sensitive toward her.

His sister, though, without a mind to his thoughts, continued ramping things up, nearing her peak performance. "With you keeping watch over us, Ichijou, we can all rest much more easily. I'm glad you're here."

She was right about the Crimson Prince's presence, as a member of the security team, being reassuring. Even Tatsuya thought as much, so one could call it an objective viewpoint—but wasn't she fanning the flames a little much?

"Yes, I'll do everything in my power to meet your expectations!"

Though it didn't matter to him, Tatsuya found himself worried about whether Masaki would be able to make it to the end of the day.

"I hope you do your best as well, Tomitsuka."

"Ah... Thank you very much for the well wishes."

Masaki's partner, flustered at having been addressed all of a sudden after being left to the side, came back with a response that was slightly too formal for someone his age.

Though she'd agreed with Tatsuya that she didn't have to be so zealous about security detail when put on the spot, Erika had no intention of acting like a spectator. She met up with Mikihiko, who had come after the Shiba siblings had left for the waiting room, then

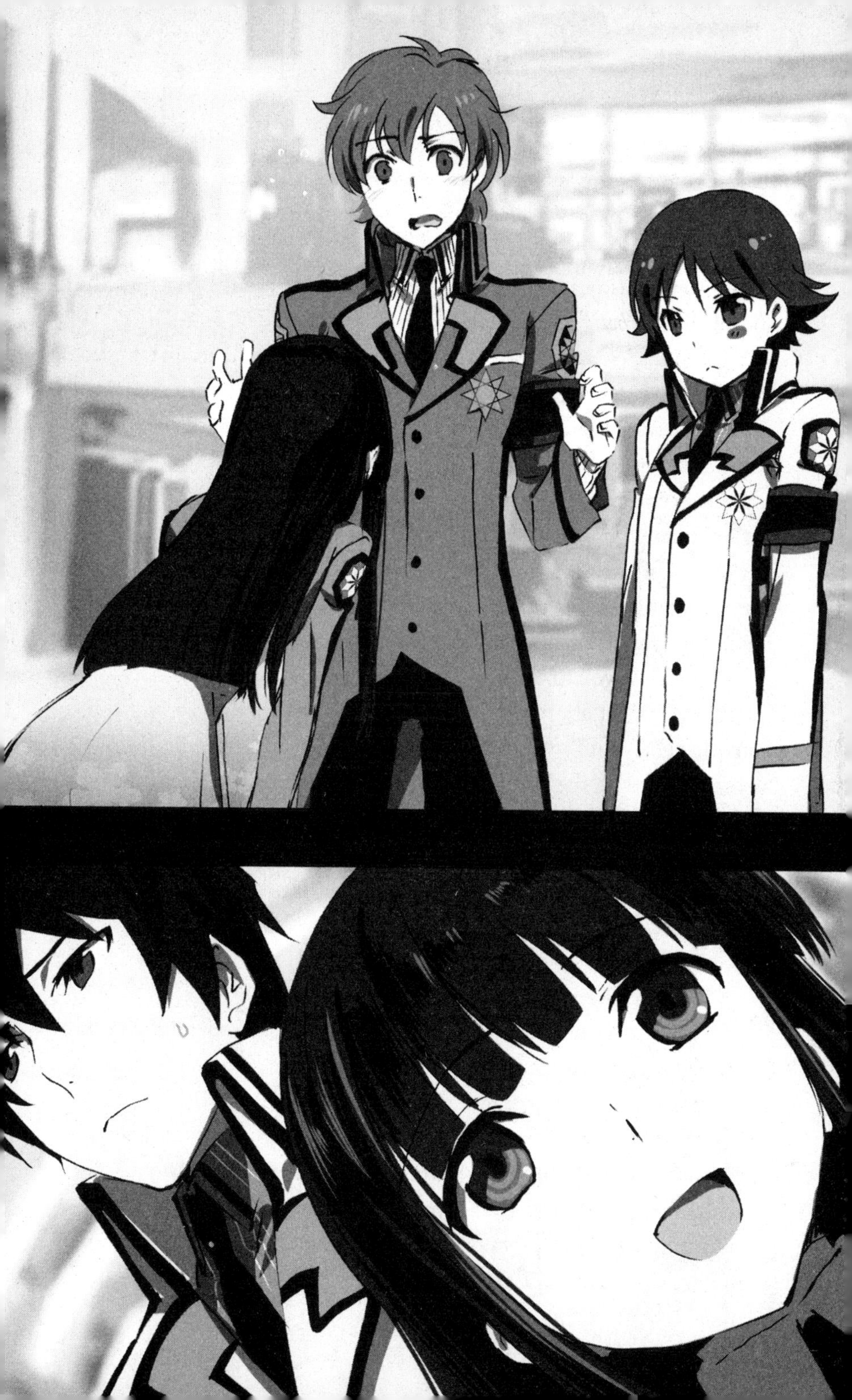

went to the lobby to grab Mizuki, who had contacted them earlier to say she'd be a little late. Even as the four of them looked for seats, Erika devoted most of her attention to spotting suspicious persons rather than finding seats with a good view.

Perhaps it should be said that her efforts bore fruit: Erika quickly spotted a familiar figure sitting in a back corner of the seats.

"Familiar"—but to her, more like someone she couldn't forget even if she wanted to. After all, she used to see him every day; and even now, with their schedules out of alignment, they still saw each other about every other one.

He seemed to notice her, too. In fact, he'd probably noticed her a little sooner. That wouldn't be strange, considering his capacity, but it got on Erika's nerves.

"Huh? Erika, isn't that…?" Mikihiko seemed to have noticed as well. He'd met the person before, so this wasn't strange, either.

"Erika, do you know him?" asked Mizuki.

"No. He's just a womanizer. Probably here waiting for a girl or something."

So before he could call out to her or someone suggested they sit together, Erika pretended she didn't know him.

Toshikazu and Erika weren't on very good terms (actually, Erika one-sidedly hated him), and Mikihiko, who knew this, averted his eyes from Leo's questioning gaze, preferring to let sleeping dogs lie.

"Miyuki, I didn't know you knew Hagane Tomitsuka."

"He's in the next class over, so I know his name and face. I'm more surprised that you knew him, Tatsuya."

After they'd found empty seats, they'd started talking—and not about their longtime-coming reunion with Masaki but about Hagane Tomitsuka, with whom they'd barely exchanged words.

…Unrequited love often happened this way.

"Tomitsuka is in Sawaki's club. But besides that, the Tomitsuka family is known for its Range Zero."

The Tomitsuka were one of the strongest families in the Hundred. One didn't have to be as connected as Tatsuya to know about the abnormal magicians born to it.

"Whatcha talkin' about?" Erika interrupted.

"Erika, are you by yourself?" Tatsuya asked. "What happened to Leo?"

She was supposed to go to the audience seating before them, and they'd been together earlier, so his question wasn't unnatural.

But Erika frowned, irritation evident on her face. "…Tatsuya, let me use this opportunity to make one thing clear to you."

Somewhat surprisingly, even Erika didn't start ranting and raving in the middle of all these unrelated outsiders. But her soft, lowered voice had more than enough punch to make up for it.

"Could you stop treating the two of us like we come as a set? All I did was give him a technique and a weapon. There's literally nothing else between us."

"That wasn't my intent…"

Tatsuya couldn't even be mistaken for an honest person, but in this particular instance, that was the perfect truth. He hadn't even purposely tried to imply anything. It seemed to him that her sensitive response meant she actually was pretty conscious of Leo, but he wasn't mean enough to say that out loud.

"Anyway, where are the others?"

Ever since the send-off party following the Nines, his classmates in 1-E seemed filled with a strange energy. He thought he remembered them getting fired up and wanting to meet here to cheer him on, once again.

"They're probably not here yet. They know you won't be going until this afternoon. Oh, but Mizuki and Miki are here. They're sitting a little farther up. You know, together."

Erika settled down into the seat next to Tatsuya and grinned.

Clearly, she didn't like people gossiping about her but loved gossiping about others.

That part of her is just like any other girl, thought Tatsuya.

◇ ◇ ◇

Nine AM. The All-High Magic Thesis Competition got started—not with a bang, but with more of a feeling of solemnity. Unlike the Nine School Competition, which—despite the military's cooperation—was a contest *among students*, the Thesis Competition was a presentation *in front of adults*: from the university, from corporations, and even from research institutions. Some presentations would determine future employment on the spot (recruiters were here). Because of this, the sponsors, too, conscious of the authority of the magic schools lined up and present, tended to adopt an adherence to formalities.

The no-fun, all-business opening greetings finished up, and the first school to go, Second High, began their presentation: "Measurement and Usages of Dark Matter Using Convergence Magic."

As the presentations got underway, people disappeared from the lobby like the tide going out. Haruka, not very interested in magic technology itself, figured that if she was going to be bored anyway, she might as well take a little nap in the tearoom.

But just as she was about to put her plan into action, an acquaintance came into the lobby from the nearest gate and said, "Ms. Ono?"

"Ms. Asuka?" replied Haruka. Because she was the counselor in charge of the mental care of First High students, she was fairly familiar with Asuka, who was the school nurse, though not to the extent of being friends outside of work.

"Did you come to listen to the thesis presentations, too?" asked Asuka. "I thought I remember you saying you weren't very interested in this."

The comment might have sounded sarcastic or caustic depending on the tone of voice, but with Asuka's smooth and gentle speech, Haruka had to wonder if she'd spoken her previous statement out loud. *She's a lot more cut out for counseling than me*, she thought, a little jealous of the woman's perception.

"Well, there was something on my mind…" she replied. "What about you, Ms. Asuka? Are you her escort?"

Asuka wasn't alone. She had a girl next to her who, while not in uniform, gave off the impression of a high school student. Haruka felt like she knew the girl from somewhere, but she wasn't one of the students Haruka was assigned to.

"Yes. Hirakawa told me she wanted to watch the presentations today. She's actually recovering right now, so her physical condition isn't great, which is why I'm with her."

By itself, that would have sounded like exceptional VIP treatment, but Haruka picked up on the last name: Hirakawa. Haruka hadn't touched the recent string of attempted information-theft incidents, but she had a general outline in her head, since she'd needed to write a report about it for her department in Public Safety.

And from a psychological viewpoint, showing Hirakawa other high school students' achievements would stimulate her and give her a goal to strive for, effectively rehabilitating her.

"I see. I appreciate your efforts," Haruka said genuinely.

Despite the slight detour, Haruka went to the tearoom as planned and idled there. Taking twenty minutes to drink her coffee didn't make her a very good customer in the shop's eyes.

She was about to think how easy her job today would be if she could use up all her time like this, but as usual, the world didn't make things that easy. In fact, the winds of karma were being rough with her.

"Might you have a moment?" somebody suddenly said.

Haruka's heart stopped.

Then, as if to make up for that, it started beating at full throttle a second later.

Of course, both of these were metaphors, but that was how surprised she was, how much her pulse and breathing had been disturbed.

Because the one to speak to her had been Fujibayashi.

"Y…es, go ahead…"

"Thanks."

The woman sat with elegant movements, then ordered a black tea from the waitress who came over a moment later.

In contrast with Fujibayashi's calm demeanor, Haruka couldn't hide her impatience.

She couldn't help it, either. Haruka had been the one supposedly watching her, but now Fujibayashi had taken her by surprise and spoken to her.

Haruka had no idea what she was after, so she couldn't get the ball rolling. All she could do was stare until the waitress came back with the tea and Fujibayashi put her lips to it, blowing slightly.

"...You know," said Fujibayashi, "it's a little embarrassing to be stared at like that."

Haruka had been so alarmed that she hadn't realized she'd been staring until it was pointed out. "I...I'm sorry." Her embarrassment amplified her distress, but the next words out of Fujibayashi's mouth froze her heart solid:

"No, I consider it an honor that Mizz Phantom has taken an interest in me."

"...I didn't think the Electron Sorceress would know anything about someone like me. The honor is all mine."

At some point they'd started speaking in a more distant, formal tone to each other, but such a change probably couldn't be helped.

The nickname Fujibayashi had used, Mizz Phantom, wasn't as widely known as Fujibayashi's alias, the Electron Sorceress. It was only whispered among those whose hands were dirtied with illegal intelligence activity—it was the code name for an unidentified female spy.

The very fact that Haruka had been pinpointed as a "Mizz Phantom" warranted treating this situation as do-or-die.

On the other hand, the ease with which Fujibayashi had spilled the grave secret told Haruka how important her business with her was. "What did you have to talk about?" she asked.

Seeing resolution instead of confusion make its way to the surface of Haruka's expression, the other woman gave a satisfied smile. "I believe you understand without me having to say any more, do you not?"

"...I'm sorry, but I've never been as talented as you are."

In actuality, Fujibayashi was right—Haruka accurately predicted what she wanted. It was just that saying "all right" and nodding would have been the same as waving a white flag.

"You're very modest. I know you graduated with excellent marks from both university and service training. Even Mr. Kokonoe has a high opinion of you."

In her mind, Haruka clicked her tongue. The Fujibayashi were a famous old magic family. There was nothing strange about her being familiar with Yakumo Kokonoe, the authority on that very old magic.

Meanwhile, it was only earlier today that Haruka had acknowledged Fujibayashi as the *target of her job*.

The cards she'd prepared had been completely beaten.

"...Look, I'm not going to make any unreasonable requests of you," said Fujibayashi.

That wasn't a compromise. It was a psychological scheme to emphasize the superior position she held.

"My only proposition is that we each stick to our own territory," she said, presenting Haruka with an unmistakable request despite not saying anything concrete.

Haruka was forced to admit she'd been completely outdone. "...I don't understand what you're talking about."

In reality, she knew what Fujibayashi's proposition meant. It was exactly what she'd predicted: She was telling Haruka to keep the Cabinet Office Intelligence Agency out of the military's affairs.

And Fujibayashi knew that she understood. "Would it be wise to state it clearly for you?" she asked anyway, with a cool face as Haruka clenched her back teeth.

This vixen! Haruka could glare all she wanted, but it was only a waste of effort now.

"It'll be fine," said Fujibayashi. "No blame will fall on you for this."

That meant she'd already dealt with the higher-ups.

Fujibayashi rose lightly to her feet, and she even had a payment slip for Haruka's coffee in her hand.

Haruka could just pay her bill at the table, so going all the way up to the register to pay was another annoyance.

Their first match had ended in utter defeat for Haruka.

...But that doesn't mean I got nothing out of this!

At the very least, the fact that this woman had come to her with this timing spoke to a relationship between Tatsuya Shiba and Kyouko Fujibayashi that needed to be kept secret.

That alone was clear.

So even realizing that she was being obstinate, Haruka inwardly swore revenge.

◇ ◇ ◇

Suzune, in First High's leader role for the day, arrived at the hall an hour early, a little past eleven. It was right after the third team, Fifth High, had begun its incredibly lofty presentation, "Controlling Tectonic Movement and the Gentle Extraction of Tectonic Plate Distortion Energy." Tatsuya was in the waiting room when she, Mayumi, and Mari arrived.

"I'm early!" was the first thing out of Mayumi's mouth.

The remark made Tatsuya want to ask *How old are you?*, and he fell into thought as he considered how to respond to her.

"What's wrong?" she asked.

"Nothing..." muttered Tatsuya. Mari and Suzune both looked fine, so he'd lose if he appeared worn out by it. He gave himself a burst of energy and decided to regroup by asking a pointless question. "Did something force you to move up the schedule?" (Meanwhile, Miyuki had completely gone into "see no evil, hear no evil, speak no evil" mode.)

Being late would have been a huge issue, but luckily, coming extra early wasn't a problem.

The waiting room they'd been given to store their equipment was more than large enough for all of them, and even this late in the game, there were still several upperclassmen aside from Tatsuya and Miyuki who fancied themselves craftspeople rummaging around, tinkering with circuitry. Three more female students wouldn't feel like a nuisance at all.

"The questioning didn't take as much time as we thought."

He'd initially thought his question pointless, but he couldn't overlook Mari's answer. "Another questioning? And today, of all days?"

He didn't have to ask who they were questioning. He knew. He was there when they'd caught Sekimoto, and he'd witnessed his hearing, which was informal at best and illegal at worst.

But that was only one time.

And not because Tatsuya had only been present once—it was because they were only able to question Sekimoto once.

After Ganghu Lu's attack, the boy had fallen into a manic state. Mari stated with confidence that it wasn't her magic that caused it, so he was probably panicking that someone was after his life. There was no way Sekimoto wouldn't realize the end goal of that attack had been his death. Because of that, even an expert official couldn't get any details out of him.

"Well, we wanted to have this done yesterday..." said Mari.

"It took a while to get approval..." added Mayumi. "And it wasn't something I could force through by using my family name, either."

I'd expect not, Tatsuya thought. It wasn't a criminal organization they were dealing with, so they couldn't do this forcibly after he was diagnosed as sick. "But why today?" he asked. "If that was the way of it, I feel like you could have just done it tomorrow."

"Well, aren't you oddly optimistic today?" said Mari.

Tatsuya thought he'd simply offered a reasonable question, but for some reason, she'd rebuked him.

"Sekimoto and the younger Hirakawa were after materials for the Thesis Competition," she explained. "And not only that, mind you! But anyway, because of that, it's not unlikely that the organization backing them would make a move on the day of the competition."

"True," Tatsuya admitted. "It's a possibility for sure."

He'd anticipated that much. But just because he'd gotten information this morning on that backing organization didn't mean they had time to take any extra preventative measures. All they could do was make up for their emergency response with the emergency responders set in place beforehand. Calling all the troops and telling them to mobilize immediately wasn't viable—even during the age of absolute monarchies, they couldn't get entire standing armies to mobilize at the drop of a hat.

In terms of venue security, they'd put together an immediate emergency response system under Katsuto's leadership that would act as quickly as possible if something happened. If Sekimoto didn't know about any concrete plans of attack, questioning him today wouldn't have been very high on the priority list.

But it wasn't Tatsuya's job to point that out.

"Yeah," said Mari. "It's only a possibility, but we can't ignore it. The more information we have, the better."

For today, it was more important that Suzune be in good form than to get information they couldn't act on, but it was already over with now. "I see," he said. "Did you find anything out?"

"Yeah. We only learned this after making him talk again today, but Sekimoto's showing signs of mind control."

"…They mean business." Leaving aside the practical applicability of mind control, Tatsuya found himself surprised at the news. "That didn't come up in the mental checkup?"

Ever since Sayaka had been placed under mind control by a terrorist organization called Blanche and made to work for them this spring, the school had begun requiring regular mental checkups for all First High students.

The fact that a magician, the kind of person who would be central to Public Safety and the JDF in the future, had been brainwashed and made into a foreign country's pawn was no joking matter. For the upper levels of their school, and even the political agencies behind it, the incident had been enough of a nightmare to forego student privacy.

If they'd discovered another victim of mind control, it would mean they weren't overdoing it so far. On the other hand, it made Tatsuya feel like their measures weren't much help.

"The mental checkups happen at the beginning of each month," said Mari. "It's more than likely he fell to it after that."

"They're good… Did they drug him, too?" asked Tatsuya.

"We don't know that much. Mayumi and I aren't experts in that area."

Tatsuya wondered if that was actually true, but he kept his mouth shut.

"The psychiatrist didn't say anything, so it must not have been a normal method," Mayumi stated. "Maybe it was a real Evil Eye."

Mayumi's opinion was a little further out than Mari's.

"An innate exotype magic user, perhaps…"

Unlike Evil Eye—a light wave oscillation–type spell developed by Belarus before the formation of the Federal Soviet Republics and given to terrorists who supported the re-separation—among the magicians who had natural talent at mental interference exotype magic, a few were said to have the power to rewrite an entire personality. If Sekimoto was one of those who had a true Evil Eye, he might be able to alter the person's behavior principles in such a short time that neither the target nor anyone nearby would realize it.

"But no matter how strong the mental interference spell is, apparently they don't go too well unless you prepare the target beforehand," Miyuki remarked.

That part was the same as hypnosis. People tended to think about human willpower as weak, but it was actually strong. Interfering with emotions or impulses without a clear direction was one thing, but when it came to interfering with firm behavioral principles, affecting a mind with magic—another mind, anyway—was, by itself, difficult.

"Sekimoto has always been unhappy with how the government

controls magic in secret," Mari bitterly explained to Mayumi. "He's an open-source advocate, so to speak. He believes magic will only truly advance when the knowledge of magic programs and activation sequences is shared throughout the world."

"Academically, he's not wrong, but it's not exactly right, given how sternly certain nations oppose one another in the real world," Mayumi offered sympathetically.

But Tatsuya said in a cutting way, "It should be called flat-out wrong." He, for one, had no interest in ideas that didn't conform with the real world.

"...That's pretty harsh, Tatsuya," Mayumi whispered.

"...Anyway, it looks like they took advantage of his idealism," continued Mari. "He firmly believes it's the duty of advanced-magic nations to give the fruits of their research to less advanced ones."

"Which less advanced nations, exactly?"

Mari's response to his question was less than favorable. "We couldn't get that out of him. It seems like he doesn't know, either."

"...In other words, they put a lock on his awareness."

I see. That's how they discovered it was mind control.

"This all means we can't predict what'll happen next," Mari offered, tense.

Mayumi agreed, her own voice worried. "I think it's possible they'll adopt a more radical method than we think, too. We'll be accompanying Rin from here on out, so I told Hanzou to keep a close eye on what's going on in the building. You be careful, too, Tatsuya. I'm serious."

"I will." Not a fiber in him was about to relax after Fujibayashi's advice anyway, but he accepted her thoughtfulness without protest.

As they were trading their not-so-peaceful words, Suzune was reading over her manuscript, maintaining perfect calm.

Meanwhile, Fujibayashi had just received a notice that indicated radical actions were more than just "certainly possible." After getting the emergency text, she hurried to look for an empty private communication booth. When she'd found somewhere discreet, she called back and said these words into her audio-only communicator:

"Ganghu Lu has escaped?! Forgive my rudeness, sir, but is that information accurate?"

"I don't want to believe it any more than you do, but it's true."

Kazama's voice didn't sound like he was joking. But it made sense; he wouldn't joke about something like that in the first place.

"The escort car bringing him to Yokosuka was attacked earlier. No survivors."

"And they didn't find Ganghu Lu's remains among them, I assume...but why would they choose today, of all days, to bring him there...?"

"Because the Thesis Competition is no more than a high school event, Lieutenant!"

"My apologies, sir!" Fujibayashi quickly straightened up at the rebuke. She'd been complaining without realizing it.

"But I understand what you mean by choosing today." Still, he wasn't the type to let slight breaches of etiquette ruffle him for long. "They carried out this operation so that they'd make it in time. We can assume they had a reason for that; at the very least, we need to put that possibility under our radar."

Kazama was a combat soldier through and through, an officer who wanted to command from the front lines. He valued quality above all else.

"Fortunately," he added, "thanks to the new weapon testing we were planning in Hodogaya tomorrow, we're all ready to deploy. We decided to move up our departure and head to you now. ETA is 1500 hours."

"Understood, sir. I'll monitor the situation carefully."

"Please do, Lieutenant."

Fujibayashi saluted to Kazama's instruction, only to realize he couldn't see her through the phone.

After Mayumi notified him that there would be a change to his duties, Hattori got Kirihara and went to see Katsuto, both to ask about the chance and to report the results of the questioning. (Sayaka was eating lunch with Erika.)

"I see," Katsuto said. "I want the two of you to form a team and keep an eye out around the building."

"Understood!"

Katsuto, who had just been in the middle of his meal, instructed them to sit down with him. As he chewed on his grab-and-go sandwich, he listened to Hattori's report and, when it was over, showed no hesitation in giving them a new mission.

Normally, that would be where it ended; Katsuto almost never asked underclassmen for their opinions on things—

"Hattori, Kirihara. Do either of you sense anything strange about this situation?"

—But this day proved to be an exception.

"Something strange?" Hattori parroted after a pause. Kirihara looked at him, curious. "...Even considering Yokohama's urban nature, it feels like there are a few too many foreigners around."

He didn't have a local's instincts from being raised in the town, but Hattori took everything seriously. He'd come to scout out the venue last week and the week before that. Compared to those times, he felt a clear increase in the number of foreigners.

"You thought so, too, Hattori?"

"Yes. Did you have the same idea, Juumonji?"

"Mm. What about you, Kirihara?"

"I apologize. I didn't notice anything about more foreigners. But..."

"No need to hold back."

"...Yes, sir. The air in the city feels strangely excited, compared to inside the hall."

"Hmm... You're definitely right about that."

After nodding, Katsuto took no more than ten seconds to mull this over, but to Hattori and Kirihara, it felt like he'd been silent for over ten minutes.

That was how heavy the silence was.

"Hattori, Kirihara. Put on bulletproof vests for your afternoon patrols."

The pair's eyes widened as they stared at their leader dubiously.

Their attitude couldn't be called courteous, but Katsuto showed no sign of concern as he picked up his short-distance wireless handset.

He proceeded to give the same order he'd given them to the entire security team.

◇ ◇ ◇

The afternoon presentations started at one, as planned.

First High would be going at three. Tatsuya and Isori, who had been trading off guard duties during the morning, were now in one final meeting to discuss minor procedures.

Each of them had one person with him.

For Tatsuya, that was Miyuki, and for Isori, that was Kanon.

The "craftsmen" who had been prowling about were no longer here. Mayumi and Mari had moved to either side of the door, too, so they wouldn't get in Suzune's way.

That was the state of the room as they heard a restrained knock on the door.

Mayumi quietly opened it to see her successor, a girl even shorter than she was, standing there.

"Oh, Ah-chan. Shouldn't you be in your seat?" asked Mayumi softly. Azusa, as it happened, had been assigned as a judge.

There was no third-party judging system in place for the competition. The audience would greatly change from presentation to presentation, so they couldn't have them judge things in the first place.

Instead, in addition to the expert judges, one student from each school would serve as a judge and score each presentation aside from their own school's, and it was tradition for that person to be the student council president. First High was no different; Azusa had been working as a judge since the morning.

"The first afternoon presentation finished early, so I came to check on everyone," she supplied.

"You came to support us? Thank you very much, Nakajou," Suzune called to her from the back of the room.

"Ah, no, I...I'm sorry, Suzune. Did I interrupt you?"

Despite how quiet her voice had been, Azusa made her small body even smaller. (Metaphorically, of course.)

Isori looked over as well and added himself to the conversation. "Which school seems most promising so far?"

Those assembled had suspended their meeting right after Azusa entered, so Isori hadn't exactly neglected Tatsuya—by changing the subject, if he had, he might have found himself blown out of the waiting room with a blizzard.

"Fourth High, as we thought. They came with a pretty elaborate setup again this year."

Isori crooked his head to the side slightly at that estimation. "It felt to me like they were trying too hard to be unique, though."

Fourth High had the second presentation this morning. It was also the one Isori had had his eyes on.

"But they still put together a system with all that complicated magic and did it flawlessly, which was amazing... Oh, sorry. The next presentation is starting soon. Please do your best, everyone."

With this, Azusa delivered the cheerleading she'd come here to do. Maybe she, too, had finally gotten used to her position as student council president.

As Tatsuya's turn came up, the usual suspects were all sitting together in the audience, waiting patiently:

Honoka and Shizuku, who'd joined up at lunchtime, as well as Erika and Leo, enthusiastic to bring their weapons inside.

"Mikihiko...how is it?" whispered Leo.

But not all of them were just sitting around.

"Nothing out of the ordinary at the moment," he answered, synchronizing his senses with the spirits he'd sent out to survey the area.

"Mizuki?" asked Erika shortly.

"I still don't see anything strange," she related, shaking her head. She put on her glasses again for the moment.

They may have been in audience seating, but they were prepared for the hypothetical enemy attack.

After Fujibayashi had warned her off and her Public Safety mission became impossible to continue, Haruka could have simply gone home. Personally, though, that was an aggravating prospect, since it would seem like running away with her tail between her legs. Instead, she sat in a corner of the lobby, idly watching the people going back and forth.

"Ms. Ono?"

And then, someone addressed her from behind.

"Mr. Tsuzura?"

She turned around to see Tsuzura, who was (supposedly) in charge of the team representing First High, standing around as though he was at a loss for what to do.

"What are you doing here?"

"Nothing in particular, really... I was just taking a short break. Should you be out here, Mr. Tsuzura?"

Tsuzura gave a complicated smile to her question. "No room for little old me in there. Our team this year is talented."

He calls himself "little old me"... Haruka thought, nodding unconsciously at the "talented" part.

"And..." he went on, "I'm getting a bad feeling for some reason."

He said "for some reason," but his tone was the opposite of vague, and it set Haruka on edge.

Tsuzura was both a magician and a magic researcher who had reached the level of assistant professor at the Magic University. His academic specialty was magic geometry, and he was known for his research in a field called polyhedron theory.

One theoretical approach in modern magic was to treat macrophenomena as collections of simple polyhedrons, such as pyramids and rectangular prisms, then grasp the changes in the phenomena via movements of those virtual polyhedrons and alter their events by constructing a magic program that would simply control that movement.

This polyhedron theory had originated as something to overcome a flaw in modern magic—namely, how difficult it was to only partially alter an event—and now it was actually considered important as a predictive technology.

Recognition systems for perceiving the world as a collection of simple three-dimensional shapes abstracted the world—with its infinitely interlacing mutual interactions—into simple, mutually interacting polyhedrons and showed that to the caster. Their recognition of this abstracted, modelized world made it easy to simulate future events from limited information.

Tsuzura was a young authority on polyhedron theory, and his "bad feelings" were, perhaps, predictions with a certain degree of accuracy to them.

"…I also have the feeling the worst won't come to pass, though."

Haruka earnestly hoped this last-minute addition wasn't empty consolation.

◇ ◇ ◇

And then, at 3:00 PM:

The team representing First High began its presentation, right on schedule.

This year, everyone's eyes were on Shinkurou Kichijouji, the one who'd discovered a Cardinal Code, but many were still very curious about First High's presentation theme, which was one of the Three Great Practical Problems of Weighting Magic, the gravity-controlled thermonuclear fusion reactor. Aside from First High's faculty and students, the venue was filled with people from the Magic University and scientists from private research institutes. The attendants all had enthusiastic eyes on the stage.

Daylight-bright lights poured down over the international assembly hall stage and the massive pieces of audio equipment on it as Suzune's controlled, clear alto voice flowed fluidly from the speakers.

Isori was next to her, controlling the demonstration machines, while Tatsuya was at a stage wing, switching between CAD monitors and activation sequences.

"…Since last century, we've known the answer to the question of what's required to create a nuclear fusion power generator."

Suzune went over to stand next to the giant glass ball. Tatsuya pulled up an emission-type spell's activation sequence.

The moment Suzune laid her hand on the CAD's access panel, the deuterium gas sealed inside the glass orb turned into plasma, then reacted with the material coating the inside to give off a brilliant glint of light.

A slight excitement rippled through the crowd at the flashy display.

"The first is to turn its fuel, deuterium, into plasma, then maintain it in that state for enough time for it to react. This problem has already been solved with the use of emission-type magic."

And yet, the sight was something that had been performed many times in the past, and so in terms of novelty, it lacked appeal.

"The main problem preventing electricity generation from nuclear fusion lies in ensuring the atomic nuclei contact one another in time for them to cause the fusion reaction, acting against the electric repulsive force of the plasmatic nuclei."

The sphere giving off light quieted, and a huge screen descended in the middle of the stage.

"Our predecessors attempted to implement nuclear fusion through nonmagic methods, and once tried to overcome this electric repulsive force by applying extreme pressure to the system."

The screen displayed both pictures of the experiments repeated up through the end of the first half of the century as well as videos of simulations, each on one half of the screen.

"However, neither increasing the gas pressure with super-high temperatures nor applying implosive pressure using the vaporization of surface materials created a stable thermonuclear reaction. There are several causes for this; one lies in the endurance of the containment vessel, while another is the issue of having to supply fuel. There was also one case where our predecessors successfully maintained a reaction, but the energy they created was too great to be used to practical effect. All of these problems, however, can be summed up as one: When it comes to drawing out the energy at the distance possible for fusion, the electric repulsive force in the system is simply too large."

The screen rose again. From behind it appeared two huge, cylindrical electromagnets, each hung from the ceiling with four ropes, facing one another—at a glance, a primitive experimental device.

Isori raised one of the electromagnets—it looked like he was pulling it up with his hands, but that was an act, as magic was responsible for lifting it—and then let go.

The electromagnet swung quickly at the other, but before they collided, the other electromagnet swung up the other way.

"Though I'm sure this doesn't warrant an explanation, the electric repulsive force between two objects increases geometrically as their distance decreases. Objects with a strong homopolar Coulomb force will increase that force when drawing near, and so they will never collide."

Suzune went over to the silently swinging experimental devices, put on a headset to protect her ears, and placed a hand on the access panel installed on a support beam.

A moment later, thundering noises, like mega-sized cymbals crashing into each other over and over again, echoed through the auditorium.

Suzune removed her hand, and the two electromagnets returned to their silent back-and-forth bouncing.

"But we can decrease the electric repulsive force with magic. We have successfully developed a magic program to lower the apparent

Coulomb force in this limited space to one-hundred-thousandth of what it should be."

Suzune hadn't especially raised her voice.

But the auditorium stirred loudly at her words.

As if to support her point, the main demonstration machine slowly rose from underneath the stage to its center.

As an analogy, it was a giant piston engine made with transparent materials. Specularly worked pistons thrust into the giant see-through cylinder from below, and those pistons were attached to a crank and flywheel. The upper portion of the cylinder contained a pair of valves; the transparent pipes coming out of them went through a cistern filled with water.

"Because of the noxious properties of neutron beams, this device uses hydrogen gas instead of deuterium gas. We will use an emission-type spell to turn the hydrogen gas inside the cylinder into plasma, then use a gravity-control spell and a Coulomb-control spell at the same time. The Coulomb-control spell will lower the repulsive force, and the gravity-control spell will gather the hydrogen plasma with that reduced force into the center of the cylinder, beginning a nuclear reaction. The time needed for this device to cause a nuclear reaction is zero point one seconds. As you all know, a nuclear reaction will never maintain itself. Without applying something from the outside to cause the reaction, it will cease immediately. Our school's gravity-controlling nuclear fusion machine uses this quality proactively.

"After the nuclear reaction stops, the machine cools the hydrogen gas enough so that the container can endure an oscillation-type spell. The heat collected from this process will be applied to the gravity-control and Coulomb-control energy. The pistons, drawn to the gravitational field created by the gravity-control spell, will experience a continuous increase in inertia, then send the hydrogen gas, now cooled to a suitable temperature, into the water tank for heat exchange…"

As Suzune continued her explanation, Isori put his hand on the experimental device's access panel. Plasmatize, Coulomb control,

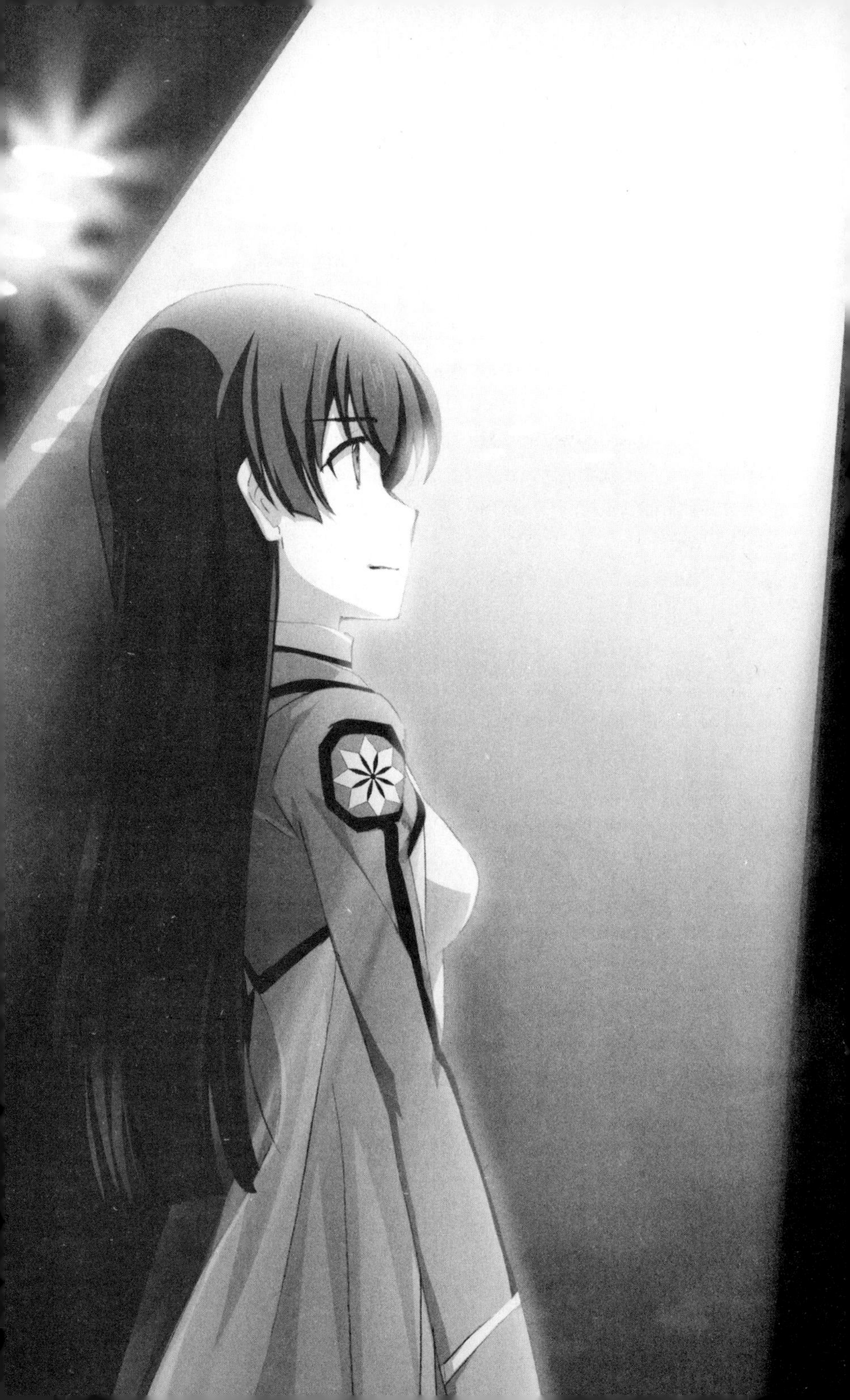

gravity control, cooling, energy collection, plasmatize, Coulomb control, gravity control... Isori continued stably activating these spells, looping dozens of times.

"Right now, a high-ranking magician is required to continuously activate this experimental device. However, with the substitution of higher energy-collection rates and stationary magic, I am certain that we can one day create a gravity-controlling magic program nuclear reactor that only needs the magician to light the fuse."

The moment after Suzune wrapped up her speech, the auditorium filled with roaring applause.

Gravity-controlled thermonuclear reactors were said to be technologically impossible because the mass of the target of the gravity-controlling spell would slowly but steadily reduce during the nuclear reaction. Gravity-controlling spells made an object's mass their target, but because that mass would change, the spell would immediately stop with a "target does not exist" error. Thus, while nuclear fusion explosions were possible, a sustained nuclear reaction was not.

But by using a Coulomb-control spell alongside one, the gravity-control spell wouldn't need to be as intense. And by abandoning the fixation with a sustained nuclear reaction in favor of an intermittent one, it could be performed using the new loop-casting technology. The idea was a beautiful one, and the spectators showed uproarious praise and applause for it.

The Thesis Competition presentations were each given thirty minutes, with ten minutes between each to switch teams. In those ten minutes, the leading team would have to clean up their demonstration equipment, and the next team would have to finish setting up their own on the stage. As it happened, this switching-out period was actually far busier for the representatives and support crew than for the presenters.

As Tatsuya was packing up the console he'd used for the presentation, the next team's controller (in other words, the assistant with the same role as him) came up to set up his own console.

"Let me just say that your presentation was amazing."

At first, Tatsuya didn't realize the comment had been directed at him. He didn't have time to be making small talk. But when he realized he was apparently being addressed, he saw Shinkurou Kichijouji there, with a fearless smile on his face.

"I suppose I should say thank you?" Tatsuya asked.

"Don't worry, I wasn't expecting any thanks."

Tatsuya shut the case with a thud and picked up the console, which was about the same size as a tabletop synthesizer. Kichijouji pointedly placed his own console case in the same spot.

Connections were installed on either side of the stage, so they normally switched back and forth for presentations. Did he have a reason for needing to be on the same side as Tatsuya?

"The gravity-control spell was an application of the general spell used in flight magic, and the spell that controlled the Coulomb force was an arrangement of a spell developed by the previous Sirius—the late William Sirius—to neutralize the bonding force between atoms. So, most of all, I was surprised by the polish of that loop casting."

"Your keen perception is astounding. I should have expected as much from Cardinal George."

Even as he spoke, Kichijouji's hands were smoothly setting things up. Tatsuya was now the only First High student left on the stage.

Meaning to withdraw himself, he began to walk backstage, his long sideways case hanging from his side.

"But we're not going to lose to you. In fact, we're going to win this time."

The voice came at Tatsuya's back. He should have rated it childish, but it didn't feel all that bad. Deciding to give a clever retort, he stopped and turned around.

And that was when explosions rocked the building.

[10]

October 30, AD 2095, 3:30 PM.

This was the time and date recorded as the start of the Yokohama Incident, the trigger for what would later be considered a turning point in mankind's history: the Scorching Halloween.

◇ ◇ ◇

First High's presentation had ended, and Toshikazu, who had been making small talk with Fujibayashi in the lobby—they'd been together all morning, and so small talk was the only topic left at this point—felt his shoulders give a jerk, and stopped mid-sentence.

The communicator-only terminal in his pocket (a police device which, in exchange for not being loaded with many information-processing capabilities, hosted powerful communication functions) had begun to vibrate, telling him he had a message.

He excused himself from Fujibayashi, then turned around to answer the terminal.

"This is Chiba. Is that you, Inagaki? —What?! ...All right. I'm heading there now."

He turned back around to see Fujibayashi just finishing up a call of her own.

"I need to go on-site," he said.

"I'll be staying here," she replied.

They each spoke with complete confidence that they'd been given the same information—and that their orders didn't, in fact, contradict.

"You'll have to excuse me! If anything happens, please call me!"

Fujibayashi nodded, and Toshikazu, without time to say any more, flew out to his car with a magic-assisted dash—from a certain angle, his feet appeared to be moving too fast.

◇ ◇ ◇

"What's the situation?!"

Three minutes after receiving the call, Toshikazu, already speeding toward the scene in his car, angrily shouted into the vehicle's hands-free communicator.

"The suicide car that rammed the control building is currently on fire. No follow-up attacks."

A voice several times calmer than his came back through the speaker with the report. Even if it had been just one car, he still had reason to worry.

The target had been the ingress-egress control building built right next to the entrance to Yamashita Wharf. There was no damage to the building itself; its sturdy construction had repelled the heat and impact from the explosion. But they couldn't let noncombatants continue working after a terrorist attack, even if they were civil servants. During their evacuation, before the police were completely in control of the port, there would be a serious security hole in surveillance of entering ships.

We were too focused on the civilians!

The government had resisted them. The public didn't like the defense force and the police being over-present, so control of ports had been put into the hands of public workers. But for an island nation, port control and border security were one and the same. The Chiba family, including Toshikazu, had long believed that if they didn't want to entrust the job to the Japan Defense Force, they could have at least stationed armed police there.

I hope our fears aren't on the mark this time, Toshikazu thought, the sober part of him already knowing it was nothing more than a fleeting hope.

"Rockets fired from a berthed cargo vessel! They appear to be from infantry launchers!"

Toshikazu nearly mishandled the steering wheel. He quickly jerked the wheel and yelled into the microphone, "Registry?!"

"Freighter registered to Australia! But its shape suggests a landing ship for mobile forces!"

Which meant the registration was fake. *What are the Immigration Bureau and the Coastal Defense Force doing?!* he fumed, fighting back the urge to wail out loud before calling someone else.

"…Dad? It's Toshikazu. A camouflaged warship of unknown nationality has invaded via the Yamashita Wharf in Yokohama. Can you request that the JDF deploy for me? Also, send over the Ikazuchi-Maru and the Orochi-Maru right away.

"…What am I doing with the Orochi-Maru? Having Erika use it, of course!"

◇ ◇ ◇

Fujibayashi headed to her car, seeking instructions from her own HQ. She'd ended up following Toshikazu out, but she hadn't been lying when she'd said she'd be staying there. She didn't need the car—she needed the communicator in it.

Still, she thought. The one to give the prediction last night had been none other than her, but she hadn't thought the situation would be quite this dire. She'd expected some spy remnants would try to kidnap people and use them as hostages to trade for their allies, and that was all.

When Toshikazu had taken her at her word and mobilized all those subordinates and equipment, she'd been astonished. Now, it looked like his efforts were well-placed. *Maybe simple earnestness does trump cunning*, she thought, honestly impressed.

◇ ◇ ◇

The hands on the clock pointed to 3:37 PM.

An explosion and tremors suddenly reached the competition hall. The spectators, unaware of what was going on, began to make noise, demanding to know what they should do.

"Miyuki!"

In their midst, Tatsuya called for the one he had to prioritize above all else.

"Tatsuya!"

He heard the reply from below the stage, and in two steps—one to jump to the edge of the stage, and the other while adjusting his power—he went down to his sister. Despite having been in the second row in the official guest seats, she'd already tried to run to him. Her reflexes were fast, too.

"Tatsuya, what on earth…?" she asked, startled. She seemed a bit unsure, but not in a state of full-out panic yet.

"I think a grenade exploded near the front entrance."

Meanwhile, confusion and panic were nowhere to be seen on Tatsuya's face. The explosion and tremor were things he'd experienced during his training with the Independent Magic Battalion time and time again. With his experience, he knew it had happened near the front entrance of this building even without accessing the Idea. The situation wasn't looking bright, but at least he'd been able to get to Miyuki right away, which was good for him.

"A grenade?! Are our upperclassmen all right?"

"I believe the official security team from the Magic Association was assigned to the front. They have experienced combat magicians, too. If this were on the level of a normal crime organization, it wouldn't be a problem, but…"

Even as Tatsuya answered her, a bad premonition came over him. That data card Fujibayashi had given him a while ago…it had said that intervention by a foreign national agency was possible.

Then, as if to lend credence to that recollection, he began to hear gunfire.

They're not full auto… High-powered anti-magician rifles!

Combat magicians had ways of neutralizing firearms. The multi-layered barrier magic of the Juumonji was one of the greatest archetypical examples. Even at the end of the twenty-first century, the main weapon of infantry was firearms. Therefore, magic to block bullets gave a person a big advantage in ground combat.

But attacks and defenses were in a constant race with one another, and even stronger attack methods would inevitably be devised to counteract the improved defense.

Magic was no exception, and magic wasn't all-powerful, either. If a moving object's inertial force was greater than a spell's interference level, the spell would fail, with no deceleration, trajectory changes, or coordinate immobilization applied at all. A physical shield could weaken the force of something piercing it, but if magic failed to alter events, then it was the same as if the person did nothing in the first place.

High-speed bullets that created high inertial force to neutralize a magician's defensive spells—that was the design concept behind high-powered anti-magician rifles. But in order to gain the speed necessary to nullify a combat-level magician's interference level, the technology for manufacturing the gun had to be two or three stages more advanced.

Small countries' official forces weren't enough to create the weapons, much less deploy them. And private criminal organizations and terrorists—private in the sense of having no national support—couldn't acquire them. But come to think of it, during the attack on the Hachiouji Special Detention Home, Ganghu Lu's allies had been using high-powered rifles. It was hard to imagine separate factions launching similar successive attacks in such a short time. The enemy was probably—no, almost definitely—hounds from the Great Asian Alliance. It could have even been the GA3 itself. *But they're making such a big show of things. What on earth could they be after?*

Tatsuya wavered. If he didn't know their goal, he also didn't know how far the situation would escalate. "Assume the worst possible scenario" was easy to say, but in reality, there was no upper bound on "worst." If he didn't know how bad the worst was, he had no way to decide how to respond.

In any case, he couldn't call this hall fit for holing up in, assuming they were going to take a standard response. That by itself would mean he should take his sister and evacuate to the waiting room.

But their friends were still in the audience.

Miyuki was the only one he had a responsibility to, but that didn't mean he took action only when his responsibilities demanded it. He was pretty sure he had the strength to cut his way through most things without needing to protect himself, but he still resisted turning a blind eye to the needs of others.

However, for better or worse, he didn't need to worry about it for long. With a tempest of clattering feet, a group bearing rifles began to flood into the auditorium.

I'm getting careless!

He'd considered the possibility of their arrival, but they still broke through too fast to thwart. As shrieks echoed through the room, Tatsuya swore to himself.

As the audience cowered in fear, it was the Third High students on the stage who showed a dauntless, courageous reaction. As though they could switch their presentation theme to anti-personnel attacks, they used the CADs they'd brought with them onstage and tried to trigger magic at the invaders.

Gunshots rang out.

Bullets riddled the back wall of the stage before the Third High spells could manifest.

Judging by the bullets' force, they were indeed carrying high-powered rifles, just as Tatsuya had predicted.

"Quiet down!"

The angry shout felt somehow unsteady. Even if they were foreigners, they must have only recently entered the country (illegally). They weren't wearing uniforms or field combat outfits, but they did sport an odd unification: They dressed in all the colors of the rainbow, but each of them had on a high-necked sweater, a blouson, and loose-fitting cargo pants. Each person appeared to be durable, too; it was certain these were no mere thugs.

Modern magic had gained enough speed to rival firearms through the speed granted by CADs, but nonetheless, they only *rivaled* firearms, and it depended on the magician's strength. Standard practice was to not recklessly resist if the opponents already had their guns at the ready.

"Remove your devices and put them on the floor."

The invaders seemed used to fighting against magicians; it was possible that they were actually magicians themselves, since only a very select handful of magicians adopted fighting styles that relied solely upon magic. A soldier carrying a gun, even though he or she was a magician, was actually a more common occurrence.

The Third High students on the stage, including Kichijouji—Masaki wasn't present among them—put their CADs on the floor, their expressions frustrated. Bravery and recklessness were two different things. Third High had apparently taught that to their students properly.

Tatsuya watched their response with admiration, but unfortunately, things got personal very quickly. The siblings happened to be the only ones standing out in the aisle, which was why they were caught in the crosshairs.

"Hey, you, too!"

One of the invaders, muzzle pointed at him, approached with careful footsteps.

There was no doubt his words had been directed at Tatsuya. There was simply no way to misunderstand that.

Guess that's it... Tatsuya thought. Six in all. Three units, front and backup. Tatsuya, without using his CAD, took aim at the terrorists or guerilla soldiers or whoever the intruders were. He didn't want to use Mist Dispersion in front of so many people, but if things got to that point, he wouldn't have a choice.

I'd rather settle this with a spell I can lie about more easily, thought Tatsuya, face impassive, as the intruder yelled at him again: "Do it now!"

Despite the aggravation in the man's shout, Tatsuya didn't move. The way he'd been raised and taught had been a bit too twisted for him to believe that his safety was guaranteed if he gave up resistance.

Without a word, he stared at the man approaching them. Actually, the expression "watching closely" would have fit his gaze better. There was no fear or distress in Tatsuya's eyes; he simply observed the man's entire body, the gun in his hands, and the muzzle aimed directly at him.

Irritated by the cold stare being directed at him, and a fear of the unknown he probably wasn't even fully aware of, the invader facing down Tatsuya squeezed his index finger on the trigger.

"Hey, wait!"

He probably couldn't hear his ally's warning. A gunshot rang out, and a scream followed.

The man had fired the bullet with clear intent to kill from just three yards away. It was more than enough to make one imagine an unavoidable tragedy.

That image made everyone's shock that much greater.

A right hand in front of his chest, closed, as though gripping something—that was the only change that had happened to Tatsuya.

Not a single drop of blood dripped from his body.

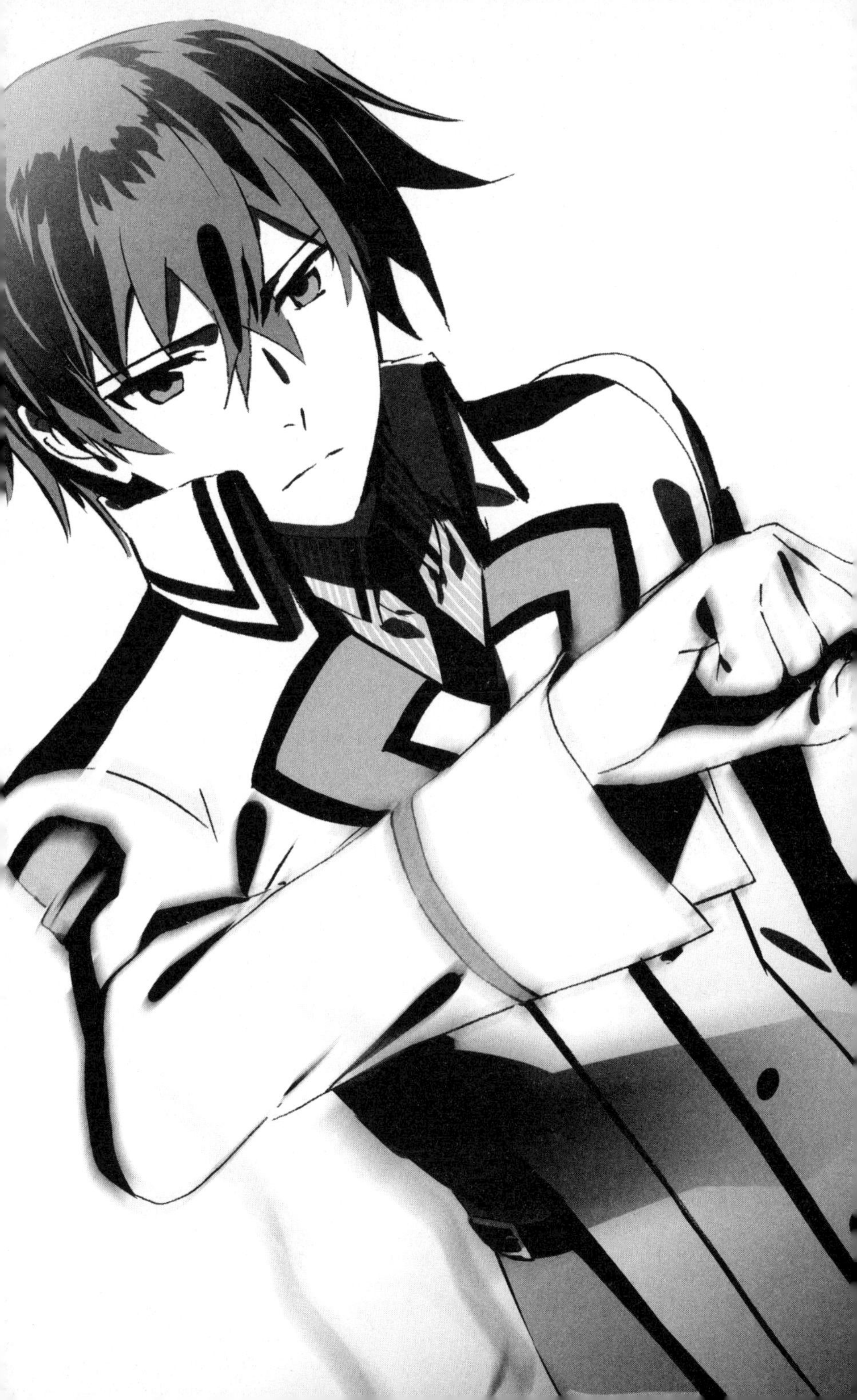

And the bullet the man fired was gone without a trace: not in the wall, not in the floor, not in the ceiling.

The man drew back as he fired a second shot, then a third. Each time, Tatsuya's right hand appeared in a different position as though he were in a time-lapse video. His hand moved too fast for any onlookers to see what he was doing. The next thing anyone knew, his right hand was in a different place, and still clenched shut as if holding on to something.

"Did he grab the bullets…?" someone muttered, baffled.

"How the hell…?" asked another, similarly confused.

"You demon!"

The man threw his gun to the side out of panic.

It would have been one thing if he'd magically blocked the bullets, but when offered the nonsensical idea that Tatsuya had grabbed them, the man came to the false conclusion that his gun would do him no good.

Still, he hadn't lost his will to fight. The fact that the man whipped out a large combat knife and came at Tatsuya to slash him spoke volumes of the high-level training the man had been through.

But the act only ushered in even more surprise.

The man approached, but Tatsuya was the one to close the distance between them. He opened his hand, straightened it, and slammed its rigid side into the arm holding the knife.

His hand then cut straight through the man's arm with no resistance.

"Gya—"

A scream sprang from the man's mouth—or was about to, anyway.

But before his voice reached that volume, Tatsuya buried his left fist into the man's solar plexus.

Fresh blood spurted out from the man's severed right arm, splattering onto Tatsuya's clothes.

That was the only counterattack the man could manage. He crumpled to the floor, and Tatsuya, without sparing a glance at him, made a light backward jump to put his sister right behind him again.

The unexpected, unimaginable sight had frozen both the audience and the invaders solid. It wasn't only their movements that had stopped—it was their thoughts, too.

With one exception:

"Tatsuya, I'll get the blood off. Please hold still for a moment."

Miyuki's soft voice reached every corner of the dead-quiet hall. Her voice hadn't even a fragment of dismay; she spoke with the severity of someone saying, "I'll dust you off."

With her voice as a signal, the frozen time began to move.

"Arrest them!"

The members of the combined security team fired a barrage of magic from both stage wings.

One or two invaders responded by dodging, but none of them were able to resist the practiced magic of nine magic schools' cream of the crop.

The magic Miyuki executed neatly took all the blood off Tatsuya.

More accurately, she separated it from my skin and clothes, vaporized the moisture, and scattered the solid parts. Despite having just fought for his life, Tatsuya didn't even bat an eye.

Actually, maybe the phrase *didn't bat an eye* wasn't accurate in this case. It was true that no confusion or excitement was visible on his face, but he *had* actually frowned at the man collapsed on the floor in a puddle of blood.

Miyuki picked up on the slight change in his expression and activated another spell. She froze the man's right hand and the severed part of his right arm, then dried up the pool of blood, making it into a dark red dust.

When Tatsuya turned around, his little sister smiled happily at him. She was too good, and before he knew it, he found himself smiling with her.

Then, for some reason, her eyes shook. But he didn't think much on it and started walking toward the front entrance.

Miyuki followed right behind him. Even as they slipped past the one-armed man, they showed a complete lack of interest in him.

And then...

"Tatsuya!" shouted two voices at once—one female, one male.

Under normal circumstances, their overlapping voices would have made these two scowl at each other, but they obviously didn't have the time for that right now.

Following Erika and Leo came Mikihiko, Mizuki, Honoka, and Shizuku, all surrounding Tatsuya and Miyuki. Honoka, though, pushed past Erika and Leo, the first ones to dash over, and asked in a fluster, "Your hand! Is it hurt?!"

It was a contrived question, but that didn't mean Tatsuya *didn't* immediately understand what she was getting at.

He obviously hadn't caught the bullets with his hand; he'd only dismantled their physical structure and movement vectors to neutralize the attack. But his friends wouldn't know that, so Tatsuya raised his right hand and opened and closed it a few times to show them it was unharmed.

Honoka and Mizuki breathed sighs of relief, but Mikihiko and Shizuku gave him questioning looks, clearly asking *How?* But Tatsuya wasn't about to answer that, verbally or not. Instead, he answered Erika's spoken one.

"This is starting to blow way out of proportion..." she said. "What do we do now?"

The words *you seem happy about this* made it halfway up his throat, but it was highly likely that saying them would just waste time. "Whether we flee or give chase, we have to clean up the enemies at the front entrance first," he said.

"You're not gonna tell us to hang tight and wait for you, right?" said Erika, eyes glittering.

Now he really wanted to point out how happy she seemed, but all he did was shake his head in resignation. "Guess it would be better than splitting up and getting attacked separately."

It was no more than a passive agreement, one suggesting it would be a tiny bit better for them that way. So when he saw not only Erika and Honoka but also Mizuki and Shizuku beaming with joy, Tatsuya had to sigh. *Give me a break...*

Still, this was an emergency. He obviously didn't have time to be sulking. He took the lead, quickly heading for the entrance.

"Wait... Wait a minute, Tatsuya Shiba!"

They were stopped by a voice—one clearly confused, and somehow desperate.

"What could you possibly need, Shinkurou Kichijouji?" asked Tatsuya, not an ounce of friendliness in his voice.

But without wincing at the obvious irritation—likely without the mental leeway to even do so—Kichijouji answered, "Wasn't that Atomic Divider?!"

Kichijouji's cry caused a stir. He continued:

"The spell to divide bonded atoms is a secret technique devised by the former commander of the USNA Army's Stars, Major William Sirius. Unlike the neutralization spell that weakens the bonding force between atoms, this dividing spell should be a USNA military secret!"

Kichijouji had completely misunderstood—because Tatsuya conveniently knew a lot about it.

"How can you use that?! Why do you know it?!" came Kichijouji's wide-eyed demands of denouncement.

"Is this really the time?" said Tatsuya to cut the conversation short, putting annoyance into his voice so that he'd sound like he was saying *No point in hiding it now* to Kichijouji's inference.

The reality was different. The spell Tatsuya had used was not the military secret magic of the USNA Army called Atomic Divider. Nor was it, of course, a certain fictional *kenpo* that could slash through body parts with bare hands.

Just as he'd dismantled the bullets, he'd simply activated his dismantling spell at relative range zero with his right hand as the starting point. But as someone ordered to protect this secret, he had no way to explain this. There was no time for it given their current situation, anyway.

"Saegusa, and Nakajou, too—you should get out of here as soon as possible. Whatever their end goal is, their first objective is probably to kill or kidnap as many high-ranking magic students as they can."

After leaving that warning with Mayumi, who had just popped out from a stage wing, and Azusa, who was sitting in the front row as a judge, Tatsuya left the place behind him.

◇ ◇ ◇

A moment after Tatsuya's group disappeared out the door, another, stronger explosion shook the hall. Chaotic screams and angry shouts muddled together, turning into a twist of sound that whittled away at everyone's nerves even more.

But the chaos hadn't extended to the front-row judging seats where Azusa was.

Not yet, anyway.

Without a doubt, though, this would escalate into a level of panic where several people would be injured. Before such a clamor, Azusa had sat frozen in place, not knowing what to do, what she *should* do.

"Ah-chan, Ah-chan…Student Council President Azusa Nakajou!"

A voice scolded her from the stage. Azusa hastily stood and looked up to the platform.

Mayumi, standing at a wing, came out farther to the front, looked at Azusa, and said, "At this rate, we'll have actual panic on our hands. Many people will be hurt. Please, calm everyone with your power."

"Huh?!" Azusa's eyes widened, though not because she didn't understand. "But that's…"

Her spell could interfere with a person's emotions, so it could quell panic. It would be incredibly effective in this situation. However, magic that interfered with mental processes was an especially tightly restricted type. It wasn't something a minor could decide to use lightly.

"Your power is for times like these, right? Not my power, not Mari's, and not Suzune's. Azusa, right now, we need you."

But Mayumi wasn't telling her lightly: "Suzune," not "Rin"; and "Azusa," not "Ah-chan."

In the past, Mayumi had normally called them Ichihara and Nakajou for more formal situations, but she could count on one hand the number of times she'd called Azusa by her first name. Azusa understood how serious Mayumi was, that she was demanding she use her Azusa Bow, her emotional interference spell, for real.

"It'll be fine. I'll take responsibility. The Saegusa name isn't just for show."

Mayumi winked comically; it was to relax Azusa. She'd said her last name out loud to ward off the adults who *should have had the power in the room* but were now watching, unable to do anything about the panic.

Azusa had known her long enough to understand that. There was no lie in her words.

She wasn't about to push all the responsibility on Mayumi, either, but she couldn't play dumb after being told all that. So she nodded firmly, turned around, and set her sights on the audience seats, which had escalated in places to shoving and jostling.

She drew in the chain hanging on her neck and pulled a locket big enough to hide a little kid's hand out of her collar. She undid the clasp and tugged it off the chain, then gripped it in her left hand.

After letting out a long breath, she poured psions into the locket.

The locket was a one-of-a-kind spell assistant device, created with only the backbone pieces of a CAD.

Its only function was to store one type of activation sequence and output one type of magic program, and so it eliminated every single system needed for switching between them, like buttons and displays. It was a miniaturized magic wand.

The magic wand built for one person alone spoke the magic words for its only spell…

…and the Azusa Bow, the emotional interference spell only Azusa could use, activated.

…The clear sound of a string passed through the hall from front row to back.

It wasn't a real sound.

A sound that floated through the sea of the unconscious rather than the air.

A wave that vibrated pushions instead of psions.

For the first ringing echo, it was like a traveler in a marshland with nothing but muddy, dirty water chancing upon a single drop of rain, then stopping and staring idly up at the sky, waiting for the next droplet. It made people long for the next echo; it tied their minds to that alone.

Once the first echo had completely faded, the second plucked the strings of their unconscious.

The people waited for the next echo even more firmly.

And at some point, the audience had stopped thinking, turning their ears to listen inside themselves.

In terms of time, it was just three seconds.

That was all it took for the panic to change into a trance.

"…*I am Mayumi Saegusa, former student council president of First High.*"

As Mayumi's voice came amplified over the speakers, it completely drew in the spectators' minds, which had stopped thinking.

"*This city is currently being invaded.*"

Those next words, spoken with an absolute grasp of the audience's consciousness, turned their daze into shock.

"*An unknown vessel berthed in the port has launched a rocket attack, and in response, guerilla soldiers secretly in the city have risen up.*"

This was too sudden to easily believe.

If Mayumi hadn't told Azusa of this earlier, she wouldn't have believed it, either.

But just like she'd said, the name "Saegusa" wasn't just for show. She was in a position to learn the truth quickest of all, and not one to make irresponsible guesses. However hard this story was to believe, it was the truth.

"*The thugs we just apprehended were likely allies of the invading forces. It's also highly likely that the explosions we've been hearing are attacks aimed at the magicians and magic technology gathered here.*"

Mayumi paused for a moment, then looked out across the crowd. The audience held its collective breath and waited for her next words.

"*As you all know, this building is connected to a train station shelter via an underground passage.*"

They stared at her, hanging on her every word.

"*The shelter should have more than enough capacity to hold us all.*"

They bent their ears to her voice.

"*However, the underground shelter is equipped for disaster and air raids.*"

Both the students and the adults…

"*It is not necessarily a perfect defense against ground forces.*"

…even the so-called authorities, who should have been used to commanding and leading the others…

"*I estimate that the invaders' ranks include a force of magicians. We cannot hope for much from the shelter if it comes under magical attack.*"

…most of the people in the hall knew who Mayumi was. Both her looks and her competitive accomplishments had shown everyone what her name meant. Not a soul in the place could laugh off her pessimistic outlook as the ramblings of a child. Even the teachers, considering the power behind the Saegusa name, had yielded the platform to her.

"*Even so, it may be even more dangerous to try to escape into the crossfire in the city. However, remaining here in the auditorium is the most dangerous option.*"

The hall was completely silent. Mayumi didn't commit the blunder of wasting time with lengthy pauses.

"*Would all school representatives please gather their students and begin moving? Whether you evacuate to the shelter or escape the building, there isn't a moment to lose!*"

A different kind of bustle spread through the hall. And the shouting, unlike before, had a certain amount of order to it.

"*For all those not related to the nine schools, I apologize, but you must use your own judgment to evacuate. Unfortunately, we don't have the strength to shoulder the responsibility for everyone's safety.*"

That declaration, which could have been seen as heartless, didn't garner any argument or denouncement. All the guests here were related to magic in some way. They were all closer to the abnormal than others.

"*If you are evacuating to the shelter, please head for the underground passage at once. If you wish to escape the building, we have reports of the Coastal Defense Force sending transport ships to the Mizuho Pier.*"

Mayumi bowed, turned off the microphone, and then spoke to Azusa again. "Ah-chan, I'll leave everyone in your hands. Would all the teachers be so kind as to support Nakajou?"

The teachers, starting with Tsuzura, all nodded, but meanwhile, Azusa's eyes went wide. "Huh? Wait, Pres— I mean, Mayumi?" she asked in a hurry.

Mayumi smiled and nodded. "See? You understand. You're the student council president of First High right now, Ah-chan. It'll be fine; I know you can do it. After all, I trained you personally."

She gave Azusa a quick wink, then turned around and ran back to the waiting room where Suzune and the others were.

◇ ◇ ◇

There was a shoot-out between rifles and magic going on in front of the main entrance.

The attacking guerillas all had Asian features. They each wore the same assorted high-necked sweaters, jumpers, and loose cargo pants as the terrorists who made it inside the hall, and they were armed with the usual assault rifles plus the anti-magician high-powered rifles.

Professional, Magic Association–sent magicians were intercepting them.

However, as one could understand from how they'd already let some of the guerillas break through the front gates, the battle wasn't looking good. The guerillas had more numbers to begin with, but likely due to their anti-magician armaments, several experienced combat magicians—who would never have let normal-equipped infantry anywhere near them—had been injured and now lay on the ground.

Tatsuya, who had been running ahead of the others, stopped behind the entrance. Miyuki, who had been following behind him, stopped along with him, but two others, seemingly in a race for third, let their zeal get the better of them.

"Stop!" Tatsuya shouted at Erika, who was about to leap out in front of him. "They have high-speed anti-magician bullets!"

"Gweh!" grunted Leo as Tatsuya grabbed his collar to drag him close at the same time.

"…Tatsuya, you have no mercy," Mikihiko muttered, sounding impressed.

"That's why he's alive," Shizuku flatly countered.

This marked the arrival of the remaining four a few moments later. The fact that his friends were still going at it at a time like this was reassuring, but Tatsuya clamped down on his pained grin before it could come out. Instead, he looked to his sister. "Miyuki, quiet their guns for me."

All his friends gave him a confused look.

"Right away. However, Tatsuya, for this many people at once, I…"

For some reason, Miyuki's answer seemed filled with an out-of-place embarrassment. The rest of the party cocked their heads at this new mystery.

"I know."

Tatsuya's next action immediately put that question to rest.

He held out his left hand, and Miyuki gently entangled her right hand in his fingers. Her bashful expression was not, from any angle you looked at it, the kind a sister would give to her brother.

But before anyone could call them out on it, Miyuki's face tightened, becoming that of an operating magician.

Her left hand now held her CAD; she had moved so naturally that nobody noticed her reaching for it.

Tatsuya raised his right hand, then pointed at the guerillas from across the door they hid behind.

A moment later, Miyuki's magic went off.

It was a spell to freeze fire.

The oscillation-/deceleration-type conceptual extension spell Freeze Flame.

Freeze Flame, which expanded the concept of freezing, was a spell that prevented combustion.

Its effect was to hold the heat retained by its target to a fixed level or below.

A gun, in the simplest terms, shot bullets using the gas pressure created by combusting gunpowder. The blasting-cap detonation that made the gunpowder combust was also a type of combustion. And the *normal concept of combustion* always accompanied an increase in heat.

If a combustible was denied that heat increase, it wouldn't be able to burn. Therefore, any firearms affected by Freeze Flame, whether it was a gun or heavy artillery, as long as it used powder to fire, would be forced into silence.

Exactly thirty guerrillas remained.

At the moment, the upper limit of how many simultaneous targets Miyuki could handle was sixteen.

A double firing of Freeze Flame targeted thirty rifles.

Without first checking to see if the spell worked, Tatsuya jumped out from behind the door.

In the blink of an eye, he was within the guerillas' ranks, swinging the ridge of his magic-enhanced hands.

The astonishing spectacle of someone cutting through body parts with his bare hands gave a far larger shock to the guerrillas than seeing their allies gunned down, because they couldn't tell if it was magic or not just by looking.

Even as their inability to use their firearms threw them into confusion, a few bravely responded with combat knives; but once five of their number had been cut down, they started to get cold feet.

They looked at Tatsuya like he was a terrifying monster.

He had purposely taken a risk and used zero-range magic instead of long-distance shooting magic for two reasons. The first was so that his friends wouldn't catch on to the real spell he was using. More importantly, though, he was trying to incite panic.

Being treated like a man-eating fiend was exactly what Tatsuya had wanted.

Their wills broken and their focus lost, the guerrillas watched as a silver wind, faster than the eye could see, swept past them from the side. Blood splattered into the air along the gale's path, and the men fell.

The silver flash had actually been a short blade, a *kodachi*—though, from its length, perhaps more accurately a *wakizashi*.

Erika had switched from her usual police baton to a guardless *wakizashi*-shaped integrated armament CAD, then run through them with a self-acceleration spell, pinpointing and slicing apart their carotids.

Like Tatsuya, she had no hesitation when it came to taking enemy lives. Part of that was because this wasn't her first battle. But more importantly, she had learned skills to take human lives, using weapons that were made for it. She knew the danger of hesitation. How arrogant and foolish it would be to hesitate to kill her opponent when they could just as easily kill her was branded into the core of her mind.

On that point, it was the same for Mikihiko. The values fostered in him by his family, which had passed down the weapon of magic for generations, wouldn't allow him to feel doubt over using magic for its original purpose.

"Tatsuya, Erika!" came Mikihiko's voice from behind, causing the two to spread left and right.

What blew through then was a true whirlwind.

The cutting air hidden in the gale shot through the guerillas, brutally tearing through their skin.

After leaving the remaining enemy troops to the magicians in the security team, Tatsuya and Erika fell back to their allies.

"I didn't even get a turn…"

Tatsuya gave Leo, who was timid for some reason, an encouraging pat on the back (which, as a result, made Leo squat down with an anguished look), then gave Mikihiko a thumbs-up, and a faint smile to Honoka and Mizuki, who were looking a little scared, with faces like they were trying not to vomit.

"I'm sorry," he said. "That might have been a little much for you two."

"…No, I'm fine."

Honoka gave a brave nod, probably an act of her feelings for him.

Whatever the reason, he was glad she was still holding tight. The truth of the matter was that Tatsuya would rather they panic or avoid him after they got out of this situation.

"Mizuki?"

"Ah…I'm fine, too."

One simple, kind word from his sister was enough to make Mizuki give a tense smile. She was as smart as the rest of them. She understood that this was not the time to act how she usually did.

"Erika, how did you even get that here?" asked Tatsuya. "It's too big to fit in your bag, isn't it?"

Still, scenes of killing weren't something one got used to right away, and the shock from it wouldn't fade quickly. Tatsuya purposely brought up something unrelated to give the two of them time to calm down.

"Yep. When it's like this, anyway." And Erika, too, replied in a more casual tone than usual because she'd guessed Tatsuya's intention properly. "But when you do this… See?"

"Ooh, now that's something…"

But the admiration that slipped from Tatsuya's lips was no act. Even Honoka and Mizuki, who had looked over on a whim—as well as Miyuki, Shizuku, and Mikihiko—had wide eyes.

And this gimmick was definitely worth the boggled expressions. When Erika pressed a switch on the bottom of the hilt, the thin, sharpened blade shrunk into a short truncheon with an elliptical cross section before their very eyes.

"Cool, huh?" said Erika. "It's a form-memory club-sword they plan on providing to the police next year."

"Oh, right," replied Tatsuya. "Your family makes close-combat weapons, don't they?"

"Actually, it's basically our main source of income!"

The conversation wasn't funny enough to warrant laughter, but the sight of them trading casual words seemed to let Mizuki and the others calm down.

"…So, what do we do now?" asked Leo, having read the mood. His tone was nearing impatience as he asked Tatsuya for more instructions.

"We need information," said Tatsuya. "Like Erika said, things have gotten a lot bigger and more serious than we thought they would. Playing things by ear might get us caught in a whole host of difficulties."

If we go to the association, we'll get information for sure. Secret lines for the Ten Master Clans' personal use ran from the Magic Association HQ and sub-HQ, and Tatsuya had been given access privileges for the Yotsuba family's secret line. If he used it, he could even obtain top-secret information from National Defense Force council meetings.

Were Tatsuya alone, it would take him less than ten minutes to get to Bay Hills Tower, where the Magic Association's Kanto branch was, even if he was caught in the middle of a city battle. He didn't go for a high-speed run every morning for nothing.

However, without roller blades or a flight device, Miyuki wouldn't be able to keep up with him. Perhaps Leo, Erika, or Mikihiko could stick with him, but it was clearly impossible for Honoka, Shizuku, and Mizuki.

"What if we use the VIP conference room?"

As Tatsuya's brow unconsciously creased into a frown, Shizuku made this suggestion, indicating the building they'd just come out of.

"VIP conference room?"

Tatsuya didn't know of any such facility. He knew of the VIP reception room, but she couldn't have simply misspoken. Besides, the room he thought of was purely for reception, and its information terminals were only hooked up to the usual communication lines.

"Yep. They use it for top-level meetings with high government officials and economic organizations, so we should be able to access most of what we need."

"There's a room like that?"

"It's not open to the general public."

"...You really know a lot about this stuff," said Erika, for once genuinely impressed.

Shizuku, a little embarrassed, said in a slightly upbeat way, "I know the encryption key and access code, too."

"Wow…" breathed Mizuki.

"Uncle Ushio really dotes on her," added Honoka.

Tatsuya nodded, convinced. Her father certainly seemed the type. And if Ushio Kitayama would use the room, then it could probably intercept police and Coastal Defense Force communications, too. "Shizuku, could you guide us there?" he asked.

Shizuku bobbed her head up and down in an unusually spirited fashion.

◇ ◇ ◇

Using Shizuku's access code to have the police's map data sent to the VIP conference room monitor, they found an entire swath of land on the ocean filled with red, indicating dangerous areas. And that red zone was expanding inland as they watched.

Nobody knew exactly how many enemies there were. But given the speed of their invasion, it seemed certain that their enemy had invested a considerable force. Hundreds, at the very least, and Tatsuya estimated that they were using a battalion-sized unit, numbering anywhere from six hundred to eight hundred. He frowned—the situation had gotten worse than he'd anticipated.

"What is this?!"

"Whoa, this is horrible."

"There are so many… But how?"

Although his scowl didn't stand out, thanks to some exaggerated reactions from his friends.

"Tatsuya…"

But though it didn't stand out, there was no way Miyuki wouldn't notice. The rippling in his mind was directly linked to his sister's unrest. The siblings' minds were connected.

After giving his nervous-eyed sister a pat on the head, Tatsuya

YOKOHAMA INCIDENT OUTLINE
1

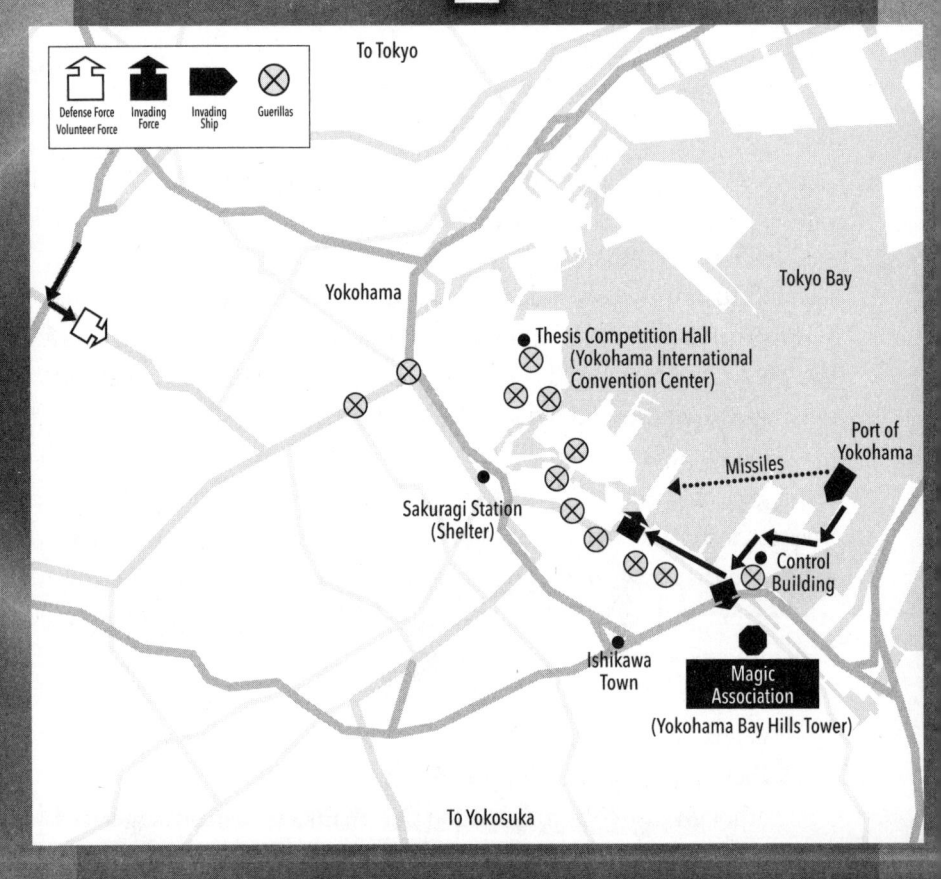

Legend:
- Defense Force Volunteer Force
- Invading Force
- Invading Ship
- Guerrillas

To Tokyo

Yokohama

Tokyo Bay

Thesis Competition Hall (Yokohama International Convention Center)

Sakuragi Station (Shelter)

Port of Yokohama

Missiles

Control Building

Ishikawa Town

Magic Association (Yokohama Bay Hills Tower)

To Yokosuka

OCTOBER 30, AD 2095
3:30 PM, COMBAT BEGINS

turned back to his friends. "I know I don't have to say it, but the situation is looking fairly bad. If we stick around here, we'll be captured before the JDF arrives. Even so, there doesn't look to be an easy avenue of escape. Not overland routes, at least. After all, the transportation systems aren't running."

"Which means we go by sea?" asked Leo.

Tatsuya shook his head. "That isn't looking good, either. Any boat they dispatched probably couldn't fit all of us."

"Evacuate to the shelter, then?" suggested Mikihiko.

Tatsuya nodded, but there wasn't much confidence in his expression. "That would be the realistic option..." he mused. "This place might be sturdy, but if they bomb the building itself, it won't last."

"Then we use the underground passage," prompted Erika, looking ready to dash off at any moment.

"Wait," Tatsuya said to her. "We shouldn't go underground. Let's keep above the surface."

"Huh? Why? ...Oh, I see," said Erika, looking convinced before he had to explain.

She really is from a family famous for its combat magic, thought Tatsuya in admiration. That wasn't the only reason he'd called for pause, though. "Also, could you give me a little time?"

"I don't mind, but...for what?" asked Honoka, cocking her head to the side. Everyone could see the situation was a race against time, but Tatsuya had suggested delaying. Still, her answer was a yes to begin with, and that spoke volumes of her feelings toward him.

"I want to get rid of the data in the demonstration machine."

"Oh, right," said Mikihiko. "Since that might be their objective."

Everyone nodded.

"Shiba, Yoshida."

In the hallway that led from the elevators to the back of the stage, Tatsuya and Mikihiko were addressed by a heavy, booming voice. They only knew one high school student with a voice that deep.

"Juumonji?"

They turned around to see Katsuto Juumonji walking over, followed by Hattori and Sawaki. All three wore bulletproof vests, the surfaces covered with small, scalelike, overlapping plates. Even Katsuto, who had a powerful magical barrier at hand, was wearing body armor, which brought the gravity of the situation that much more into focus.

"The others are with you? I thought you'd all evacuated earlier." *Evacuate now* was written across his face.

"We were headed to the demonstration machines to wipe the data so they can't steal it, just in case. The girls, well, I figured it would be better than all of us moving independently." Tatsuya had vacillated over how to explain why he'd brought them here without telling him they'd essentially hacked into the private conference room, and decided to fabricate a fake reason. (The first half, though, wasn't fabricated.)

"But all the other students are already headed for the underground passage."

This from Hattori.

Tatsuya scowled in response, and Sawaki, sharply picking up on that, asked, "Is it dangerous down there?"

"Not dangerous, really…but it's not a straight line, so they could run across another group. Depending on the situation—"

"You mean they could encounter the enemy?!" demanded Hattori without letting him finish.

"The underground passage will restrict their movements," explained Tatsuya. "They won't be able to run away or hide, and they could be forced to face them head-on. That was why I decided to go aboveground."

Katsuto's verdict was swift. "Hattori, Sawaki, go after Nakajou at once."

"Yes, sir!"

"Understood."

After watching the two of them speed off, Katsuto looked down at Tatsuya with a trace of criticism in his eyes. "Shiba, for someone so resourceful, it seems like you have poor footwork."

Tatsuya, of course, understood what he was trying to say. That wasn't to say he accepted it, but for now, he wouldn't argue.

"Well, fine. Let's hurry."

"Understood."

This time, it was Tatsuya following after Katsuto.

There weren't enough words in their exchange to show that Katsuto had acknowledged what Tatsuya was trying to do and decided to help him, but Tatsuya knew he had.

"What are you doing here?"

Upon returning to the stage's rear, where they'd left the demo machines, a remark that completely ignored the question of his own presence was the first thing that slipped out of Tatsuya's mouth. Suzune and Isori were here, fiddling with the machines, while Mayumi, Mari, Kanon, Kirihara, and Sayaka surrounded them in defense.

"Wiping the data."

Tatsuya could tell what they were doing just from looking. What he'd really wanted to ask was why they were still here, but when Suzune purposely came back with a literal answer to the question, he found himself at a loss for words.

"You all haven't evacuated yet?"

"With Rin and Isori doing their best, we can't very well run away before them, can we?"

Katsuto had given voice to what Tatsuya wanted to say, but with yet another person—Mayumi—responding as though their behavior was entirely natural, he couldn't say anything more, either.

"We'll take care of things here, so could you do the ones still in the waiting room, Shiba?"

"If you can, destroy the equipment the other schools left, too, please."

"Once we're done here, we'll head to the waiting room. Then we'll decide what to do from there."

After successive requests (instructions?) from Isori, Kanon, and Mari, Tatsuya and Katsuto both turned on their heels.

By the time Tatsuya, with Miyuki, had gone around to the other schools' waiting rooms and returned (he hadn't brought the other members with him, since he didn't want them to see him using his magic to dismantle the patterns recorded in the information and empty the storage media), Suzune's group had already finished up their work onstage and come to the waiting room.

"You're back early."

"How'd it go?"

"The data has been destroyed from all the abandoned terminals," Tatsuya answered succinctly.

"Really…? How?" asked Kanon, having predicted the answer but being unable to hide her surprise anyway.

Tatsuya's answer was brief: "It's a secret."

"Kanon, you can't just ask other magicians how their secret spells work. It's not polite."

Those words belonged to none other than Isori. Protest was written all over Kanon's face, but she backed down honestly.

"So, what do we do now?" asked Mari, getting the ball rolling by looking at Mayumi.

"One enemy ship in the port," said Mayumi. "Nobody's spotted any others in Tokyo Bay. We don't know exactly how large the force they landed is, but it looks like almost all of the coastline is under enemy control. All aboveground transportation facilities are frozen. We probably have the guerillas to thank for that."

"What could they be after?" wondered Isori.

Mayumi and Mari exchanged glances. "This is only a guess, but…" Mayumi answered. "They're targeting Yokohama, so I'm wondering if their objective is a certain something they can only find here. Though there is one in Kyoto, too."

"The Magic Association's sub-headquarters?" blurted out Kanon without waiting for Mayumi to get to the answer.

"More accurately, the association's main data banks," replied Mari with a dry grin, supplementing her answer. "The important data is all centrally controlled in Kyoto and Yokohama. It's still possible that they're after the academics who came to the Thesis Competition, though."

"When will the evacuation ships arrive?" said Mari, less a question than a prompt for confirmation.

Mayumi made a face like she wasn't sure. "The Coastal Defense Force transport ships should arrive in ten minutes. Apparently, they can't guarantee it'll be enough to cover everyone evacuating, though."

Her information matched what Tatsuya's group had gotten on the floor above. Which meant it was certain that not everyone would be able to evacuate.

"As for Nakajou and the others who headed for the shelter, it unfortunately looks like your worries were on the mark, Shiba," said Suzune in Mayumi's place. "They've been stopped in their tracks by guerillas. But it doesn't seem like there are many of them, and Nakajou contacted me to say they would eliminate them soon."

"And that's the situation," said Mari. "We don't know how much space the shelter will have, but unfortunately, we probably won't be able to get on that boat. I think the only thing we can do now is head for the shelter. What does everyone else think?"

Mayumi, Mari, Suzune.

Isori, Kanon, Sayaka.

Tatsuya, Miyuki, Erika, Leo, Mikihiko, Mizuki, Honoka, and Shizuku:

Those were the fourteen left here. Katsuto had already taken Kirihara, who had still been guarding Suzune, with him to start searching again for anyone who hadn't escaped yet.

The three seniors all had their mouths shut. They must have wanted to make their remarks after hearing what their underclassmen had to say.

"...I agree with Mari's viewpoint."

Kanon and the other juniors seemed to be under the impression that they didn't have a choice.

The freshmen's eyes all fixed upon Tatsuya.

Mari also looked at him for an answer...only to see his eyes pointing in an entirely different direction.

With lightning-fast motions, he brought his silver CAD up and pointed it at the wall.

"Tatsuya?!" came both Miyuki's and Mayumi's surprised voices at once.

Without answering, Tatsuya pulled the trigger.

Many from a third party were here in this place, and Tatsuya hadn't forgotten about that for a moment.

But he didn't have enough time to deal with the situation while protecting his secrets.

He'd noticed it almost by coincidence.

Maybe it was his Yakumo-trained intuition that told him. The man had instructed him over and over not to rely too much on just Elemental Sight.

Tatsuya, who had been overcome with a powerful sense of danger and expanded his "sight" beyond the wall, had picked up on the information of the massive object plunging toward them.

If Katsuto had been here, the situation would have been different.

If soldiers had jumped in, he could have left it to Mayumi, Mari, and the like.

Had she the time, he could have had only Miyuki deal with it, too.

But at that moment, the only thing that could respond to the big truck covered in armored plates crashing into the room was Tatsuya's magic.

Four yards high, three yards wide, and weighing thirty tons.

The truck, one allowed to be significantly larger due to advancements in road standards and to which many heavy protective plates were also attached, fell completely into Tatsuya's aim, and he triggered his dismantling spell, Mist Dispersion.

A moment later, the truck turned into dust and vanished.

The driver was flung out of the disappeared driver's seat, slammed into the ground, and collided with the wall.

Propelled by inertia, a powder of metal and plastic pounded the hall's wall, the only proof that the large piece of transportation machinery had ever existed. The outer wall only suffered minor scratches, with no damage to the inner wall.

But unfortunately, things were never so easy. Someone realized what had happened.

"...What was that?" asked Mayumi with much trepidation.

Tatsuya wanted to click his tongue in frustration. He was right to worry—Mayumi had witnessed the scene. She'd probably looked where he was looking, then peered beyond the wall with her perception-type spell Multiscope.

But fortunately—though it was still just putting off the problem—he didn't need to answer her.

Because Mayumi, who had left her expanded vision active, paled at a new sight:

A swarm of small missiles sailing toward them.

Tatsuya, who had also left his vision expanded, spotted them as well.

Looks like the invaders recognized everyone still in here as dangerous to combat, thought Tatsuya. With the capture of their forces in the hall, the battle outside the front entrance, and the truck being destroyed a moment ago, it looked like they'd changed their combat objective from point securing to annihilation.

As one part of his mind calmly analyzed the situation as though it was someone else's problem, another part was building up a spell to intercept the rain of portable missiles coming down.

But this time, he didn't need to do anything. A magical barrier, several layers thick, formed on the outside of the room's wall.

Before the missiles struck the new wall, a sonic boom fired into them from the side, and they exploded in midair.

"Sorry for the wait!"

Suddenly, a voice addressed them, and Tatsuya and Mayumi both returned to normal vision.

As though she'd timed the moment—and he wanted to believe she wasn't mean enough to do something like that—a woman had entered the waiting room.

"Huh? Wait, is that you, Ms. Kyouko?"

"It's been a while, hasn't it, Mayumi?"

Her sudden appearance completed, Fujibayashi greeted her old friend Mayumi with a smile.

◇ ◇ ◇

Katsuto had spotted the missile rain because he'd sensed the presence of powerful magic. Magicians perceived the usage of magic by the reactions of event alterations; however, the spell he'd sensed barely had any reaction at all.

Nevertheless, Katsuto knew that the world had just undergone a significant alteration.

It wasn't like Tatsuya had a patent on understanding the world beyond the traditional five senses. Katsuto used magic that altered spatial properties, so he possessed an acute awareness of changes in space.

Gravitational force was equivalent to the distribution of

mass—one of the most basic properties of space. By perceiving fluctuations in mass distribution, Katsuto could ascertain the movement and changes in objects. Even if the object with a lot of mass wasn't as big as a boat or a building, his senses had clued him in to a quantity of mass, which could only be called enormous, suddenly dispersing.

Katsuto didn't think he'd ever seen such a smooth event alteration on such a large scale. Rather than feeling threatened, he felt himself grow curious, so he paused his search for people who hadn't escaped yet and jumped to where the mass had dispersed.

Though difficult to imagine given his large frame, he was very good at spells that helped him move at high speeds, too. Leaving Kirihara behind, he leaped through the air as if sliding across it, then rounded a corner by altering his movement vector, and finally arrived at the wall outside the waiting room.

Had that been good luck or bad luck?

According to Mayumi or Mari, one could call it good.

One wouldn't know what Katsuto himself thought without asking him.

Because the moment he landed there, he was welcomed by portable missiles.

His reaction was almost a conditioned reflex.

In the blink of an eye, he constructed a multilayered wall—one that wouldn't even let air through, and one that could withstand heat up to two hundred thousand degrees. The heat wave from the missiles, which had blown up in midair for some reason, hit the barrier Katsuto had made, not leaving a single burn mark on the actual wall behind it.

Katsuto whirled around to where the shock wave that had blown up the missiles had flown in from. He saw an open-top military vehicle and a JDF captain standing in it, holding what looked like a missile launcher.

"A supersonic launcher... Would you happen to be from the 101st?" he called out to the vehicle as it neared, speaking politely.

The captain jumped out from the car, which had approached with almost complete silence—it seemed to use a hybrid system—and saluted Katsuto with a smile that looked like a sticker on his face.

"Shigeru Sanada, captain of the Japan Defense Force's 101st Brigade, Independent Magic Battalion. I'm much obliged that the current leader of the Juumonji would know who I am."

Katsuto's eyebrow twitched. But that was all, and that could be said to be due to his exceptional mental prowess for an eighteen-year-old.

"Apologies. We should both probably refrain from pointless chatter."

"...That fault is mine."

"Again, much obliged. Next leader of the Juumonji family—shall we go?" said Sanada, heading for the conference hall.

Katsuto had no idea what they wanted with him, but he decided that, for now, he shouldn't take his eyes off this soldier—since he clearly knew the secret circumstances in the Juumonji family.

The two lined up (one behind the other) and entered the assembly hall from the nearest entrance.

◇ ◇ ◇

Fujibayashi wasn't alone.

From behind her military field uniform (featuring thin slacks and short boots) came a man in the prime of his life, also wearing the uniform of the Japan Ground Defense Force—one with a major-rank badge on it.

The major came before Tatsuya, who was standing there bewildered, and clasped his hands behind him.

"Specialist, information control is temporarily revoked," said Fujibayashi from beside the colonel.

The bewilderment vanished from Tatsuya's face. He straightened and responded with a salute to the man in front of him.

Everyone else present, save for Miyuki, and including the just-arrived Katsuto, stared at him, unable to hide their shock.

The soldier answered Tatsuya's salute with one of his own, then looked to Katsuto and walked over to him. "Harunobu Kazama, major of the Japan Ground Defense Force. Please forgive me, as circumstances dictate I withhold my attachment."

Sanada had already revealed their attachment; Kazama was more considering the fact that Mayumi, Erika, and the others were listening.

"I see—so you would be Major Kazama. I am Katsuto Juumonji, representative agent of the Juumonji of the Ten Master Clans."

In response to Kazama's self-introduction, Katsuto openly stated his own name and public position in the magic world.

Kazama bowed slightly, then turned so that he could see both Katsuto and Tatsuya at once. "Fujibayashi, explain the situation to them."

"Yes, sir. In terms of our forces, the Hodogaya garrison is currently in combat with the invading forces. In addition, one battalion each from Tsurumi and Fujisawa are making their ways here posthaste. The Magic Association's Kanto branch has also assembled a volunteer army, which has begun taking action for self-defense."

"Thank you. Now then, Specialist…" After curtly thanking Fujibayashi, Kazama looked at Tatsuya and used the term *Specialist*. "Considering the uniqueness of the present situation, we've just received orders to join the defense despite being deployed on another mission in Hodogaya. In accordance with the special duty bylaws of the Japan Defense Force, I hereby order you into action."

The power of his stare, more than his stern words and grave tone, cut off any argument from Mayumi, Mari, and Kanon.

"Specialist, the MOVAL suits you designed are in the trailer," said Sanada. "We should hurry."

Tatsuya nodded to Sanada and turned back to his friends. "Sorry, but you heard them. I want all of you to evacuate with our upperclassmen," he said, lightly bowing in apology.

"Specialist, our team will accompany them," said Fujibayashi in support.

Tatsuya was honestly thankful for her—and the Major's—good offices in assigning some of their most elite for the sake of his friends in this situation, despite how few they had. "I would be grateful for that, Lieutenant."

"Roger that. You do your best, too, Specialist."

Tatsuya bowed to Fujibayashi, then followed Kazama out.

He'd apologized to his classmates, while completely ignoring his upperclassmen, but either both groups had a good enough grasp on the situation or were simply too baffled to stop him.

"Tatsuya, please wait a moment."

Instead, the one to call out to him, face tormented, was his sister, Miyuki.

Tatsuya looked at Kazama in silent question, and the man returned a nod before leaving ahead of him.

Miyuki went before her brother and reached her hand out to his cheek.

Her goal wasn't to stop him. Miyuki understood Tatsuya's position and duties just as well as he did. In fact, her biggest fear was to be an impediment to him.

What she was trying to do now…

Was something she had no right to do.

But Miyuki, on her own judgment, taking full responsibility, decided to do it anyway. She had resolved herself to undo the chains binding her brother.

Tatsuya saw the determination in her eyes.

His sister looked up at him with eyes full of confusion, understanding, and gratitude, all mixed together, and nodded. Tatsuya knelt down on one knee in front of her—like a knight bending before his princess.

Miyuki put her hand on his cheek, then brought her brother's face, his eyes closed, up to face her.

* * *

Then, she bent down...

...and kissed her brother's forehead.

Her lips parted, her hand pulled away from his cheek, and Tatsuya hung his head once again.

The change happened suddenly.

Particles of light, bright enough to burn one's eyes, seethed up from Tatsuya's body.

They weren't photons but rather the particles that were the wellspring of magic, wrapped in a light that wasn't natural.

Tatsuya opened his eyes and stood.

The psions, energized to the point of impossibility, raged around him in a whirlwind.

He was like a high king of storms, veiled in tempests and attended by thunderbolts.

The inconceivably intense radiance dimmed quickly, but the vast field of psions was still quietly swirling around him.

As everyone staggered one or two steps away from Tatsuya, Miyuki, with a graceful smile, pinched her skirt and curtsied to him.

"Use it as you like."

"I'll be back soon."

And with his sister's gaze—replete with every emotion imaginable—seeing him off, Tatsuya departed for the battlefield in the city of Yokohama.

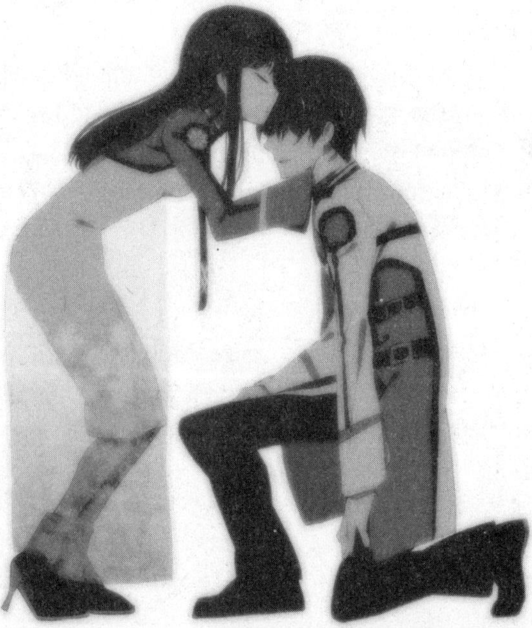

[11]

The battle between First High's band of students, faculty, and attendees who were evacuating through the underground tunnel, and the armed guerillas who had followed them, was nearing its end.

The evacuees numbered more than sixty. Given that the venue had been attacked right after First High's presentation, the number of students from the school who'd offered support was at a maximum.

While lamenting their unfortunate stroke of fate, Azusa managed to keep at least a facade of calm as the student council president.

Roars rang out farther up the passage, an exchange of gunshots and shock waves. It was the sound of Sawaki on the front lines, knocking over the handgun-toting guerillas.

They'd gotten everyone to cooperate in disabling the enemy's main weapons—assault rifles, submachine guns, and the like. Azusa had personally used a spell that placed an air mass inside a gun's muzzle to make it burst apart, disabling two rifles alongside their users.

She could see the results in front of her. Though this was a tunnel system, it wasn't the kind of secret passage from premodern times. It was very brightly lit.

And with all of their destruction, guerillas lay on the underground passage floor, covered in blood.

She wanted to squat on the ground and close her eyes from the gruesome sight. But she desperately held back her fear, keeping in mind the duty bestowed upon her as a representative of the student body.

Azusa had little knowledge regarding magical warfare techniques and combat command, but she didn't need to in the end: The members of the security team, carefully selected from the club committee and disciplinary committee, formed the main part of the group, thus far preventing the enemy from closing in.

Azusa fought back the bile rising in her throat and watched as Hattori and Sawaki, who had come running to them earlier, routed the guerillas. Watching was all she could do, but she felt it was still her duty to see this through to the end.

The enemy hadn't been numerous, so thankfully, none of their group had died.

However, magicians weren't immortal.

If you cut them, they would bleed, and if you shot them, they would die.

Magic-based defenses weren't all-powerful, either. If a bullet's kinetic energy was higher than a magical barrier spell's event-altering force, it would pierce right through.

So she felt it an unforgivable betrayal to avert her eyes from her allies, who were putting themselves at the forefront of risk to protect the students like her, who weren't cut out for battle.

Azusa watched carefully as Sawaki punched and kicked down the sporadically appearing guerillas and as Hattori offered magical support fire from behind him.

One guerilla fighter popped out from behind an obstacle, and Sawaki knocked him out before he could do anything.

Their enemies were informal soldiers of East Asian descent; their garb wasn't immediately distinguishable from civilian wear. You could tell them apart right away, once they brought their assault rifles and other big firearms to bear, but with them hiding handguns and combat knives as they approached, it was difficult to tell them apart from the civilians who had fled from the surface with them.

So, Sawaki gave up any pretense of trying to tell them apart. He hardened his defenses and struck down anyone who came to attack. But he could only adopt such a recklessly violent tactic because of his strength and heightened defenses.

Air Armor, a composite convergence-/movement-type spell: It constructed a layer of compressed air at relative coordinates one to two inches from his body's surface, which would bring any approaching object's relative velocity to zero.

This layer of air, formed along the curved surface of the human body, could cause high-speed, low-mass bullets to stray from their paths if he turned his body to lessen the angles of approach.

He immediately calculated the bullet's trajectory by the barrel's direction, then took the necessary evasive maneuver.

It wasn't only magic, and it wasn't only martial arts. His speed and technique were a fusion of both, and it made his foolhardy tactic of counterattacking bullets possible.

A fresh enemy lunged at him, slashing with a large knife.

Sawaki used a multicast to trigger an acceleration spell on himself.

His fist sped up to the speed of sound.

Then his fist, veiled in a layer of air, slammed into the sonic barrier.

The guerilla flew away with a boom.

The force behind the attack seemed excessive, but it was also to ward off new enemies.

It started to look like, for all the enemy's repeated threats, they were getting absolutely nothing out of attacking the students.

But just as human stamina was limited, so, too, was their determination. Sawaki's attack had hit two guerillas—the second having tried to slash from behind his ally—and smashed them into the underground passage wall together. And that, at last, was enough to break their morale.

It was when he saw out of the corner of his eye a mean-spirited classmate hurl a statically charged vapor mass after the fleeing rogues that Sawaki finally released the armor magic protecting himself.

◇ ◇ ◇

Fujibayashi's team was a small one, not even amounting to a squad. It consisted of only two off-road vehicles plus eight people (including Fujibayashi), but all of them had an air about them that intimated considerable skill.

"Mayumi, unfortunately…not everyone can fit," said Fujibayashi with an apologetic look.

The veteran air each individual soldier gave off had been overwhelming Mayumi. "Ah, no, I was planning to evacuate on foot to begin with…"

"I see. You won't be able to go very far like that. Where are you fleeing to?"

Fujibayashi had probably spoken to Mayumi rather than Katsuto because she was a familiar face, but Mayumi wished she'd consult him instead. He was doubtlessly more accustomed to these situations than her.

"The Hodogaya force has made Nogeyama their base of operations, and they've split into platoons to mop up the guerillas," explained Fujibayashi. "We haven't seen any movements from the camouflaged enemy ship in Yamashita Wharf yet, but it will almost certainly land a task force very soon. When that happens, the coastal regions will be caught right in the middle of the combat, so I think you would be better off fleeing inland."

"Umm…I think evacuating to the station shelter as planned would be a better idea," said Mayumi, unable to drive the doubt from her voice. She looked at Katsuto.

"Yes," said Katsuto, nodding immediately. "That would be best."

Mayumi sighed in relief.

The corners of Fujibayashi's lips turned up in amusement, but nobody, Mayumi included, noticed her modest smile. "We'll shore you up with cars in the front and back, so please come with us. We'll drive slowly, so you'll be fine," she said, heading for one of the vehicles. Mayumi and Mari followed her.

But Katsuto, instead of starting to walk, called out from behind. "Lieutenant Fujibayashi?"

"What is it?" she answered with no pause whatsoever, spinning around. The act looked swift enough to imply that she had expected this.

"I understand this is incredibly selfish, but would I be able to borrow one of your cars?"

That's crazy, thought all the assembled freshman ears. The group only had two cars, and they weren't just for ferrying people—they were for carrying weapons and ammunition.

But surprisingly, Fujibayashi only asked, "Where would you be taking it?"

"The Magic Association branch," Katsuto replied without hesitation. "As a member of the Master Clans Council, though only a proxy, I must fulfill my duty as a staff member of the association."

His tone reverberated to the pit of their stomachs. It was well beyond youthful heroism; it contained the resolution of someone with a mission.

"All right."

Fujibayashi's answer to that was truly a simple one.

"Sergeant Tateoka, Corporal Otowa. Escort Juumonji to the Magic Association's Kanto branch office."

Instead, Katsuto was the one unable to hide his bewilderment as Fujibayashi named two subordinates and lent him one of the vehicles. Then, she got in the other one, stood on its bed, and called out to Mayumi's group, "Let's get going. There's no time to waste."

◇ ◇ ◇

Third High's representatives and cheering group had decided on their course of action: to evacuate using the bus they had come in.

"Why did it have to be this far away...?"

"We can't help it. That's just how the city's made."

Their bus was parked in a large-vehicle lot a good distance away from the international assembly hall. When Masaki complained about it, Kichijouji rebuked him rather sharply.

It was already fortunate simply that they'd planned to have the driver wait here so they could go home after the competition instead of staying the night. The parking lot might have been far away, but it was still closer than the pier at which the evacuation boat would arrive, so Kichijouji considered complaining at this point reprimand worthy.

If there was one thing that made him feel uneasy, it was that the parking lot was south of the hall. In other words, it was near the pier where the camouflaged combat vessel was berthed. Still, the Third High students had a strong militaristic sense, so they were actually in high spirits, wanting to "kick the asses of those low-life invaders."

Having been forced to disarm themselves on the stage earlier seemed to have just kindled the flames even more.

That optimistic stance made Kichijouji nothing but more uneasy. "Strong militaristic sense" was easy to say, but only a handful of students had any real combat experience, with Masaki being at the top of the list. Kichijouji himself had no combat experience he could call real, and the teachers supervising the trip were all academic types.

In this world, only the feelings you wish were wrong turned out to be right.

The resignation that a certain mid-twentieth-century ship captain had felt upon discovering this unamusing rule must have felt like this, thought Kichijouji, because:

Immediately after arriving at the parking lot and laying his eyes on their bus...

…it took a direct hit from rocket artillery.

Fortunately—the only fortunate part about this—the rocket landed near the bus's back end, so the driver panicked and rolled out before he could get burned. The bus was actually made using the same kind of anti-heat, anti–shock wave armor plating and materials as military vehicles, so despite the glass breaking and the surface charring, it had no holes in it.

One of the tires, however, was done for. The heat and fragments had torn it apart.

"Bastard!" burst out Masaki from next to him.

In an attempt to be cautious and calm, Kichijouji turned his thoughts to assessment. To change the tire, they'd have to keep the enemies away from them. He decided to let his friend *break loose as much as he liked*.

He left Masaki's side and went to where the teachers were. "Sensei."

"What is it, Kichijouji?" asked one, his voice almost trembling, but nobly attempting to stay strong.

If Kichijouji didn't have so much faith in his classmate, he would have certainly sounded the same way. "Let's leave the enemies to Masaki while we get ready to change the tire."

"Get ready to? How…?"

"This parking lot is reserved for large or otherwise unique vehicles. They have a facility for doing simple repairs, so they should have spare tires there."

"I—I see! All right, anyone free, go with Kichijouji and look for a replacement tire!"

His teacher included "anyone free" because several others had gone straight into battle mode alongside Masaki.

Kichijouji, who was the calmest here despite being a freshman, took the initiative naturally. The other Third High students—classmates and seniors, and even the teachers—obeyed his instructions. They would make it out.

◇ ◇ ◇

The First High gaggle, led by Azusa, arrived at the underground shelter after the other schools.

They were late because they had more people than the others: sixty in all.

Normally, that wouldn't have been a big number. But it was a lot to keep so many evacuees together and secure, not to mention cautiously advancing while taking down attackers. The task was definitely a double-edged sword.

During a disaster, even doors were a problem, with enemy soldiers running rampant. Many evacuees were already inside, and they would have to persuade them to unlock any given door.

As they were waiting in an antechamber for the door to the underground shelter to open for them, Hattori and Sawaki were doing a roll call to make sure nobody had gone missing.

The faculty were performing their adult roles; Asuka was going around to look at the injured; Haruka was talking to students who looked uneasy; and Tsuzura was standing guard at the end of the line with Tomitsuka.

And from his position, Tsuzura was the first one to notice an abnormality.

"Everyone, cover your heads and get on the ground!"

A strange noise rang through the ceiling—the concrete was creaking.

The lights went out, and a curtain of darkness descended.

And then they heard cracks run through the ceiling and walls.

All of it happened before anyone could take a breath.

Some screamed.

Others just cowered.

And some threw together spells to hold up the iron, concrete, and dirt.

But whatever power they tried to use, they couldn't stop the underground tunnel from collapsing.

At the time, Azusa had been negotiating with the wired terminal on the shelter entrance, trying to get it open quickly.

When she'd reflexively turned around at Tsuzura's warning, she couldn't avert her eyes from the catastrophe happening right in front of her.

She couldn't shut them, either.

The ceiling collapsed, and the walls peeled away.

There was no danger of her getting caught in the collapse.

She was outside the door, but this part of the passage was covered in sturdy alloy.

But the other students…

"…Huh?"

However, when the dust settled and the lights from the passage leading to the shelter illuminated the hallway's collapse, no tears came from her eyes—instead, she muttered in surprise.

The First High students hadn't been buried alive.

The concrete fragments had formed an arch.

By some coincidence, the big concrete fragments had locked together in the shape of an archway, supporting one another's weight, leaving a space underneath tall enough to stoop inside.

No, there's no way this can be a coincidence… thought Azusa. The chances of this happening purely out of luck were infinitely close to zero.

…I see! Polyhedra Control! It's Mr. Tsuzura's spell!

Polyhedra Control, the name she'd shouted in her mind, was a spell that abstracted something's structure to a conglomeration of simple polyhedrons, then "controlled" those simple 3-D shapes—the structural elements—to manipulate large-scale changes.

Permanently changing one part of a single thing—that alone was considered to be one of modern magic's difficulties. If you wanted to stop the event of the underground passage collapsing, you would normally need to mark the entire passage as your target, but of course the fragments were each their own targets.

But by perceiving a single thing as a collection of multiple structural elements, Polyhedra Control could change one part of that single thing and thereby affect the entire thing.

Of course, you would need the analytical prowess to break up a single structure into multiple, smaller elements to do that, but magicians who could would be able to purposely demonstrate miracles created by impossible coincidences—just like now.

Tsuzura had probably realized that, for whatever reason, there was an immense pressure weighing down on the passage, and that a collapse was unavoidable. He'd used the dirt's pressure to control the falling fragments billiard-style and have them fall into an arch.

But this arch was still no more than rubble. It wasn't as sturdy as natural stone.

"Quickly, everyone! Over here!"

After Azusa shouted to the others, she immediately got back to work, desperately trying to open the shelter door.

As Asuka left to examine the injured, Chiaki, all alone in the midst of their group of sixty, was one of those who had simply cowered, unable to scream.

She knew the ceiling had collapsed. Parts of the walls were broken, too. So why wasn't she buried alive right now?

Chiaki nervously opened her eyes. The sight that flooded into her vision stunned her. The reinforcing bars and concrete fragments had come together like a complex jigsaw puzzle to create a small tunnel. She sank to the floor at the impossible coincidence.

Then—

"What are you doing?! You need to get out of there!"

A voice admonished her and someone grabbed her hand.

Her body lurched backward in surprise, and she reflexively tried to bat the hand away. But it was soft so that it wouldn't cause her pain, yet still firm enough that it would never let go of hers.

"Hurry!"

Without showing any concern for Chiaki's initial rejection, the hand pulled her away. She didn't hear any voices or feel anyone behind her. In her daze, she had apparently been the last one left. There was a weak light shining up ahead that must have been someone who had already escaped the rubble tunnel and was pointing a light in for her.

Right now, Chiaki's mind was blank. She just let herself be pulled along, in her painful half-risen posture, but kept running, never letting her feet stop.

The light grew in intensity, and she saw the end of the tunnel.

…And then she heard an ominous *grrrk*.

Part of the rubble was starting to collapse.

A vision of the end unfolded before her in slow motion.

The boy pulling on Chiaki's hand tugged her into an embrace. Then, he smacked his right hip with an empty hand.

Chiaki rocked, then felt an impact like her body had been uprooted.

As she flew, she held on as hard as she could to the chest at the base of those arms.

She realized her grip had only been from inertia once they'd made it out from the crumbling rubble and into the shelter.

After seeing Tomitsuka safely rescue the girl who'd fallen behind, Azusa heaved a sigh of relief.

But when she saw the girl's face, her heart, which had regained its calm, once again started pounding wildly.

Hirakawa's little sister…

As a fellow member of the Nine School Competition engineering team, she was friends with Koharu Hirakawa. The calm, elder Hirakawa was one of the easier upperclassmen for Azusa to get along with, and since they both excelled at engineering, they could talk on the same wavelength.

When Azusa had first heard that her younger sister had attempted sabotage, she'd doubted her ears. She'd never directly met her before, but from what Koharu would sometimes say, she didn't seem like the sort of girl to do that—so it shocked her more than the others.

Seeing her flustered, then looking down in embarrassment but glancing up at the boy's face now and again, she looked like a regular freshman.

I hope we wake up from this nightmare soon… Azusa thought.

Chiaki, having escaped a live burial by the skin of her teeth, breathed a sigh of relief now that she was under the sturdy alloy roof.

And finally, she calmed down enough to realize what state she was in.

"!"

Was that reaction time a personal best? she thought, mind still fortunately muddled. Fortunate in the sense that if her mind weren't muddled, she'd have been hallucinating.

In any case, she moved her limbs at full speed to escape the boy holding her. She couldn't bring her gaze up because she was too embarrassed, but at the same time, she couldn't help starting to wonder what his face looked like.

As a result, she ended up repeating the fairly suspicious act of keeping her head down but glancing up at him every once in a while, but the boy didn't seem particularly bothered by it.

"Are you okay? You should get inside."

The voice was worried about her.

She suddenly felt like she hadn't heard a voice like that in quite a long time. In her "partnerships"—in which she used others and was used in return—there was no caring for the other person, nor being cared for. Once she'd been caught without fulfilling her goal, it felt like everything anyone else said to her had been criticism.

But somehow, she could feel it from his voice—how nonchalantly this boy was worried about her.

"Ah, wait…"

As the boy was about to slip through the door ahead of her—as even then, he was looking at her, guiding her in—she unthinkingly grabbed his jacket.

"Umm…thank you…"

For now, that was all she could manage.

"Hm? You're welcome."

The fact that this boy, whose name she didn't even know, had plainly accepted her gratitude made her feel happy enough that even she thought it was strange.

◇ ◇ ◇

When Mayumi's party—with Fujibayashi's subordinates taking the lead—arrived in the plaza in front of the station where the underground shelter was set up, the disastrous scene there put them at a loss for words.

The plaza had completely caved in.

Giant hunks of metal swaggered atop where it had been.

"Upright tanks…? Where on earth did they come from?" came a groan from Fujibayashi's lips.

Mobile humanoid gun turrets, covered in compound armor plates. Their lower halves consisted of two short, stumpy legs with roller skate–like tracks on the feet, while their upper halves had long arms and neckless heads attached to one-person compact cars with all sorts of weaponry equipped to them.

They stood at a total height of about twelve feet, a ground-to-shoulder height of about nine feet, a width of about six feet, and a length of about eight feet. The machines were weapons originally developed in eastern Europe for the purpose of efficiently stamping out infantry in urban environments.

And there were two.

With a full ammunition load and a troop inside, it weighed about nine tons in total. Although the two of them would add up to eighteen tons, that wasn't enough to cause the paved, reinforced road to cave in like that.

Clearly, the upright tanks had delivered some kind of attack aimed at the underground shelter, or at the underground passage.

"You…!"

"Kanon, you can't use Mine Origin!"

In a moment recovering from her stupefaction, Kanon attempted to execute a spell, but Isori grabbed her arm and stopped her.

They didn't know what state the underground was in. Using magic to vibrate the ground in this situation could easily magnify the tragedy.

"That's not what I'm doing!"

Kanon shook off the hand and went to trigger her spell again.

She set her aims on the targets…

…when they suddenly filled with holes and froze into white ice.

"Ah…"

"As expected of Mayumi and Miyuki. We didn't even have time to act," praised Fujibayashi with a bit of a dry grin, as Kanon, next to her, stared in awe. Mayumi and Miyuki both returned a bow, Mayumi blushing a little and Miyuki with a slight smile.

"…It looks like those who went underground are safe. No traces of anyone being buried alive."

That report came from Mikihiko. He had his eyes closed, and his expression was distant. He'd probably been searching underground, giving over part of his senses to the spirits.

"I see. If someone from the Yoshida family says so, it must be true. Excellent work."

"Oh, no, it wasn't anything at all!"

Mikihiko, after Fujibayashi commended him, popped his eyes open in a fluster and gave a quick bit of deference. There were plenty of members in their group who would have loved to tease and make fun of his innocence, but…

"…So now what do we do?"

...what actually came was Erika, on point.

The fact that Fujibayashi didn't react a bit to the challenging tone must have simply been her years of maturity. "If they've gotten upright tanks this far inland, then the situation is escalating faster than we thought. I would personally recommend evacuating to the Nogeyama encampment."

"Won't that make us a target for the enemy forces, though?"

"Mari, they don't care whether we're combatants or not. It won't be any less dangerous to separate ourselves from the army. In fact, I think it would be more dangerous."

Mari had asked the question to keep things formal, but Mayumi gently shot it down.

"Do you think we should head for Nogeyama, then, Saegusa?" Isori's question also seemed natural.

But Mayumi shook her head. "I plan to call in a transport helicopter for the civilians left behind," she said, looking toward the station. There, the number of potential civilian losses under the crushed shelter entrance was increasing by the minute. "First I want to clear away that rubble, secure a landing zone, and then wait here for the helicopter to arrive. Mari, you take everyone and go with Ms. Kyouko."

"What are you saying?! You plan to stay here alone?!"

Her unexpected declaration, of course, made Mari lash out. But Mayumi's response was firm: "This is my duty as part of the Ten Master Clans. Under the Clans, we enjoy many conveniences. Officially, Japan has no aristocratic rank any longer, but for all intents and purposes, the clans can sometimes act freely without being restrained by the law. The price for that is needing to use our strength to help out in times like these."

"...Then I'm staying here, too," Isori answered. The determination in Mayumi's words appeared to have strengthened her resolve while losing Mari hers. "As a number-holding member of the Hundred, we get a lot of conveniences from the government, too."

"If Kei's staying, then I'm staying! I'm one of the Hundred, too!"

"Guess I'm sticking around, too. I *am* a daughter of the Chiba, after all."

"I will stay as well. I cannot sit idly by when my brother is out there fighting."

"M-me too!"

"I'll contact my father to see if we can send the company helicopter over, too."

"I'm not part of the Ten Master Clans or the Hundred…but if girls younger than me are saying they'll stay, I can't exactly tuck my tail and run."

"The same goes for me. I'm confident in my muscles."

"I'll stay, too. I'm not as strong as Eri or Kirihara, but I at least want to repent."

"The Yoshida aren't part of the Hundred…but we're alike in that we get favored treatment just the same."

"Umm, I don't know if I'll be any help, but if I can at least be everyone's 'eyes'…"

"Ichihara. Our underclassmen are all saying they'll stay here. We're not going to be the only two evacuating, are we?"

"Well, leaving Mayumi by herself would make me uneasy, too," Ichihara noted. "She can be surprisingly dull-witted sometimes."

"Hey!" Mayumi objected. "Still…I suppose we're all stupid." She sighed in a suffering way for real, not only as an act. Her pretty features now colored with resignation, she turned back to Fujibayashi.

"We've made our decision. Our kids are just so disobedient…I do apologize for letting your goodwill go to waste."

Mayumi bowed deeply while the rest of the group behind her looked away awkwardly. Fujibayashi, looking serious on the surface at least, was clearly amused. "How dependable. I'll leave a few of my people here, then."

"No, the situation doesn't call for that."

That voice didn't come from the First High side but from someone behind Fujibayashi.

"Oh, Chief."

YOKOHAMA INCIDENT OUTLINE 2

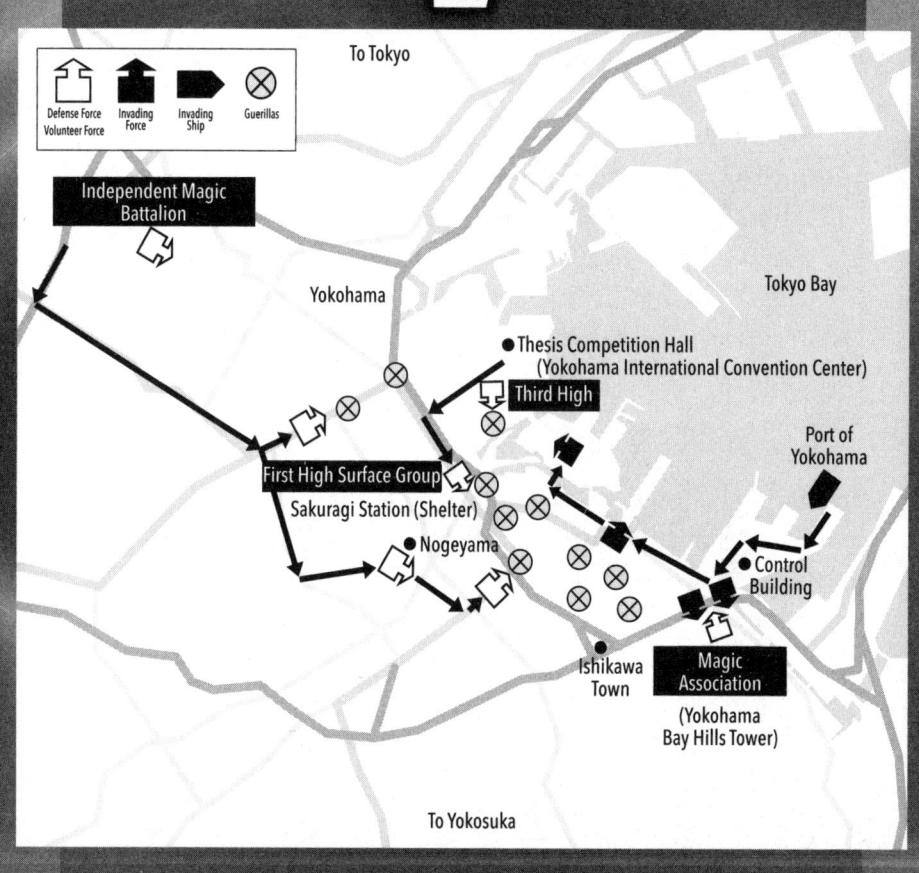

Legend:
- Defense Force Volunteer Force
- Invading Force
- Invading Ship
- Guerillas ⊗

Map labels:
- To Tokyo
- Tokyo Bay
- Yokohama
- Independent Magic Battalion
- Thesis Competition Hall (Yokohama International Convention Center)
- Third High
- Port of Yokohama
- First High Surface Group
- Sakuragi Station (Shelter)
- Nogeyama
- Control Building
- Ishikawa Town
- Magic Association (Yokohama Bay Hills Tower)
- To Yokosuka

OCTOBER 30, AD 2095
4:00 PM, PRESENT TIME

"Kazu?!"

Two different greetings for the same person.

Chief Chiba turned to face Fujibayashi, the former speaker. "The military's goal is to eliminate outside threats; securing civilians is the police's job. We'll stay here. Ms. Fujibayashi…er, Lieutenant Fujibayashi, please go join the main force."

"Understood. Chief Chiba, I'll leave the rest here to you."

One's appearance was too well-timed, and the other's words sounded rehearsed.

But without touching on either of those things, Fujibayashi made a crisp salute and ran off gallantly.

"Hmm…what a nice woman."

"Ah, it'll never work, Kazu. She's too good for you."

Upon receiving a merciless retort to his serious mutterings from his sister, Chief Chiba deflated just like a balloon and fell silent.

◇ ◇ ◇

The Third High students taking up arms against the guerilla fighters in the large-vehicle parking lot had dwindled to fewer than half their numbers—all unable to fight because they were unable to stop themselves from retching.

"Ichijou, go a little easier on them!" balked one upperclassman.

"No! Would you all please stand back?"

The cause of all this—Masaki—wasn't hearing any criticism.

His reddish, handgun-shaped specialized CAD pointed at the guerillas from a nation unknown…

…and a crimson flower blossomed and scattered.

The sound of another wet groan reached Masaki's ears.

Every time he sent an enemy to the grave, both their morale and the enemy's continued to fall.

If this is enough to scare them, they shouldn't have thought to stand on the battlefield to begin with, Masaki told himself, coolly ignoring the verbal and visual remarks the others were giving him.

His claim was right; it was a correct argument that left no room for complaint.

But how many soldiers were out there who could stay calm at the sight of human bodies bursting apart into showers of fresh blood (red blood cells, to be precise)?

The Ichijou family's secret technique, Burst: a spell that instantly vaporized the fluids inside a target.

Used on a human, the spell would cause blood plasma to vaporize; the pressure would burst out of a person's muscles and skin, and the solid components of blood—the red blood cells—would blossom into a flower of scarlet and crimson.

His fellow freshmen and upperclassmen, save for a handful of exceptions, had learned the true meaning behind "Crimson."

◇ ◇ ◇

Despite the camouflaged landing ship cleanly and successfully pulling off a surprise attack, the mood on the ship's bridge—its command center—was far from smooth sailing.

"We've lost contact with the agents who were headed to secure the shelter. No response from the upright tanks."

The captain of the camouflaged landing ship, also the commander of the invading forces, frowned at his communications officer's report. Their strategy had planned for the agents already on the inside to secure hostages, then send all their mobile troops in.

The losses among their casual-clothed agents were a lot more severe than they'd expected. The forces they'd sent to the international assembly hall and the large-vehicle parking lot, in particular, had taken heavy damage.

Unfortunately, the captain decided, they'd have to change the plan. The diversion could no longer be sustained by their undercover agents alone.

"Send in the mobile troops."

Thus, he ordered the mobilization of his upright tanks and armored cars—deployed *in the country that had made them.*

◇ ◇ ◇

"...So? What are you doing here, Kazu?"

In a corner of the station plaza, the Chiba siblings were busy having a not-exactly-heartwarming time enjoying (?) each other's presence. (At the very least, the brother was enjoying it, so that statement was half-correct.)

They were in a corner because neither Erika nor Toshikazu was fit for the jobs of cleaning up the upright tank wreckage, dragging out the pilots and interrogating them, or preparing the road so that the helicopters could land—though it was suspicious whether Toshikazu, the acting chief of police, was cut out for interrogation.

In any case, both of them were out of work. (Though one might add that, in order to protect their honor, so were Kirihara and Sayaka.)

But at the very least, Toshikazu didn't seem bothered by being treated as useless—which Inagaki had already done—and instead seemed to be enjoying his conversation with his quick-tempered, bellicose sister.

"You wound me. Why is it strange at all for a kindhearted brother to want to give his dear sister a hand?"

"Kindhearted?! The freaking nerve you have to say that, you hypocrite..."

"Come on, Erika. A girl shouldn't be using vulgar words like 'freaking.'"

"Who! Gave you! The right! To start telling me to behave like a proper lady after everything you've done?!"

"My, my, how sad… This is what I get for all my love for my little sister."

That must have been too shameless, and Erika's flared emotions cooled right down. She turned around, then glared at him coldly.

Toshikazu sighed, fed up. "I really did come to help you," he said in an uneven tone, face unamused. When his sister snorted at him, he gave her a mean smile. "Should you really be acting like that, Erika?"

"What?"

The girl appeared to flinch a little. Her sense of weakness against people who were strictly stronger than her—which she has had with him since she was a lot younger—wasn't something she could wipe away that easily.

"I brought you a nice present."

"A present? Hmph, I don't need it."

Still, her tough talk—her pride—wasn't broken. To her, Toshikazu Chiba was someone she couldn't yield to a second time.

For Toshikazu, that was a good thing, something he'd wanted from her when she was little.

"Don't say that. Today it's something you need."

To Toshikazu, little Erika was his cute sister who always made him want to tease her. But right now, she was even stronger than back then, which made her even cuter. As he thought about how it would make him sound like a villain—or defeated—if he said something like "I'll do you a favor and leave it at that for today," he took a long, slightly curved object out of the station wagon he was lounging against.

When Erika saw the object's silhouette, her eyes went wide and she couldn't say anything.

Toshikazu took off the long, slender bag and offered the extra-long sword to her.

Its length of seventy inches was far more than Erika's own height. Just the blade itself was fifty-five inches.

But for a katana, it had a mysterious lack of curvature.

"The Orochi-Maru? Why did you bring it here…?"

"Why? That's a silly question, Erika. The Orochi-Maru is a sword for creating the Mountain Tsunami, and you're the only one who can do that. Neither our father nor Naotsugu can use the spell. They can trace its form, but you're the only one who can say she can actually *use* it. That means the Orochi-Maru is the katana for you."

Erika's hands quivered as they took the long sword offered to her. She gripped it tightly to prevent her body from tipping over from the weight, and her trembling finally stopped.

The strongest weapon ever created by the Chiba family. A secret weapon they claimed to be their masterpiece, along with the Ikazuchi-Maru, a sword-shaped, integrated armament device.

Even if it was only for a short time, Erika never thought she'd be allowed to wield this katana freely.

"You seem happy."

Her face pricked up at her brother's voice.

Her heart had been taken by the Orochi-Maru to the point where she had forgotten to be rebellious against him.

Because this katana was…

"Are you that happy about holding your favorite sword, your other self, Erika? Heh…I knew it. No matter what Dad thinks, or what Naotsugu thinks, you are a daughter of the Chiba."

"…Hmph! I guess I'll thank you this one time."

"I told you, girls shouldn't be talking like that…"

Without listening to her brother's pronouncement all the way through, Erika spun around.

She swiftly left, the Orochi-Maru in hand.

Toshikazu smiled gleefully at his sister's transparent attitude.

"Find anything out?"

Isori, who had his upper body inside the upright tank's cockpit item from which they'd dragged the pilot, pulled himself out in response to the voice, turned around, and shook his head. "Nothing. I'm not very knowledgeable about weapons like these, but I think it's an old model they sell in used marketplaces. I couldn't find anything on it to pinpoint what country it's registered to."

"They have marketplaces for used weapons?" asked Mayumi, surprised.

Isori smiled and nodded. "There's a market for used fighter jets, too. Even World War II weapons are still around for pocket conflicts."

"Huh," said Mayumi, impressed.

Isori began to smile even wider, but then something disturbed the air next to him. He didn't have to turn around to know who it was. He tightened up, loosened his expression, and looked at Mayumi once again. "Of course, even in used marketplaces, it's easiest to get weapons from allied nations. This upright tank seems to be from eastern Europe, so I'd say the chances are high that these agents are from the Great Asian Alliance… But to know the mastermind for sure, I don't think there's any option but to make the pilots tell us."

"But will they tell us the truth?" Kanon asked.

Mayumi shrugged. "That's where we rely on Mari's skill."

"Then I'm going to go help them clear the space out," Isori offered with a bow.

As she watched him leave with Kanon right behind him, Mayumi went over to Mari and the others who were going to be doing the interrogation.

Aside from minor freeze wounds on their faces, the two tied-up pilots had no notable injuries.

Inagaki was interrogating one while Mari was questioning the other.

"How's it looking?" Mayumi asked simply, upon approach to the latter.

Mari seemed a little irritated. "Nothing. If I knew it was going to come to this, I would have brought stronger perfume…"

"It's not your fault. Our condition for questioning Sekimoto today was not to use chemicals."

Known as a personal-combat specialist, Mari was more skilled in the use of small firearms and chemical weapons than magic or swords.

One of her special techniques was to control airflows in order to nasally administer volatile medicines only to enemies. She also had a more secret technique—a wicked (actually, outright illegal) method of having a specific target smell mind-altering perfume. Just now, she'd tried to sneak some of that perfume onto the person they had tied up, but unfortunately, she'd seen no effect.

"Guess we'll just have to torture him," Mari muttered.

"Wait, you can't just do that…" Mayumi protested.

"It's fine," Mari replied. "I'm confident I can give just the pain and none of the injuries."

"That isn't what I mean! Ugh…Mari, why don't you take a break?"

"…Yeah, I guess. I'll do that."

She probably felt somewhat like her mind had melted into soup.

Mari waved to Mayumi, then walked over to where Suzune was sitting on a bench with a map spread out in front of her.

On the pavement in front of the bench Suzune was sitting on was a highly precise map of the area enlarged to three by four yards. Suzune had called up the map on her terminal, and Honoka was refracting light to project it.

The map showed a detailed view of the coastal area from Sakuragi Town to Yamashita Town. Then, Honoka projected ships, crowds of people, and buildings onto it.

"Hey, that's really something."

"Oh, Watanabe!"

The image projected on the road shook and collapsed but soon returned to a clear image.

Suzune's fingers danced busily on the keyboard of her fully

opened notebook terminal, until finally pressing the Enter key to finish. She looked up. "Did you find anything out?"

"Unfortunately, no." The answer put a bitter look on Mari's face as she shook her head. But then, Mari went right back to her brimming-with-curiosity expression. "But this looks pretty hopeful."

"Yes. Thanks to Mitsui, I have a good grasp on the current enemy troops and their movements… Mitsui, that's enough."

Honoka smiled widely at Suzune's praise and nodded. At the same time, the map on the road disappeared.

"Even for light-controlling spells, isn't this level of precision kind of unusual?"

"Yes. I have no memory of anyone being able to display a clear, low-altitude reconnaissance plane image just by bending light. As it is, we should consider it a different kind of spell than normal light-refracting ones."

Honoka's face reddened at the flatly spoken praise from Suzune. "No, I… Compared to Tatsuya and Miyuki, my magic isn't much."

"You don't need to be modest, Mitsui. Sure, those two are pretty strong, but sometimes information can change a battle more than attack power."

"That's right, Mitsui. Getting a comprehensive grasp on the situation like this is extremely meaningful. We don't have any way of communicating with unmanned reconnaissance craft or stratosphere cameras, so this spell only you can use is incredibly beneficial."

"Thank you!" said Honoka, blushing even more.

The two seniors grinned at her. With all the insolent (?) underclassmen around, such an unspoiled reaction felt fresh.

◇ ◇ ◇

Although coastal roads were the quickest way from the international assembly hall to Yokohama Bay Hills Tower, where the Magic Association's branch offices were, using a more inland route wouldn't be too much of a detour. The enemy forces set to storm the building consisted of a landing team dumped out by a war vessel of unknown affiliation. The troops who had been hidden throughout the city were also very active along the coast.

But when asked whether they would take the long way around, Katsuto shook his head.

And now, the army vehicle he occupied was heading for Bay Hills using the shortest possible ocean-side route—straight through the crossfire.

The closer they got to Bay Hills—technically, the closer they got to Yamashita Wharf—the heavier the enemy's armaments became. The frequency at which he spotted invading mobile weapons (upright tanks, to be exact) was rising steadily.

"It's not that their forces are concentrated here but that they're still expanding outward as we speak," explained Sergeant Tateoka from the passenger's seat.

Katsuto returned a wordless nod. Not because he looked down on the low-ranking officer but because he was devoting most of his focus to magic.

A moment later, a small group with a multibarreled missile launcher came onto the street from a side road in the direction they were going. They weren't the ones in civilian dress. Nothing on their clothing made it clear what country they were from, but they all wore field gear of uniform design. It was unmistakably part of the enemy landing force.

The small unit fired four portable missile shots, probably anti-tank missiles, at the vehicle Katsuto was on.

It was essentially point-blank range. However slow the missiles started out, an off-road car wouldn't have been able to avoid it like that.

But Corporal Otowa, gripping the steering wheel, showed no dismay as Sergeant Tateoka stationed an automatic rifle over the windshield.

The missiles struck the air five yards in front of the car. Explosive flames licked at a hemispherical barrier covering the vehicle.

Bullets fired from within mowed the enemy soldiers down.

They wouldn't let any outside attacks penetrate, but every attack from inside got out.

This clear, directional barrier was, needless to say, Katsuto's area-of-effect spell.

He altered the properties of a thin hemispherical space centered on him to disallow penetration by large foreign objects with more than a fixed amount of heat and oxygen molecules.

Even with the car moving quickly, Katsuto's defensive spell never wavered.

During this short process, Fujibayashi's subordinates had already realized firsthand what his nickname, the Iron Wall, meant.

◇ ◇ ◇

The Independent Magic Battalion was graded a "battalion," as a strategic unit that operated independently, but in terms of numbers, it was only as large as two companies. Today, they had sent out fifty of them for their original mission—field tests for magi-tech weapons. There was enough new equipment packed into the two large armored trailers for that many.

"...How does it look, Specialist?"

"Amazing as always, sir. I take my hat off to you."

Sanada, standing in front of a hangar, on which was what looked like a single-piece riding suit with protectors on it, nodded proudly several times. "The size should be just right. Hurry up and get changed."

At Sanada's request, Tatsuya removed everything he was wearing. Female officers and soldiers were in the trailer, but no one involved was bothered.

In a sense, all the soldiers in the Independent Magic Battalion were test subjects, and full-body inspections were nothing unusual.

Not only would male soldiers see the female soldiers stark-naked, the reverse happened sometimes as well. You couldn't make it in this line of work if that petrified you with embarrassment.

Tatsuya quickly put on the special underwear, then briskly got into the black one-piece—the MOVAL suit. He wrapped a thick belt around his waist, then clicked it into the suit's joints. After placing his personal CADs in the holsters on either hip, he slipped on his full-face helmet, which had a removable mask.

"No problems, looks like."

"None, sir. Errors are within acceptable bounds."

Tatsuya's voice came over a speaker inside the trailer. Realizing the communicator was set to On by default, he manipulated the helmet and took off the mask covering his mouth.

"In addition to the usual bulletproofing, heatproofing, and shock absorbing, we got the simple power assistance in there just as specified. And of course, the flight unit is packed into the belt. It's also made to be used in tandem with the shock absorbers as a reaction canceler, so you'll be able to shoot from the air."

"All I can say, sir, is wonderfully done. This has higher specs than my design."

"Hey, you let me do a good job on it." Sanada sought a handshake from Tatsuya, and as their hands tightly gripped each other's, Kazama arrived.

"Sanada, satisfied now?"

As his subordinate silently saluted, Kazama gave him a stare, then moved his gaze to Tatsuya. "Let's get right to it. Specialist, I want you to meet up with Yanagi's team. They're holding off an enemy unit in front of the bridge connecting to Mizuho Pier."

"You can display Captain Yanagi's position on your visor."

"Understood, sir."

Tatsuya placed his mask back on, and after confirming his position relative to the Yanagi team, he headed out of the trailer.

He jumped out without using the ramp, and while he still had momentum, he hit his belt buckle.

It was the switch for the flight magic CAD.

Tatsuya lightly kicked off the ground and dashed off, up into the sky.

◇ ◇ ◇

The invading army of unknown affiliation that had landed a mobile force at Yamashita Wharf was split into two units.

One was their advance force, which would head straight to Bay Hills, where the Magic Association was. The other would advance north along the coastline.

Instead of joining the guerillas stalled by Third High, the northbound force took a detour around them, moving to chase down the civilians trying to escape via water.

Their movements were known to the Independent Magic Battalion—an advance force of six-wheeled armored combat vehicles with a focus on mobility.

As they reformed their ranks into two lengthwise lines, their armored vehicles flooded toward the bridge and Captain Yanagi grinned from beneath his helmet.

He was the definition of an anti-personnel combat magician.

His specialty was a close-combat skill where he predicted his opponent's movement vector, then used a combination of martial arts and magic to guide, amplify, or reverse the enemy's course. An armored unit like this was something he'd rarely been up against before—at least, before being assigned to the IMB.

Because the IMB's leader was a user of old magic, they had a relatively large number of old-style magicians compared to the rest of the 101st Brigade, but Yanagi was a model old-style caster even among them.

Yanagi had inherited physical movement skills where he substituted symbolic hand gestures with the actions in kata themselves as a trick to utilize magic in the midst of a swordfight or brawl. He even kept well away from having to handle his CAD, wary of the time loss that created.

But even he had to admit how practical specialized CADs were for building large-scale spells that could flip over huge weights of many tons at the mere flick of a trigger. If he'd wanted to trigger this kind of spell using hand gestures or some substitute ritual, it would have taken him at least five seconds. With the enemy right in front of them, he didn't have that kind of time.

I don't like this, he thought, though his lips were still twisted into a smile.

A bestial smile carved into his face under the mask, Yanagi jumped out from behind his cover and toward the front of the armored-car lines.

As a man in a full-body black armor suit.

A man who was alone.

The armored cars' turrets didn't fire, probably out of surprise at such an unexpected enemy. Or perhaps they planned to run over the lone soldier with their giant wheels.

There was far too much of a discrepancy in defense between an armored car and an armored suit. And Yanagi had no intention of sticking around in front of their guns in the first place.

He pulled the trigger of his bayonet rifle–shaped CAD, saw the spell go off, then dived behind cover again.

Immediately, dust appeared to spring up and engrave a line into the road.

Any armored-car wheel that touched that line was sent into the air.

A series of earth-rattling tremors told Yanagi the result of the magic he'd used.

A line of armored cars turning over, colliding with nearby cars…

Upon closer inspection, he could tell that the vehicles proceeding east were ending up on top of the vehicles heading west, and flipping.

The acceleration-type spell Floor Flip: By severing the earth's gravity on a north-south axis for a moment, the spell's targets would have their eastern part lifted up by the planet's centrifugal force, causing them to topple to the west.

Bullets rained down from the sky, aimed at the armored cars' undercarriages. The attack came from his team members, who had risen into the sky in tandem with his spell. The bullets fired from their rifle-shaped, integrated-armament CADs had added penetrative effects, and they easily pierced the landmine-equipped armored-car bottoms.

The cars, their fuel tanks shot through and now on fire, bounced upward, pushed from below.

It seemed the defensive personnel inside the invaders' attack vehicles specialized in repulsion. Their strong barriers brushed aside the ten-ton objects, and they would doubtlessly nullify most shots from normal firearms. They were very clearly strong magicians—or perhaps just loaded with systems that amplified magic.

Another barrage of bullets showered down from the sky.

The influence of the spell to strengthen the bullets, and the spell to reflect them, dug into one another and canceled each other out.

The armor-piercing ammunition dug into the armor but didn't penetrate.

The armored cars' machine-gun turrets angled upward, then loosed a volley of large-bore bullets into the sky.

Two of his team members lost their posture and fell to the ground. One appeared to have been hit in his leg, the other in his gut. Thanks to the bulletproofing on their suits, the attack didn't result in wounds that tore their bodies completely apart.

Yanagi, who saw all that from behind cover, jumped out in front of the enemy again, then pulled the trigger three times in succession.

His Floor Flip spell cut off the earth's gravity. It didn't interfere with the information attached to its targets.

So regardless of the defensive spell on the enemy's vehicles, the gravity-severing magic activated.

Their armored cars rocketed over backward.

The magical barrier protecting them must have ceased from the impact of their fall, because the bullets from above began to pierce the armored-car hulls, sending the last three of them up in crimson flames.

◇ ◇ ◇

The speed that flight magic could output depended on how trained the magician was with the spell. Tatsuya, who had built the spell from square one, understood it better than anyone. For the flight magic he used, the distance between IMB's mobile HQ trailer and Yanagi's position was practically within hailing range.

The scenery flew by. Tatsuya had honed his perception of moving objects quite a bit in training, but given that flying in the sky wasn't something humans could naturally do, he wasn't confident in his motor functions. He was paying close attention to obstacles in flight by using his physical eyes, along with Elemental Sight as a kind of radar.

And thanks to that, he noticed something:

A small flying object about three feet long. The canard craft, painted all in black, had to be a low-altitude unmanned reconnaissance craft. It was circling the air above his destination—the area in which Yanagi's unit was currently engaged.

To avoid magical detection, Tatsuya first ascended high above the craft, then brought his CAD to bear in his right hand and turned off his flight magic.

He dropped, upside down. When he'd gotten the closest he could to the craft, he cast his dismantling spell, Mist Dispersion.

The unmanned reconnaissance craft instantly turned to dust and scattered into the wind.

Tatsuya reactivated his flight spell and prepared to make landfall.

◊ ◊ ◊

When one of the video feeds from their unmanned recon craft suddenly ceased, the invading army's command center didn't quite turn into a panicked mess, but the chaos that ensued was close to it.

It wasn't as though that one craft they'd lost their link with had been their only one, but the small planes were expensive, so they didn't bring any extra. They'd doubtlessly lost an invaluable "eye."

Launching an attack deep into enemy territory meant, on the flip side, isolating yourself in the middle of enemy territory. The fact that they'd lost a means of keeping track of the situation put no small pressure on them.

◊ ◊ ◊

When Tatsuya joined Yanagi, the initial battle had already ended. Yanagi was overseeing the treatment of the injured.

"Perfect timing, Specialist."

Before Tatsuya could address him, Yanagi had spotted him and called him over.

After crisply saluting, Tatsuya peered at an injured man lying on the ground with his suit off.

"The bullet went through. Can I leave this to you?"

Nothing worthy of calling an expression was on Yanagi's face as he took off his helmet, but his eyes couldn't completely hide what he felt deep down.

"Yes, sir" came the definite reply as Tatsuya rejected the man's guilt and pulled out the silver CAD from the holster on his left hip.

The injured soldier's low groaning stopped, and instead, Yanagi heard the slight sound of teeth grinding from inside Tatsuya's closed mouth.

◊ ◊ ◊

Suzune, having gotten a bird's-eye image of the invading army with Honoka's magic, realized their forces were smaller than she'd expected.

"Maybe, but doesn't it seem like the battle lines are expanding pretty quickly?" asked Mari.

"There is no real battle line at the moment," replied Suzune without reserve. "The internal battles are happening at points. The guerillas that infiltrated are wreaking havoc on transportation and communication, and the landing force is heading straight for their objective of taking control... I believe this is a fundamental strategy invaders tend to use."

"If you say so, Rin... But what is their objective, then?"

As Mayumi cocked her head, Suzune pretended to think about it for a moment. "...One possibility is your prediction—the Magic Association's Kanto branch offices. That one is for certain; their other objective appears to be going after civilians trying to escape by sea, but I believe they may want hostages."

"Hostages?" repeated Mayumi reflexively.

Suzune's answer was careful. "It doesn't seem like killing civilians is their objective, in and of itself. If it were, I think they would have invaded with artillery ships rather than landing ships. They could be after a prisoner exchange, or a ransom... I don't know their end goal, though."

"Which means they probably won't be in danger of artillery and missiles suddenly coming at them," said Mari, analyzing the situation under Suzune's lens.

"Most likely. But if they want hostages, it's highly possible this is one of their targets," said Suzune, looking behind her at the group of civilians gathered in the hall in front of the ticket gates.

"Going by what Ms. Kyouko said earlier, reinforcements from Tsurumi should be arriving soon," Mari added. "Considering their route, they should be going to secure the civilians at Mizuho Pier, then have their remaining forces start mopping up."

"Yes, I think so, too," Suzune agreed.

"If they're after hostages, they'd naturally end up here, where defenses are thin… I'll— Hmm. I'll go join Kanon's group," Mari proposed.

"Yes… They may not have many people, but Miyuki is there," Mayumi agreed.

"Yeah. That girl's freezing magic is practically on a tactical level." Mayumi and Mari exchanged dry grins. Both of them were probably thinking, *Just like her brother…*

"…But, Mari," Mayumi cautioned, "don't do anything rash. You won't have an easy time against mechanized units."

"I know that."

After watching Mari run off at a trot, Honoka, who was standing nearby, nervously spoke up to Mayumi, who had remained. "Umm, should I intercept them, too? I can't stand at the front, but I think I could back them up."

Honoka probably had to muster every ounce of courage to make the offer, but Mayumi smiled and swung her head left and right. "I'll need your help when the helicopter arrives, Honoka. And Miyuki and Kanon's job isn't to intercept—it's to keep watch. We're not professional combat magicians; we don't need to expose ourselves to danger for it, and we shouldn't be fighting anyway. In fact, we should think about running away."

Mayumi ended her sentence with a mischievous tone to discourage her.

But Honoka was more than half-certain Miyuki and Erika wouldn't ever run away. She looked over at Shizuku, unease wavering in her eyes, and saw that her friend had the same look as she did.

The team that Mayumi had mentioned keeping the watch—in reality an interception team—indeed decided to split into two groups along the invasion paths Suzune had predicted. When they arrived at the fork, Kirihara abruptly said to Sayaka, "Look, Mibu…I'd rather you stay in the back."

Sayaka was more confused than surprised as to why he'd say that at this point. "Kirihara, I'm a swordsman, too. I'm prepared for a true battle or two."

"Just stop!" Kirihara blurted. Sayaka opened her eyes wide in confusion and froze. "Mibu, please, don't talk about battle that lightly!"

"...Kirihara?"

"Kirihara...what are you mad about?"

After the sincerely perplexed questions from Sayaka and Erika, who had been watching, Kirihara calmed down enough to get his thoughts in order. "I just...don't want your sword to get blood on it."

Taken aback by the unexpected words, Sayaka gave him the argument that scarcely needed saying. "But...swords were originally made for—"

"I know all that!" he interrupted. "Swords are tools for fighting people. Unlike spears and bows, they were made with the intent to kill people from the start. You're right—anyone who uses them needs to prepare to draw blood one day."

Kirihara accepted what Sayaka was trying to say. But then, he attempted to reject that reasoning: "But *kendo* doesn't need to be an art that uses real swords, does it? Isn't it okay for a killing form to create a sport?"

Sayaka and even Erika felt enough passion from their classmate that they listened intently.

"When I... In middle school, when I saw Mibu's swordsmanship, I thought it was amazing. Amazing that the art of wielding a sword could be polished that much to turn into something that beautiful. The art of the sword— No, the *way* of the sword, without any of the terrible killing aspect, purely for bettering oneself. A beautiful form, one that I couldn't imitate. I remember thinking that I wanted her swordsmanship to stay that beautiful, to keep ascending in that beauty. So, well... Agh, I can't find the right words!"

"I understand, Kirihara."

As Kirihara wracked his brain over how to properly express himself, Erika responded in a different tone than usual.

"During club recruitment week, Saya's swordsmanship had been advancing in the *correct* direction, but you didn't think so, right? It might have been right for a sword, but wrong for *kendo*." She paused. "All I know about swords is how to kill people with them, even more than you, but that wasn't how it looked to me."

"Eri..." said Sayaka worriedly; Erika's tone was more gloomy than usual. Kirihara, meanwhile, was struck dumb with surprise.

"But, Kirihara, Saya has to be the one to decide," Erika added, piercing his gaze with a firm look of her own. "Real battle is definitely different from practicing together. I don't think you're wrong to want to keep blood off Saya's hands, and her sword. But I think Saya's feelings are just as correct. She doesn't want the one she likes to be in danger, and she wants to fight for him."

Sayaka and Kirihara were both blushing. The phrase *one she likes* probably embarrassed them. But they seemed to know full well this wasn't the time to act bashfully or feel teased by it.

"...Aha, listen to me. I don't even sound like myself."

In fact, it was Erika herself who couldn't endure the embarrassment anymore, but neither Sayaka nor Kirihara criticized her.

"Time for the third wheel to step aside, huh? Talk it over and decide what you'll do."

At that, Erika walked off in a hurry.

Sayaka and Kirihara exchanged a glance, and then calm returned to them.

◇ ◇ ◇

Masaki and Kichijouji of Third High didn't know that the enemy line didn't go very deep for lack of any bird's-eye recon tools.

The total invasion force consisted of one landing ship (or rather, one ground troop transport) disguised as a large cargo vessel and the guerilla fighters who had infiltrated beforehand. After all, the goal of their military action wasn't to spread out their forces and continuously establish points of control.

"Is it over already…?"

Masaki, who wasn't aware of that, was dubious of the enemy waves running out, and it wasn't only because he liked to fight.

"There's no way for us to know if that was it. We don't have any way to get information."

Masaki's mutterings received an answer from Kichijouji, who had walked up to him from behind.

He was the only one around him. There were no allies at his sides, and only blood-covered corpses in front of him.

"If we're going to escape, we have to do it now."

Masaki put his handgun-shaped CAD with its glossy, reddish sheen back into his pocket and turned around as Kichijouji continued, face serious.

"We're finished changing the tire, so we should hurry back to the bus."

Masaki looked around; most of the students who had been engaging the enemy were clustered near the bus.

"Let's go," urged Kichijouji. "We should leave as soon as possible."

But Masaki shook his head.

"What is it?"

"I'm going straight from here to the Magic Association."

"That's crazy!" Kichijouji cried, eyes widening. "For what, even?!"

Masaki drew closer with an oddly cold look. "To join the reinforcements. The association's magicians won't be sitting around in this situation. They'll obviously be putting together a volunteer force to add to the defense."

"But that doesn't mean—"

"And I'm an Ichijou."

The quickly spoken words made Kichijouji suck in his breath. "...Are you bothered by what happened before? Nobody meant anything by it. They just aren't used to this, that's all. It wasn't like you were—"

"That's not bothering me," Masaki interrupted, shaking his head. "I wanted to throw up the first time I went out on a battlefield, too. I didn't actually do it, though," he added with a wry grin.

Kichijouji felt like he saw loneliness cross his face.

"Plus, here we've been thrown into the battle without any preparation, good equipment, or reliable officers. This was the worst first battle I can think of."

"Exactly! Nobody means anything by how they were acti—"

"I said that's not why," Masaki interrupted again as Kichijouji desperately rationalized it—though knowing that's what he was doing stung Masaki a little. "I can't say anything specific, but the Ten Master Clans have a responsibility to the Magic Association. I can't pretend I didn't see anything and run away. Not as the eldest son of the Ichijou."

Masaki clapped his friend's shoulders, then headed in the direction opposite the bus.

"Then I'll go with you!" Kichijouji managed to shout, stopping him. "I'm your adviser. If you're joining the volunteer force, then I will, too!"

"George, you make sure everyone escapes safely," said Masaki, turning his head to look at him from the side. "This city is still a war zone; we don't know what'll happen. To be honest, I'd be too worried about you getting out safely with just our teachers and seniors to focus on fighting." He turned back around.

"...All right, Masaki. I'll take responsibility for getting them out safely, so you come back safely, too." *Because you're the only "general" I have,* he added reluctantly to himself.

Masaki answered by raising one of his hands, back still turned to him, and headed for farther battlefields.

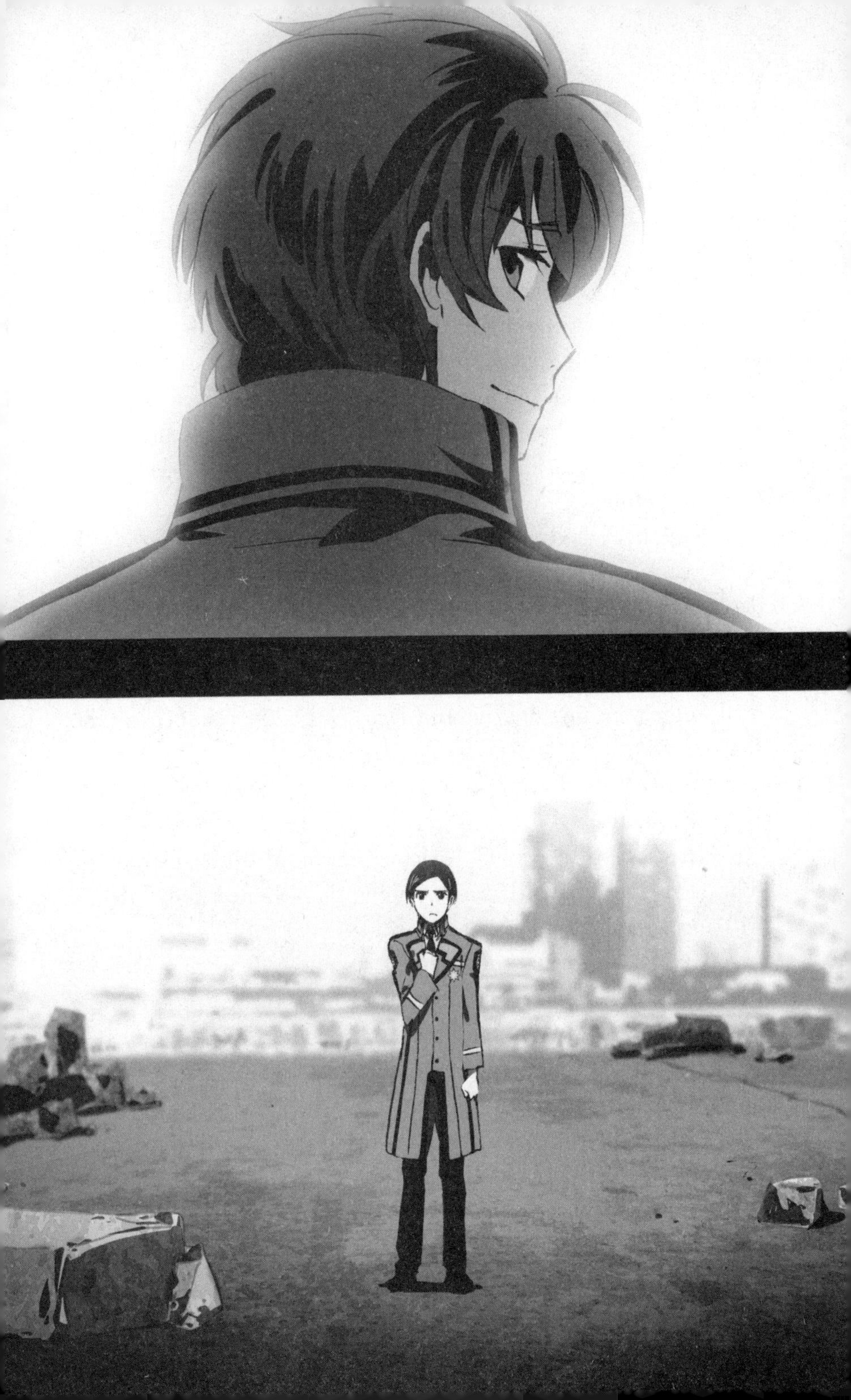

◇ ◇ ◇

"…They're here."

The first one on the First High watch team to notice enemies approaching was Mikihiko. The spirits roused by the paper talismans he'd scattered to the winds had sent him an image of the enemy.

"Upright tanks… But different from before. They're moving much more humanlike."

"Humanlike?" repeated Erika, who had momentarily removed a set of sound-dampening earmuffs.

Upright tanks were simply tanks made to enter narrow roads, with tracks on the end of short legs to make it easy to climb stairs or rubble, and with a set of mounted, swivel-type gun turrets. They hadn't been developed as combat mechs. With current military technology levels, at least to Erika's knowledge, there were no combat mechs that could replicate a human's movements.

"We'll be able to see them soon… There!"

But she didn't have time to be thinking about how far removed from common sense it was.

At Mikihiko's signal, upright tanks came out from behind a building.

Short legs equipped with tracks. A long torso front to back. Those parts were the same as regular upright tanks.

But the chainsaws equipped to the right hand and the gunpowder-type pile drivers attached to the left were never seen on regular upright tanks. If you'd set out to make a piece of heavy machinery intended for removing obstacles at disaster sites into a human shape, it might take on this form—but these had grenade launchers on the right shoulder and heavy machine guns on the left.

"Combat mechs?!" cried Erika, feeling like fantasy had infiltrated her reality.

Next to her, Miyuki pointed an icy stare at the sinister mobile weapons' forms.

As soon as these new weapons entered their fields of view, Miyuki triggered a spell.

It was over in an instant.

The three machines stopped their advance.

Their tracks frozen, they now stood immobile.

But they didn't tip over forward—a testament, perhaps, to excellent balance-control systems.

But their legs weren't the only things frozen; Miyuki's spell wasn't nearly that trivial.

Anyone with enough military knowledge to control an upright tank would immediately know the freezing had been a magical attack. And they would have instinctively known the magic user in question was the girl standing defiantly in their path, long hair fluttering in the wind.

And yet, neither their machine guns nor their grenade launchers spouted any flame.

This wasn't just a freezing spell but Freeze Flame—Miyuki's magic had both limited their movements and forbidden any increase in heat.

As the ice continued to spread, Leo rushed out into the fray.

This reaction speed, this sharp nose for any chance at victory—it could only be compared to a wild beast.

The weapon in his hand: a short stick that looked like a double-headed hammer.

Its length: twenty inches; its grip: about twelve.

The tip protruding from the hammerhead was quite a bit wider than the grip, at four inches in length. Its vertical-horizontal proportions might have been close to a Latin cross.

The noise of a motor turning on came from the hammerhead portion, and the stick's tip shot out a black film.

Thin, very thin—a black, see-through film.

When the sound of the motor stopped, the film turned into a straight blade two yards long.

It was a superthin blade with a perfectly flat surface, one invisible if looked at from the side.

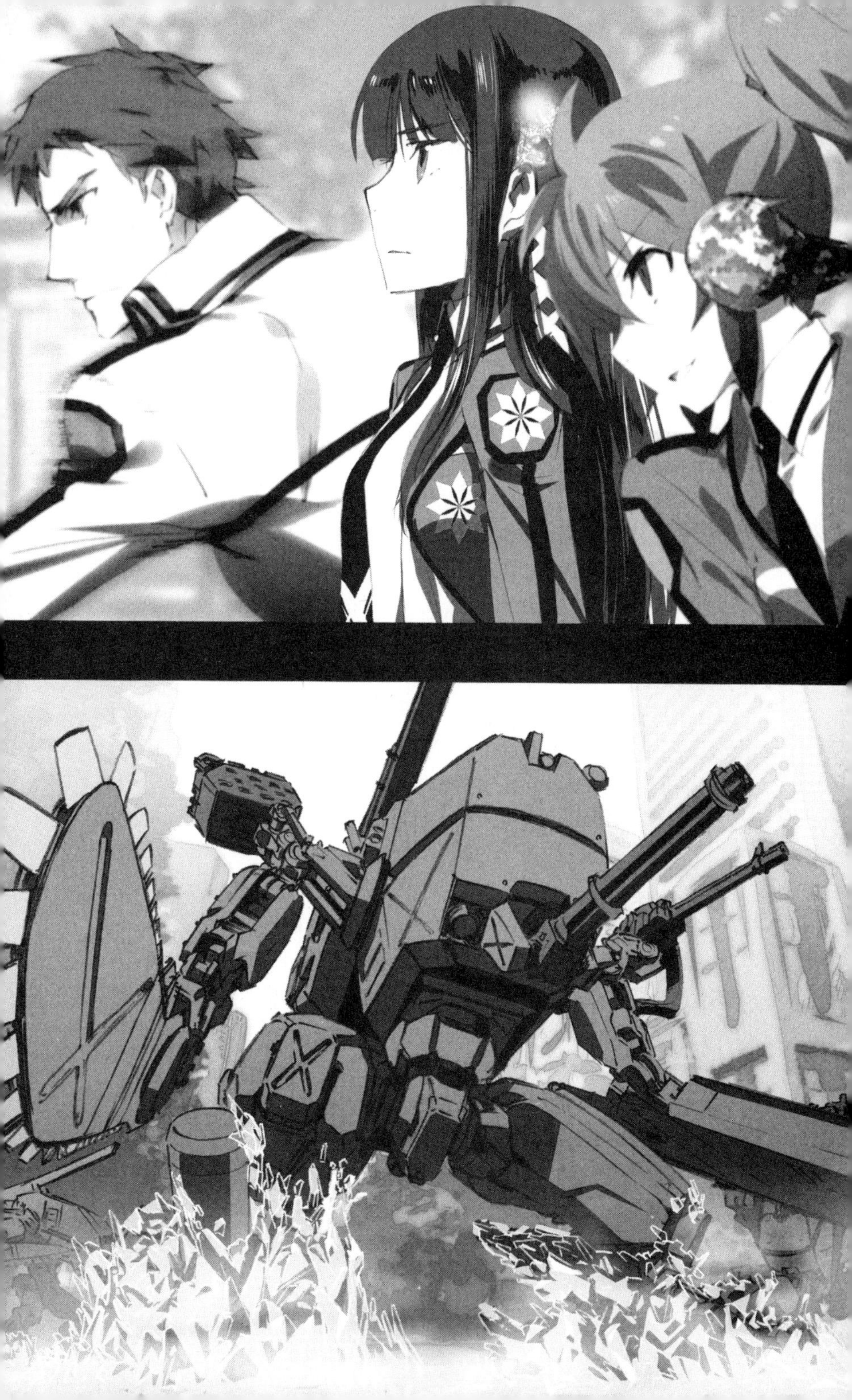

This was the secret art of the Chiba: *Usuba Kagerou*, the Antlion.

A carbon nanotube sheet blade, stabilized into a perfectly flat surface with hardening magic. The Antlion was both the name of the spell and the name of this unique armament device.

Leo's right hand flicked the *Usuba Kagerou*.

The superthin sheet, five nanometers thick, made of woven carbon nanotube, was a sharper blade than any sword, than any razor, and easily cleaved through the frozen armor plating.

The front armor was slashed through diagonally.

The line was so slender that you couldn't even tell it was cut.

But red soon dripped out of it.

This was the power of his trump card, that which had taught him *to kill*, the fruit of his short but dense training.

Leo quickly jumped back, and as if chasing him, the upright tank's body fell onto the road.

Leo had gotten a slight head start in terms of reaction, but Erika might have been the first to actually finish off her prey.

She slid her muffs back into position, then grabbed the hilt of the Orochi-Maru, which had been resting on her left arm, and loosened it from its sheath.

As she moved her left hand from the sheath to the hilt, the sheath popped open, hinged on the back, and the long blade appeared.

Leaving the inside of her hand where it was, Erika used her right index finger to press the button just under the guard. Then, she hefted the six-foot weapon onto her shoulder.

The spell had already activated by then.

She easily swung out the long twenty-two-pound katana. And then, a moment later, she disappeared.

At least, it looked that way to Miyuki, who had been next to her.

A crunching sound thundered.

It was the sound of crushing and tearing metal that one might hear in an old scrapyard.

Erika reappeared, now in a posture of having already swung the blade.

The upright tank, its front armor severed like a bamboo shoot, fell over as though it had been clubbed down.

The red fluid mixed with motor oil whetted her blade. The red was, without a doubt, the fresh blood of the pilot.

The weighting-type inertia control spell, Mountain Tsunami: a secret sword technique where the user minimized the inertia on herself and her blade, approached the enemy at a high speed, and at the moment of impact, added the erased inertia to amplify the blade's inertia as it struck the target. The longer the approach, the greater this false inertial quantity would be, reaching ten tons at max.

The speed gained from eliminating inertia—and the weight gained from increasing it: At maximum power, Mountain Tsunami was like dropping a giant ten-ton guillotine blade from high in the sky.

At this point in time, there was probably no armor that could withstand its force.

The timing to gauge when to switch from inertia cancellation to inertia amplification; the footwork to run in an unstable state with no inertia; the blade work to keep the cut straight; and above all, the perception, speed, and athleticism to handle such speed in that inertialess state: These were the necessary requirements for Mountain Tsunami.

It was a sword technique made possible only by Erika's natural speed and the days she'd been made to spend training for this skill alone.

Erika looked toward her next target.

Leo had already closed in on his.

But Mountain Tsunami activated.

An instant later, in front of the smashed upright tank, Leo released the *Usuba Kagerou* once more and then doubled over, covering his ears.

The other part of the halved watch team—actually an interception team—had plunged into combat against upright tanks as well.

Here, Isori had built a wall to block geological vibrations up to ten feet underground, making Kanon's spell, which used the ground as a medium, possible. His underground circle also served the purpose of searching for enemies aboveground.

The spell constructed a pattern with effects that assisted magic activation (in other words, a magic circle) by channeling psionic threads through a fixed surface. It was Kei Isori's forte as the gifted child of the Isori family, who were authorities on seal magic—and it looked eerily similar to the spell circles in the old magic Mikihiko used. As a result, it basically confirmed that modern magic and old magic were both truly expressions of the same system.

So in a way, it was only natural that they'd be tasked with the same types of battle responsibility.

"They're here."

At Isori's voice, Kanon expanded an activation sequence. Even though Isori had it covered, if she didn't clearly know what state the underground was in, she couldn't use overly powerful vibration magic.

Two strange-looking upright tanks appeared.

Kanon wasn't very familiar with types of weaponry, so she wasn't overly surprised by their oddity. So without getting caught up in unneeded consideration, she simply sent out a spell as planned.

The paved road broke into dirt-sized pieces, and water seeped from the subtly vibrating ground, forming a pool.

The upright tanks got one head shorter in height. Their feet had sunk into the ground.

Their endless tracks were for running over beach, swamp, and plain. But the road, turned to quicksand, easily absorbed the little caterpillars.

This was Vibrating Landmine, one of the variations of the Chiyoda family spell, Mine Origin.

Its effects were as demonstrated here: It turned the ground fluid to stop enemies in their tracks.

The upright tanks' tracks squealed as they scooped out muddy water, but soon sand got stuck in them and they froze. Then, abruptly, the moisture was gone, and the liquefied road re-hardened around them. Kanon had continued the ground liquefaction until the water molecules had vibrated themselves into evaporation.

Everything up until this point of capture was a single process for Vibrating Landmine. Though somewhat different in composition than that of roads from the previous century, paving materials were fundamentally concrete—but that didn't mean they had reproduced the effects of the chemical mixture process, so it was just like moist sand had simply hardened. Therefore, despite the term *capture*, it was really only a temporary restraint, but if they were unable to move with the enemy right there, even for a moment, that spelled doom.

To either side of the forlorn upright tanks, Toshikazu and Kirihara showed up.

Toshikazu attacked from the air.

The enemy pilot had no hope of reacting.

With the force of a peregrine falcon, he descended, slashing deeply into the pilot's seat.

The secret sword technique Zantetsu: a movement-type magic that defined a katana as a singular concept of existence, then moved it along a slashing path set by the magic program—at least, that was what it would have been, had he been using anything but the Ikazuchi-Maru.

Triggering Zantetsu with the Ikazuchi-Maru included the caster himself, not only the sword, as the magic's target. Along with defining the katana as a single concept, it defined the entire sword-wielding person as a collective Idea, allowing for perfectly straight high-speed approaches and slashes.

And what movement was it that could be used so perfectly that it was part of a spell? Only full-body-slashing practice consisting of thousands, tens of thousands, hundreds of thousands of both solo swings and kata drills hammered into him could make this skill possible.

In fact, Toshikazu personally considered Naotsugu to be the genius, not himself.

But because he wasn't a genius, as a result of repeated secret, honest kata practice, he had attained the Zantetsu of the Ikazuchi-Maru—the Jinrai Zantetsu, named for its lightning speed.

Because it was a master's technique, he could only use the Jinrai Zantetsu in practice, a practice he could never show anyone. As such, many misunderstood him as a lazy man, but in reality, at the end of his endless endeavors, he had gained this secret technique.

Its console cleaved in twain, the upright tank fell dead silent.

As Kirihara leaped off the ground to approach, the upright tank's upper body swiveled to face him.

One more step until he was in blade range.

A machine-gun barrel aimed at him—

But nothing fired from it.

Because a small katana that flew in from behind Kirihara plunged into the gun, tearing it free of the tank's shoulder.

Sayaka, who stood diagonally behind him, threw another *kodachi*, and the grenade launcher tore away in the same manner.

The two *kodachi* curved through the air in an arc, then returned to Sayaka's hands.

A sword-throwing technique.

Sayaka belonged to the kendo club at school, but her father had used *kenjutsu* in actual combat before. Her family had initiated her into *kenjutsu* techniques as well, and among them, she was best at this throwing technique. Not with shuriken or throwing daggers but with *kodachi* and *wakizashi*.

Being female, she would always lag behind in strength if things came to physical blows. Kirihara's specialty, the High-Frequency Blade, was something he swung using force, for example. Similarly, controlling the blade's motion to the point necessary for magic was difficult for her. But with throwing techniques, physical strength had nothing to do with it, since the idea was to cast the spell during her throwing motion. That had been the idea during her training.

Because of the huge opening left behind after the throw, she couldn't use it against fast opponents. But against large, slow-moving targets, it demonstrated its maximum efficacy.

Seeing that the firearms had been disabled, Kirihara took the final step in.

A giant chain saw swung down from overhead.

But he could tell where it was going.

Kirihara put his body into a natural slide, his katana slicing through the tank's left leg as he went.

The High-Frequency Blade.

This was the spell he was most skilled with, and it had easily ripped through the armor plating, which had been devised for landmines and anti-tank rifles.

The machine leaned forward and began to fall.

Retreating, Kirihara cut its pile driver free from the base, then went around to its side and thrust his blade into the pilot seat.

The sensation of penetrating flesh rang through his hands, and his face changed slightly as he pulled the blade out. But he still managed to leap back and put distance between him and the falling upright tank.

The expression he had made was certainly not a smile.

◇ ◇ ◇

Tatsuya, who had been rummaging through what remained of the armored car, removed from it a one-foot cubed box to the side. "Is this it, sir?" he asked, pointing the box at a camera.

"Yes, that's it. Just hold it up to the analyzer… Hmm, that's definitely it" came the reply from the display hooked up to the camera. "That's a Sorcery Booster."

"It looks like just a box, sir."

"One hundred percent of its connection and control are done through magical circuits. It won't have a mechanical terminal," Sanada explained through the display while Tatsuya frowned dubiously at the box, which was flat save for the handle.

"Does this mean they used this Booster to amplify their defense magic?" Yanagi added.

"Well, it's only speculation, but I think that's on the mark," Sanada agreed.

"Guess we know exactly who they are now. Even though there was really no other possibility to begin with."

"It's weak evidence, but we're neither policemen nor judges. Still, knowing this doesn't change our response."

The two captains traded a dark smile between one side of the display and the other.

"Sir," Tatsuya broke in, "should I sink the camouflaged GAA warship?"

"We can't do it in the harbor" came back Sanada. "It'll impact its functions too much."

Tatsuya knew that, of course. He'd only been joking, but when he received a more serious reply than expected, he started to feel a little apologetic.

But it was then that Kazama pushed Sanada out of the way to get into the frame. "Then should we go aboard and seize it, sir?" Yanagi asked the newcomer.

Tatsuya got the feeling that they'd long since decided to attack the enemy ship, even with this few people. It reminded him that these friends of his—well, his commanding officers, at the moment—didn't understand jokes, or at least use them in daily life on a regular basis.

"*That comes later. Helicopters have been prepared to evacuate the civilians in the station plaza, courtesy of some civs themselves. Once we've handed over monitoring your site to the Tsurumi advance unit, go to the station and help them escape.*"

"Understood, sir." Tatsuya saluted next to Yanagi, impressed that civilians had the courage to maneuver themselves to safety like that. He thought that the stance of taking civilians left behind with you as you escaped was praiseworthy, but then…

"The names of the civilians who called the helicopters are Mayumi Saegusa and Shizuku Kitayama. If either of them requests it, I want you to do everything you can to help."

Upon hearing those all-too-familiar names, Tatsuya nearly cleared his throat despite himself.

◇ ◇ ◇

At about the same time, people in another location had arrived at the same conclusion as to the enemy's identity.

The wreckage Erika was responsible for was a far cry from its original form, so Miyuki, Erika, Leo, and Mikihiko all gathered before the other upright tank, mostly unharmed save for the pilot seat Leo had sliced through. Mikihiko had called the rest of them there.

"About this upright tank… I don't think it was moving purely by mechanical control."

"Do you mean they were using some sort of magic in parallel?"

"Yes, I believe so."

It wasn't unique for a male student to address Miyuki formally. But whether he was acting in line with that or not, Mikihiko just couldn't seem to loosen up when talking to her.

"These three were moving oddly, like humans. The pilot seat takes up all of an upright tank's torso, so its internal structure is nothing like a human. Even if you tried to make it move like a human being, you couldn't make it act as a human being does. If you tried too hard, I believe you would only end up losing power for it."

"And they still tried too hard?" asked Leo.

Mikihiko nodded unfalteringly. "I can only think pistons, gears, and wires weren't the only things contributing to its power source. It must have had a power that directly made the limb movements look lifelike."

"So with magic?" asked Erika. "What kind of spell would that be?"

Mikihiko's answer was fluid. "It's probably an application of the Paper Soldier spell."

"Paper-whatta now?" Erika balked back, cocking her head in confusion.

"Is that the onmyoudou spell that uses a human shape? I hear it was originally from Taoism."

But when Miyuki answered her instead, Mikihiko nodded, unable to hide how impressed he was. "Yes. You cut a person shape out of paper and house any old spirit in it. That's the Paper Soldier spell." The latter half was his explanation to Erika.

"So we're dealing with the Great Asian Alliance, then?" Erika, however, breezed past his explanation and got straight to the heart of the matter.

"Isn't it too early to jump to conclusions? If it's an onmyoudou spell, they could simply be Japanese defectors, too."

"No, in all likelihood, Erika's correct." Though Leo had proposed an unusual caution, Mikihiko shook his head and supported Erika's opinion. "This may sound odd, but there are fads among old magic spells, too… Even if you honor tradition, some techniques see booms in certain times, while others are abandoned. No form of old magic in the country has used *shiki* with physical forms for over ten years now. Paper Soldier was abandoned in this country. If you wanted to control the saws and pile drivers on the upright tanks' arms, there are many other options that are more efficient. If it were me, for example, I'd put a spell on the driver and saw myself. We old sorcerers aren't stubborn enough to purposely bring out an abandoned technique if we knew it was uneconomical."

"Hey, I'm not trying to call anyone stubborn here." Leo waved his hands, flinching somewhat from Mikihiko, who seemed a little irritated—too conscious—of it. "The point is, we've got GAA magicians controlling these upright tanks, right? Got it. Makes sense."

"Ah, well, I... You're right." Mikihiko realized he was letting frustration into his voice, too, and clammed up, embarrassed. But soon his face tightened, and he said something the other three did not expect:

"Huh? You want Shibata over there?" Mayumi asked into the air, unintentionally shouting her reply to her voice communicator. "...I see. Well, you have a point, but... Yes, I understand. But let me clear it with her first... Yes, it would be better if you explained directly. Shibata?"

Mayumi took her face from the terminal and held it toward Mizuki.

"Um, what is it...?"

"Miyuki and the others want you to go to them. She wants to explain the reason directly, so listen to what she has to say and decide for yourself."

Mayumi and Mizuki had barely ever spoken. Mayumi offered her the voice unit in a rather businesslike tone, and Mizuki awkwardly—no, outright nervously—decided she had no choice but to take it.

"*Oh, Shibata?*"

"Yoshida?" Once she knew Mikihiko was on the other end, she gave a look of relief. If it had been Erika, she wouldn't know when the bomb would be dropped on her, and even now, she was unreasonably nervous whenever she spoke to Miyuki. Still, as to why she was relieved it was Mikihiko—she herself didn't quite understand that yet.

"*I want you to lend us your strength.*" Meanwhile, Mikihiko's voice sounded rather hurried—or excited, perhaps.

"Huh? My strength?"

"*The enemy is moving their armored weapons using an old magic spell called Paper Soldier. It's not the same kind that I use, so I can't really figure the spell out. But with your eyes, you'd be able to catch sight of enemy movements faster than me, since they always have the spell active. And you* should be able to figure out where their magical cores are located. *If we find that, I can disable their Paper Soldier spells with my magic. So I want you to come here, Shibata. I know it's more dangerous than over there, but I promise I won't ever let you get hurt.*"

"...!" Mizuki, dumbstruck, felt her cheeks heat up. She knew he didn't mean anything by it, of course, but...

"Isn't that nice, Mizuki? Yoshida-kun says he'll protect you."

"...!"

"...!!"

Miyuki's remark cut into their communication, and now both of them were at a loss for words, which they could each feel through the waves. Time stopped during that awkward silence, where she could easily imagine his face, down to its own bright color.

"*...Not only Yoshida, of course. We'll all do our best to back you up.*"

Time started moving again with Miyuki's bald-faced follow-up. Mayumi, who had been listening in, said to herself, *I knew Miyuki was an A-plus catch...*

"*R-right! We'll all make sure you're well defended!*" cried Mikihiko, desperate in more ways than one.

Mizuki, for her part, nodded. "All right. I'll go over there now."

She lowered the communication terminal from her face and breathed a sigh of relief. Then, after returning it to Mayumi and bowing, she quickly ran off at a trot to the front line, where Mikihiko and the others had taken up position.

[12]

Current time: 4:30 PM. The situation was already showing signs of a turnabout.

The invading army probably hadn't planned for long-term battle to begin with. The only ship at their command was the one disguised as a large cargo vessel, and their coordination with their black ops wasn't very careful. Central hadn't even followed up on its attack of one of their original objectives, the Thesis Competition hall, so the only result to this point was some partial damage to the building.

Nevertheless, if the individual invaders had only a police force to go up against, they had more than enough troops to control vital facilities and capture scores of civilians. Unfortunately, the haste with which the Magic Association assembled a volunteer army to resist had been a huge miscalculation on their part.

The Japan Defense Force's response had also been swift, of course. Not even an hour since mobilization and they'd already supplied significant reinforcements to serve as a shield for the evacuees.

It wouldn't be long before the enemy's retreat and the inevitable switch to a mop-up campaign to restore the peace on the home team's part. The situation had improved to the point where civilians escaping wasn't even considered necessary.

YOKOHAMA INCIDENT OUTLINE 3

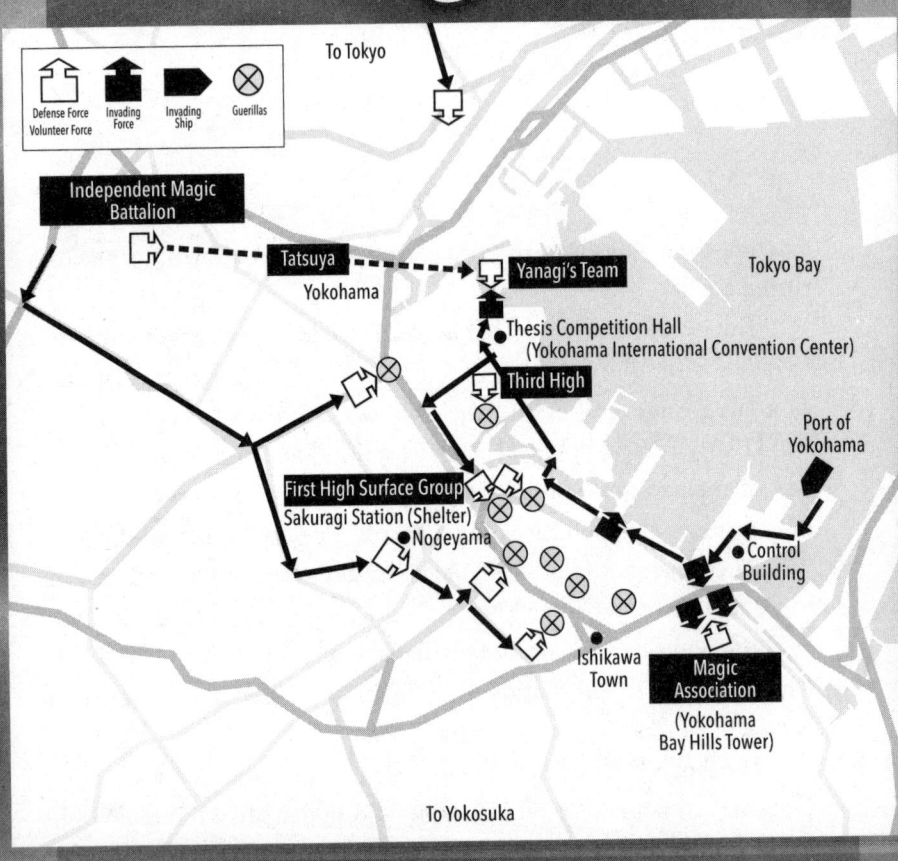

Legend:
- ⇧ Defense Force Volunteer Force
- ⇧ Invading Force
- ▶ Invading Ship
- ⊗ Guerillas

To Tokyo

Independent Magic Battalion

Tatsuya
Yokohama

Yanagi's Team

Tokyo Bay

Thesis Competition Hall
(Yokohama International Convention Center)

Third High

First High Surface Group
Sakuragi Station (Shelter)
Nogeyama

Port of Yokohama

Control Building

Ishikawa Town

Magic Association
(Yokohama Bay Hills Tower)

To Yokosuka

OCTOBER 30, AD 2095
4:30 PM, PRESENT TIME

However, the boys and girls who had placed themselves in the middle of it all had no way of knowing any of that.

◇ ◇ ◇

"Ms. Kurosawa? ...Yep, that's right... No, not at all. Thanks."

As Shizuku took the comm unit away from her ear, they heard a helicopter approaching. For some reason, the one she'd been talking to in order to procure this was her family housekeeper. "Saegusa, our rides should be arriving soon."

Mayumi, who had been giving her information terminal a difficult stare, looked up and gave a fake smile. "Understood. Kitayama, please prioritize gathering women and families with children to yours. Mr. Inagaki, please go on that helicopter and support her. Also, Mr. Inagaki, could you instruct the people on who will evacuate first? Ichihara and I will help you. Mitsui, you keep watch on our surroundings."

After a crisp series of instructions, Mayumi sighed to herself. The civilians whose evacuation was getting put off wouldn't be happy, naturally. There were already teens holding the initiative here; quite a few of the adults felt this objectionable. Nobody was acting out at the moment, probably because they wouldn't be allowed onto a helicopter if they did, but the longer it took for the second helicopter to arrive, the higher tensions were sure to rise.

Having both of them land at the same time would be ideal, but they obviously couldn't tell the first one to wait around up in the air.

What's taking them so long?!

For now, the only thing Mayumi could do was try to stem the tide of her irritation.

◇ ◇ ◇

With the situation getting worse by the minute, the invading army's commander could no longer hide his dangerous expression. Because this operation was for a single ship to land a force in an enemy nation, their chances for success were dependent on achieving their goals and retreating before the enemy could put together a response. The plan they'd used had gone well up through the first phase.

Though the enemy had answered quickly, that was within their predictions. The civilian troops' resistance, however, was far stronger than they'd expected. Originally, they would have already been in the retreat phase by now, but while they'd been dealing with the civilian resistance, the enemy had closed an interception force around them.

The route north along the coast was already contained by a force from Tsurumi. It was no longer possible to take any of the evacuees hostage.

"All unmanned recon craft signals lost."

The commander stopped caring what his subordinates heard and swore to himself. They'd shot down the last scout craft. Now he'd have to command based solely on prior information. Privately cursing Xiangshan Chen, who had gotten behind enemy lines but didn't bother to contact them, he ordered their north-bearing forces to change course.

Inland—toward the station plaza awaiting helicopters.

◊ ◊ ◊

As a wheeled armored vehicle turned at an intersection, it lost its grip and slid sideways into a spin.

Thanks to Isori using his Road Extension to overcome the reflecting spell on the vehicle, the armored car crashed into a streetlight and stopped, its wheels still spinning.

"Kanon!"

"Leave it to me!"

As a result of them pushing their point of interception forward, Kanon no longer had to consider the students who had evacuated underground. She activated Mine Origin, synonymous with the Chiyoda family.

Severe tremors thrust up from directly under the armored car, propagating through it as though laughing away the shock absorbers on each wheel and causing vibration fractures at several points. The car, with no damage to its armor up to this point, broke apart beyond usage, its driver's brain and semicircular canals shaken.

Large machine-gun bullets chipped away at the wall the two of them were hiding behind. It was an attack from a follow-up car.

Kanon yelped, and Isori held her to him as he built up a vector-reversing field along the wall's surface.

When the reflected bullets made the armored car go silent, Mari, hiding across the street, triggered a spell that decreased oxygen density. But the car was airtight, as though built for anti-biochemical-weapon warfare, so it was too hard for her to alter the air composition inside it. Her spell ended in failure.

Mari tsked and released her influence over the oxygen density information, then sent heated air into the car's grenade launcher barrel. A grenade, set in the launcher just before she fired, exploded, taking the machine gun along with it.

The armored car, with no more attack power, then fell under assault from Kirihara.

He pierced its armor, his High-Frequency Blade plunged into the driver's seat.

The car's back hatch opened, and a soldier with a handgun dodged out.

A short arrow flew at him: After the crossbow bolt shot him through the right shoulder, Kirihara's blade sliced his throat.

After getting back behind cover, Kirihara asked worriedly, "Mibu, are you okay?" Sayaka had been the one to shoot the soldier going for him. His condition, when she said she wanted to come no matter what, was not to kill anyone with her sword techniques. The only time she would use a sword would be on inanimate objects and for self-defense if it was absolutely called for. Therefore, he'd let Sayaka bring a small, mechanical crossbow armament along with her *kodachi*.

"I'm fine. This is a battlefield. I'm prepared," she answered, her face pale but her voice firm.

The ground rumbled again.

This time, it was Kanon's spell; she'd cast one against the upright tanks coming on the heels of the armored cars.

The tanks quickly backed up and fired grenades from their back line, forcing the students behind cover.

The enemy line was denser now, and they were holding Kanon and the others in place.

Miyuki's magical influence prevented all enemy magic. Even if it was amplified with a Booster.

Meanwhile, *Usuba Kagerou* assailed the frozen armored car.

There were twenty-two yards of superthin carbon nanotube sheet stored in the hammerhead-shaped winder. That meant Leo had a blade he could extend and retract freely to a maximum of twenty-two yards.

Still, the longer the sheet got, the more difficult it should have been to use magic to harden it into a blade, but Leo effortlessly created one twenty-two yards long and sliced horizontally through the armored car.

"Incoming on the right! Core's in the same place!"

Mizuki located an enemy upright tank as it came around from the side, and Mikihiko used his spell-breaking technique on it.

The enemy appeared to slam into an invisible wall, and its arms fell limp to its sides.

Then, with speed too fast to be seen, Erika carved into it with Mountain Tsunami. The Orochi-Maru's long, slender blade crushed the mechanical soldier that was easily twice her height.

With Mikihiko and Miyuki providing support fire, Leo and Erika worked as a team to destroy one enemy combat vehicle after another.

"Mizuki?"

Mizuki suddenly heard her name called when things had calmed down for a moment, and turned around.

"Can you tell what state Chiyoda's group is in?" Miyuki asked about the other team. She didn't know Mari had gone to reinforce them; Mizuki hadn't had time to tell her yet.

"Umm…it looks like they moved. They're still engaged."

The point where their seniors had intercepted the enemy was a little ahead of theirs. They were positioned to block off the two main routes to the station.

"What's wrong, Miyuki?" asked Erika, the Orochi-Maru on her shoulder, as Miyuki frowned. "What's there to think so hard about at this point?"

"Doesn't this seem strange?" answered Miyuki. "Why is the enemy always coming to where we're waiting for them?"

Erika frowned, too.

"Don't they have to pass through where we are to get to the station?" asked Mizuki. Indeed, the upperclassman and freshman groups had taken up position based on Suzune's reading of the map.

But Mizuki's answer didn't satisfy the Shiba sister. "That's only if they're using main streets, Mizuki. They must have a way to communicate with each other, and there are only ten of us, so you'd think they could easily slip past us."

"…Maybe they're holding us here," said Erika.

At that same moment, Mizuki gave a start.

"They're here!"

But with the new enemy attack Mikihiko reported, they were forced to leave their guesswork for later.

◇ ◇ ◇

The double-rotor transport helicopter Kurosawa was flying—amazingly, the housekeeper could pilot helicopters, not just cruisers—appeared in the sky, and as it was lowering its altitude to land, it happened:

Suddenly, a black cloud came flying in. The abrupt appearance, which could only be described as "appearing out of thin air," was actually a huge swarm of out-of-season locusts.

They may have only been locusts, but they could still clog the engines. And besides, they'd appeared in such an unnatural way that they couldn't have been an innocent natural phenomenon.

Shizuku, who had gone out to greet the helicopter, made a snap judgment and took her CAD out of her pouch. It was a silver one in the shape of a small handgun.

It was the second of the Silver models she'd bought right after the Nines. The activation sequence installed on it was a loop-cast Phonon Maser.

She pointed it into the air and pulled the trigger.

A sonic heat wave cut down a swarm of locusts.

"So…many…!"

That swarm vanished, as though they'd vaporized rather than burned to death. But that was only one part of a bigger cloud. She activated Phonon Maser again and again, shooting away the locusts nearing the helicopter, but nevertheless, one group got around her and cut in.

Honoka noticed it, too, but her magic wasn't suited for intercepting enemies like this. Afraid she'd cause a conflict with Shizuku's spell, she was unable to help.

Then, as the swarm of locusts reached the helicopter…

…a wind of destruction blew in.

The huge black cloud's outline collapsed as though it were a mirage, and its color thinned until it had disappeared completely.

Shizuku and Honoka looked into the sky.

Mayumi and Suzune, having noticed the emergency later, directed their eyes skyward as well.

They saw a figure wrapped in black floating there, a silver CAD at the ready.

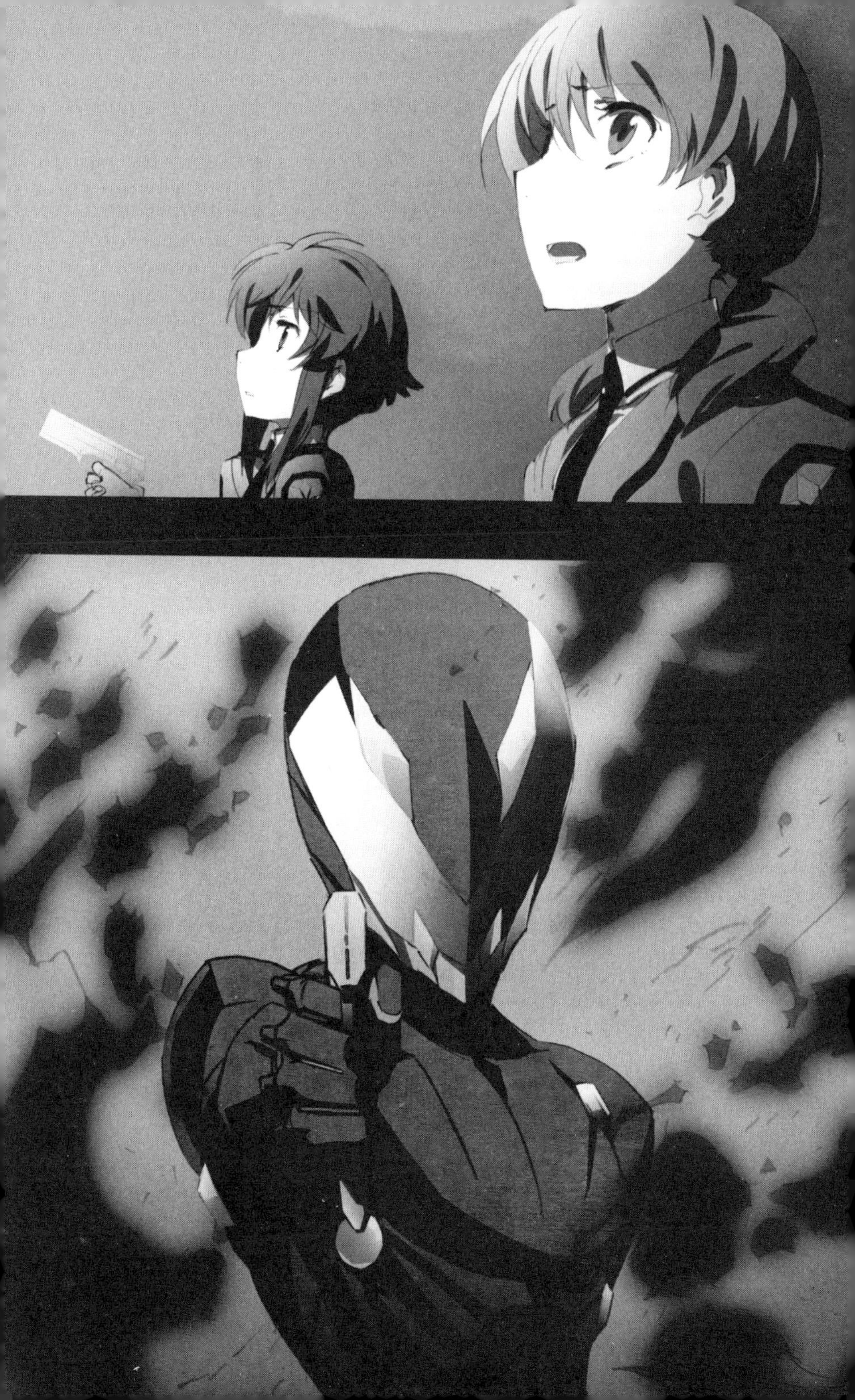

"Tatsuya...?"

Had it been Shizuku or Honoka to mutter that?

A group of other figures in entirely black suits flew in, then took up positions to protect the helicopter.

Once more, the transport helicopter began its descent.

◇ ◇ ◇

"Compound-form attack prevented. Protecting the helicopter's descent."

"Leave its escort to the others, Specialist. Search for the caster and eliminate them," Yanagi instructed.

"Roger."

Tatsuya peeled away his gaze, looking for the one who had created the familiar.

He hadn't dismantled each individual locust when he intercepted the swarm; instead, he'd aimed his dismantling spell at the magic program that had created the compound locust form. Once the spell creating the false body had been dismantled, the matter imitating locusts returned to psionic particles.

During that process, he'd seen where the magic program had come from. At that range and with this much time elapsed, he could easily trace it while maintaining his flight magic.

Over there.

Tatsuya could just go over and eliminate them, but it would be easier to apply his spell if he saw the person directly.

He moved to a spot over the fleeing caster's head.

◇ ◇ ◇

A soldier in black holding a large, silver handgun-shaped CAD flew behind a cluster of buildings, as quick as a comet.

His companions, with their rifles, formed a circle in midair as the helicopter inside their ring landed. The sight of the flying soldiers all in black, whose faces were hidden, exuded a certain ominous air.

But nobody, not Honoka, nor Shizuku, nor Mayumi, nor Suzune, felt uneasy about them.

"Who are they, exactly?" asked Inagaki, sounding creeped out.

But he only got a short answer from Mayumi: "They're allies," she said with a smile.

They were Tatsuya's allies, and Fujibayashi's as well—a unit in the Japan Defense Force.

Mayumi didn't know any more than that, but it was enough.

They kept a sharp lookout in midair even as the civilians climbed aboard the helicopter.

The soldiers had been floating for over ten minutes now, and yet none of them seemed the least bit exhausted. Clearly, each and every one of them was a high-level magician.

She'd heard rumors before about an experimental unit in the Japan Ground Defense Force made up of rather unique magicians prominent in specific fields.

If you looked at each individual magician's rank, they wouldn't seem like all that much. But when this group of combat magicians entered battle, they were a very strong strike force.

Now that she thought about it, those conditions fit *him* perfectly.

"Reliable reinforcements," added Mayumi, watching the last few people board the helicopter.

The helicopter that now held Shizuku and Inagaki safely lifted off, and after watching it ascend out of reach of ground sniping, the flying soldiers of the IMB guarding the perimeter scattered to nearby buildings.

A sense of relief settled over the remaining civilians. The strange, unnerving feeling from the strike force remained, but the JDF was keeping watch over their surroundings. Even if they felt it was a much more reliable situation than leaving everything to kids, nobody could have blamed them.

"It's finally here…"

Despite not having to worry about any panic thanks to the reinforcements, Mayumi still wanted to quickly escape the pressure from the civilians who desperately wanted to escape. When she'd heard the sound of rotors indicating her helicopter's arrival, she'd gotten impatient. The thought *finally* was her perfectly truthful impression of the matter.

What arrived was a military twin-engine helicopter. It was a good deal bigger than the one Shizuku had prepared. All the remaining civilians should have been able to board it without a problem.

Plus, more than one helicopter had come. A second one, a combat helicopter, was accompanying it.

"Miss Mayumi, are you safe?"

Upon hearing her ring tone and putting her communication unit to her ear, Mayumi heard the voice of her bodyguard, Nakura. "There are no problems here. Mr. Nakura, which one are you in?"

"I'm currently on board the combat helicopter. The master has bid me to ensure you and the other helicopter escape."

"…Understood." Mayumi had been about to say "I'm staying here," but quickly gave up the idea. Unfortunately, Nakura was a cut above her in close combat. And she couldn't shoot at a helicopter that came to rescue them, obviously. In many ways, resistance would be pointless.

"In any case, let's hurry the civilians inside," she said to Suzune, after her call had ended.

Suzune turned around in response—

And that's when it happened.

"Don't move!"

A young man wrapped an arm around Suzune's neck from behind and used his other hand to point a knife at her.

He had a rifle pointed at him from the top of a building, but another man took a step forward and held a hand grenade out in front of him.

"…I see. Now your opening move makes sense."

The quiet remark was from Suzune, who had the knife to her neck.

"You're a quick thinker," said the guerilla, who was disguised as an evacuating civilian. But he knew something was off; she seemed too calm.

"Drawing our combat forces to the front with your mechanized unit, but even then only securing the target once there were as few people waiting to escape as possible. A very well-thought-out plan," she continued.

"We didn't want to let any of you escape to begin with. We just came up with a plan where it wouldn't hurt if some of you did."

The man seemed to have been hooked by Suzune's chatty calm.

"Did you choose me as your target to stabilize your energy supply?"

"Not just that. More importantly, a lot of our friends are behind bars. You'll be a good hostage to set them free."

"I won't be much of a resource by myself, you know."

"That's not true... I told you not to move!"

The man sharply picked up on Mayumi trying to secretly use her CAD behind her back, and waved his knife. Mayumi gave up and put her hands in the air.

"Taking you as a hostage will force the Saegusa to act. I bet it's more effective if their daughter's friend is taken hostage rather than her."

"You're right. After all, Mayumi is too soft."

Although she felt like she was being unfairly criticized, Mayumi found herself unable to do anything. This was probably why they called her soft, but that didn't mean the *hostage* had to be criticizing her, too, did it?

"After that, do you plan to kidnap me and bring me to your country?"

"Yeah."

"But that wouldn't make sense for a hostage exchange, would it?"

"Well, we— What did you do?"

Finally, the man noticed that he was talking too much. In fact, he couldn't believe that he was speaking freely like this among the enemy, even with a hostage.

"Your plan wasn't a bad one."

The knife slipped away from Suzune's face.

"But you chose the wrong target."

The arm around her neck simply came off.

"I'm only average at using magic with a CAD, but I'm better than both Mayumi and Juumonji at using it with a medium."

She walked around the man holding the knife, over to in front of the others, and slowly pulled the grenade out of the other man's hand.

"I paralyzed the motor center controlling your voluntary muscles. You won't be able to move for a while."

Just as she said this, though they began to sweat and make slight motions, the men's arms and legs didn't make any meaningful movements.

"The spell directly influences your body. Once, this type of magic was forbidden—probably because it required human test subjects."

As they listened to Suzune, the men desperately tried to regain control over their bodies, but they couldn't even squirm.

"The difficulty is in how long it takes for the effects to appear, but thankfully you were talkative. Oh, and let me say this—magic wasn't what made you loosen your tongue. You were simply being imprudent."

Suzune's smile was ice-cold.

◇ ◇ ◇

The Magic Association branch's attack on the enemy had gotten fiercer. It was the result of the invading army realizing they were nearing the limit of their offensive, and launching a decisive battle instead.

Katsuto was listening to the reports flying in left and right from the association.

The JDF had launched a counterattack from Sakuragi Town and

Kannai; and as for Ishikawa Town and Chinatown, the volunteer force with the Magic Association at its center was just barely holding out.

"...Do we have any spare combat clothes?"

A female staff member opened her eyes wide at Katsuto's question and cried, "You can't possibly plan on going out there yourself! You mustn't!"

"We do have one, don't we?"

But when Katsuto repeated himself to get his point across, the staff member nodded, feeling the pressure. "But the Juumonji family head himself..."

"Please take me to it," interrupted Katsuto as she hesitated.

Awkwardly, the woman stood.

◇ ◇ ◇

The other Ten Master Clans member had joined the volunteer force in front of Chinatown. He'd walked alone, right into the middle of where enemies were going back and forth, causing crimson flowers to blossom. Eventually, he'd managed to join up with the group battling the invading army.

Hiding behind cover, he gripped his CAD with the reddish sheen in his left hand, gasping for breath. The protector he wore was something a wounded man had given him.

The exhaustion was from repeatedly firing Burst. Plus, now that the enemy's attacks had switched from mechanized weapons to magic, that wear and tear had started accumulating twice as fast.

Wraiths approached in a rank. A wraith was neither a metaphor *nor the true thing*. They were illusions created by old magic.

Instead of using the specialized CAD in his left hand, Masaki used the multipurpose CAD on his right arm.

An emission of interference.

The illusion of the wraith herd disappeared, leaving a single wooden dummy behind.

Having to apply Area Interference over a wide horizontal area to cover the entire rank quickly ate away at his stamina. And anyway, Masaki's Burst spell vaporized the fluids inside an object. There had to be fluids inside the target or else it wouldn't work.

The enemy had been quick to react to him, and this was the result. As soon as they saw an entire group of upright tanks crushed by Burst, they'd assembled a force of false wraiths and sent them into battle.

Burst was meaningless against illusions with no form created by old magic. And even without a physical form, the illusions still had attack power. It probably worked under the same logic as hypnotism. If you were cut by an illusion, red scar lines would appear and you would still die. Magicians could nullify the false slashing by covering themselves with Information Boost. However, the non-magician volunteer soldiers couldn't.

Masaki, fighting alongside those civilian soldiers, desperately continued to search for the enemy magician as he withstood the illusory attacks that had stopped his own advance cold.

◇ ◇ ◇

The civilians had finished boarding the transport helicopter.

"Rin, I'll leave them to you."

"Mayumi, please don't do anything reckless."

With this, the first helicopter lifted off.

The soldiers in black followed the helicopter up into the sky and formed a perimeter around it. Once they saw it ascend to a safe altitude, they dispersed, heading toward the coast.

"We should go, too. We'll pick up Miyuki and Mari's groups, then make our escape."

"…Understood."

Nakura looked like he had something to say about her order, but in the end, he nodded respectfully and went back to the copilot's seat.

The combat helicopter with Mayumi and Honoka on it lifted off as well.

Meanwhile, Mayumi noticed a single soldier standing on top of a building, seeing her off.

In his right hand was a specialized silver CAD.

Honoka was looking out the other way, so she didn't notice.

Without letting anyone in the helicopter see, Mayumi stuck out her tongue.

◇ ◇ ◇

Tatsuya saw Mayumi's gesture perfectly from behind his smoke visor.

…*What a delightful person.*

That was the only way he could express it.

Still, to think that Ichihara was one of the Ichihana…

The spell Suzune had used was the reason the Ichihana had their number stripped from their name and made an Extra. While their current name retained the *ichi*, it was no longer the character for *one*, but *city*.

He was pretty sure the spell relied predominantly on her genetics as an Ichihana.

Not only had magic that directly interfered with the human body been forbidden at the time, it was heavily restricted even now outside medical usage. It was dubious whether Suzune understood her circumstances, but he was almost certain she had Ichihana blood in her.

Of course, he thought, *my magic deserves the same number-stripping, doesn't it?* He didn't even give a dry grin for that one, just said it to himself flatly, before flipping the call switch in his helmet. "Mayumi Saegusa has boarded the helicopter. It's headed toward the coast at a low altitude. It appears they'll leave the area once they've picked up her classmates."

"Roger. Once you've confirmed your escort target has withdrawn from the combat zone, join up with the rest of us."

"Yes, sir."

Not much longer now, thought Tatsuya as he cut the line. Yanagi hadn't said it, but he knew without asking that they'd be going on the counteroffensive.

First, he had to make sure Mayumi and the others escaped safely.

Tatsuya, standing on the edge of a rooftop, pointed his CAD downward and casually pulled the trigger. A flame erupted at the corner of the building, then vanished just as quickly. He saw a missile launcher fall to the ground, but he didn't pay it any heed. The portable weapon was constructed well enough not to misfire just from that.

He repeated the same action five times.

Once he knew all the ones aiming for the helicopter were gone, he turned around.

One man was there, holding an unsheathed katana.

It looked like the katana was just hanging from his side, but it was a perfectly guarded formless stance.

"...Who are you?"

The man was the one who'd asked. Considering he'd climbed all the way up here—not through normal means but by dashing up the space between buildings, kicking off one wall to another—it was a dull question.

"JDF 101st Brigade, Special Duty Officer of the Independent Magic Battalion, Ryuuya Ooguro."

"What?"

The man with the katana, Chief Toshikazu, probably hadn't expected Tatsuya to answer so readily. That took him aback more than the unfamiliar unit name had, creating an opening in his stance.

Tatsuya lightly kicked off the roof.

He didn't jump for Toshikazu, but away from the building altogether.

With his left hand on his belt buckle, his body released from the fetters of gravity, and with his right-hand CAD still warding off the interloper, Tatsuya blasted off to heights where handgun bullets couldn't catch him.

◇ ◇ ◇

The Magic Association's volunteer army was being forced into a slow retreat.

The enemy ground unit they faced was clearly the main force.

The mixed unit of armored cars and upright tanks that had gone north was, if anything, mainly armored cars, but the force that attacked the association was mainly composed of the special, close-quarters combat upright tanks, further unique because several magicians were with them.

A beast resembling a dog turned into a ball of flame and burst apart. It was an old spell that created a compound form imitating a magical beast known as a Huodou.

No sooner did that happen than a bird resembling a one-legged crane scattered sparks and vanished. It was the same type of spell, this time creating a magical beast known as a Bifang.

Old magic from the mainland assailed the volunteer force.

These were no longer beings of unknown affiliation. Maybe they'd abandoned any pretense of hiding their identities, because unique spells and upright tanks with anti-magic defenses applied were trampling down the volunteers' lines.

The association's magicians replied with fast—in other words, less troublesome—modern magic, but eventually they couldn't hold out against their numbers anymore.

"Urgh. Retreat!"

"Retreat and reform the defensive line!"

The voices didn't sound like they'd lost the will to fight. But behind their spirit was the fact that they'd gone on the defense.

"Don't retreat!"

Just then, a voice thundered over the volunteers' cowardice.

The birdlike compound form shooting fire everywhere slammed

into the ground, splintered, and vanished. It was a sight like a giant hammer had come crashing down on it.

"Raise your spirits, all you who use magic. Protect our motherland from these foul invaders!"

A fire-spitting dog, a flame-winged bird, and other old magic familiars modeled after various mythical beasts were crushed to these words, one after another. And then, a large figure stepped out to the front of the volunteer army.

Clad in what looked like medieval armor with a sturdy protector and a helmet was Katsuto. He raised his right hand, then brought it down.

The act didn't have much force behind it. But as he swung down, one of the enemy's upright tanks was destroyed.

It was clear to everyone what that meant.

He repeated the same thing again—

—and a mechanized weapon that they thought was protected by magic was smashed like a toy made of paper.

Voices were raised.

They were the whoops of the volunteer soldiers put at a disadvantage, suddenly freed from that burden.

Katsuto shut the lid on the embarrassment in his mind and locked it.

He wasn't young enough to believe in absolute justice.

He also wasn't old enough to understand this as a temporary stopgap.

But he knew his role.

It didn't take very long for the enemy to snap out of its reverie.

They probably still didn't know what Katsuto had done, but even those with slow wits could tell that the magical attack on them had come from him.

Upright tank machine guns aimed at the youth, and tracks

groaned. And not just one but three had formed a line to press the attack, speaking to the skill of the enemy for not over-relying on their equipment.

But in the end, none of them could fire even a shot, nor advance even a yard.

Katsuto stuck out his right palm. That was the only warning he gave.

But that was all it took to turn the upright tanks into scrap.

This was the multilayered barrier spell Phalanx.

Such magic wasn't only for stopping the enemies; its true value actually lay in this kind of crushing attack.

The Phalanx spell constructed layer upon layer of barriers, so if the barrier in front went down, it would push the next one to the front, then add a new barrier to the back.

Instead of fixing the wall in front of himself, he slammed dozens of them into the enemies at high speed.

This was the true offensive casting of the Phalanx. He could expand an attack barrier simplified down to be opaque only to objects, even if other magic was trading back and forth. The magically created barrier both targeted objects and forbade any other magic with its influence.

Its flaws were that its range was short and that it only worked against physical forms or materialized phenomena. Despite that, this anti-object, anti-magic defense spell that doubled as a planar attack was incredibly potent against close-range combat such as a clustered enemy.

For defense, it deployed multiple barriers with multiple properties simultaneously.

For offense, it fired multiple barriers with a single property with rapidity.

Just as its name suggested, Phalanx was at once an attack spell and a defense spell.

And so in response, flames and lightning assailed Katsuto.

YOKOHAMA INCIDENT OUTLINE
4

Legend:
- Defense Force Volunteer Force
- Invading Force
- Invading Ship
- Guerillas
- Evacuation Ship

To Tokyo

Tokyo Bay

Independent Magic Battalion

Tatsuya

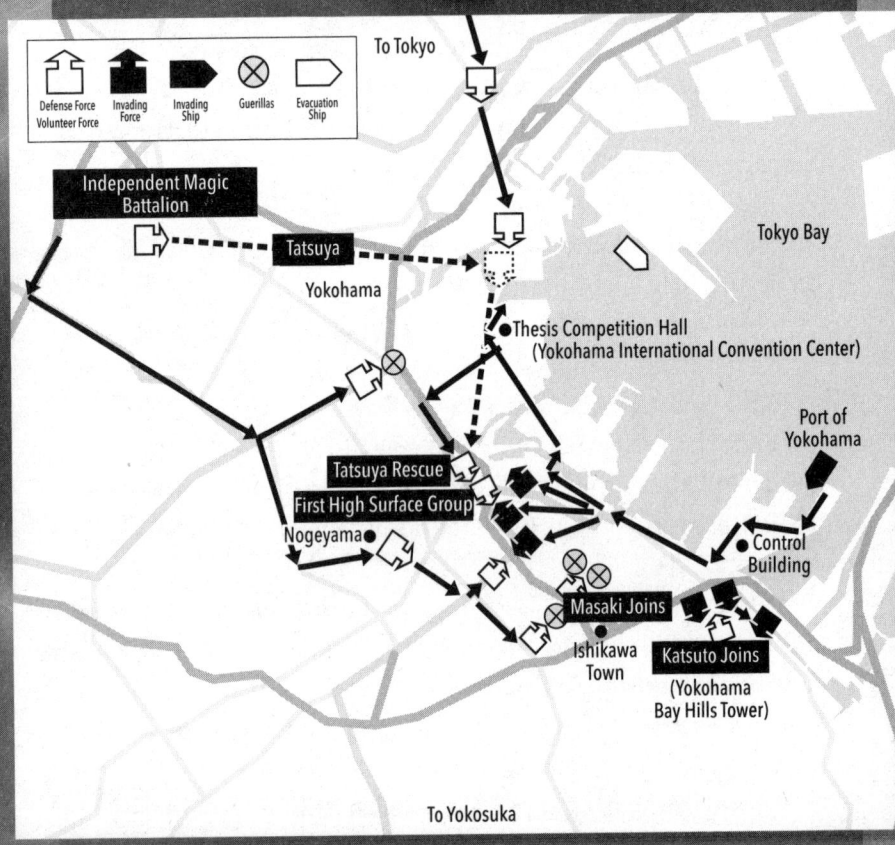

Yokohama

Thesis Competition Hall (Yokohama International Convention Center)

Port of Yokohama

Tatsuya Rescue
First High Surface Group

Nogeyama

Control Building

Masaki Joins

Ishikawa Town

Katsuto Joins (Yokohama Bay Hills Tower)

To Yokosuka

OCTOBER 30, AD 2095
5:00 PM, PRESENT TIME

But such old-style magical attacks—ones that couldn't immediately alter events and only manifested their processes as natural phenomena—were easy opponents for Katsuto to deal with. He constructed heatproof and shockproof walls in midair to protect himself and the volunteers around him.

But it wasn't just defensive. This act blew away the enemy magicians, along with the foot soldiers escorting them at the front of the line.

With just a single new addition to the battlefield, the situation reversed.

◇ ◇ ◇

Masaki, his hands full with the illusory attacks, was in the middle of a change of plans.

He stopped looking for the enemy magician and transitioned toward massacring all the enemies at once.

Until now, he'd feared civilian collateral damage, so he'd stuck to using spells that attacked single enemies. But he decided that letting the battle drag on like this would make the civilian damage worse—though he couldn't deny losing his temper, either.

Masaki aimed for the most focused group of three-man cells spread among the enemies, then designated a square area as an execution ground. Fifty feet to a side. Just to be sure, he left the cube at six and a half feet. (There were no signs of the enemy having made it into the building yet, so this would prevent potential casualties of civilians who were hiding.)

Using the CAD on his left arm, he activated a spell. A force sprang into effect that would alter events even behind cover, regardless of physical obstacles.

The initial change was a small one. The enemy troops would have only felt a slight rise in body temperature. But it would quickly become a stinging heat, then such an intense pain that they would have to roll around on the ground, until finally, after thirty seconds, the agony would turn them into white-eyed corpses.

A spell that heated via fluid particle oscillation, Screaming Inferno.

Dispersion magic that vaporized fluids was the Ichijou magicians' specialty, but that didn't mean they couldn't use other magic, of course.

In reality, though he wouldn't say it to his friend, Masaki was skeptical of the Cardinal Code hypothesis. He knew through his senses, rather than his mind, that the four families and eight types of magic were seamlessly connected, that they were fundamentally one thing. He *felt* that the type categorization of magic was nothing more than a convenience.

Screaming Inferno could be called a lesser version of Burst. Rather than instantly vaporizing body fluids, as Burst does, Screaming Inferno would heat them up over time (though that "time" was a little under a minute).

In exchange for its weaker power, the spell's target expanded from a "thing" to an "area."

From within the cube he'd summoned the cauldron of hell into, he felt an extreme disturbance.

Screaming Inferno also directly interfered with objects' interiors and people's bodies. It wouldn't work very well against a magician wearing Information Boost.

Which meant anyone still alive in that execution ground was a magician.

Found you!

Enemies still remained, but Masaki's gut told him that the magician still standing was the illusionist he was searching for.

He jumped out from behind a building and charged straight into what was left of the execution ground, now a blank area in his mind.

His allies' support fire silenced the guns aimed at him.

Switching his handgun-shaped CAD back to his right hand, he ran up behind the fleeing enemy magician—

And pulled the trigger without waiting for him to turn around. A crimson flower bloomed.

The enemy magician died at Masaki's hand with no time to surrender.

◇ ◇ ◇

Small thunderbolts danced madly across the street, putting a stop to the gun-wielding enemy troops.

Miyuki's group was encountering the enemy sporadically, and they'd stopped seeing new upright tanks and armored cars. The five soldiers disabled by Mikihiko's lightning magic all gathered behind a building.

"Saegusa says she'll come for us in a helicopter," explained Miyuki, who had received a call. "She's procured one just for us, aside from the one to evacuate civilians."

"How magnanimous of her," Erika admired drily.

"I don't think it's generosity, really… I think it was to make sure they got themselves out of here."

"Still, I'm not gonna complain!"

"You're right. Thanks to her, we should be able to escape, too."

Mikihiko, Leo, and Mizuki, respectively, could talk like this because the enemy's attacks had gone silent.

"Oh, isn't that it?"

Erika pointed it out, and they all turned to the sound of rotor blades. They'd taken up position only ten minutes' running distance away. When using a helicopter, other than landing and taking off, long distance travel was trivial. But the helicopter wasn't showing up. They could hear the sound of cutting winds from directly above them, but there was no shadow, no helicopter, nothing.

A call sign came. Miyuki put her comm unit to her ear.

"Miyuki? Sorry, but it's a little too narrow for us to land. We'll lower ropes, so could you grab on to them?"

Without waiting for a reply, five ropes appeared out of thin air and were lowered down to them. The ends wavered like a mirage.

"...Rarefaction— No, I suppose I should call it optical camouflage. Very clever, Honoka," said Miyuki to herself as she grabbed a rope and placed one foot on the last hold. She gave it a little tug to indicate she was ready, and the rope began to smoothly wind back up.

The other four hastily followed suit.

Once they got into the helicopter, everyone but Miyuki could clearly tell what Honoka was doing.

She was projecting a refracted image of the sky onto a semi-globular screen. Controlling the spell left her no room to speak; if the scenery was more variable than just sky, she wouldn't have been able to maintain the optical camouflage while moving.

"This is the perfect spell for ambushes, isn't it?" Mizuki asked.

"It is. I don't think I could keep up such complex processing, though," Miyuki stated.

"You think so, too, huh?"

Honoka didn't appear to hear much of what her friends were saying.

"We'll arrive soon, but if it's too hard on you, you can let it go," encouraged Mayumi.

"I'll be fine" was all Honoka could muster.

But unfortunately, they couldn't pick up Mari's group quickly.

Perhaps one should call it a last-ditch effort. From where Mayumi and the others had an aerial view of the situation, it appeared the center of battle had shifted near Chinatown, and they could tell that not many enemies were left.

However, Mari's group was currently under a fierce attack from foot soldiers—a number of magicians using rifles and missile launchers as their main weapons. Mayumi and the others hadn't been informed that Toshikazu was making his way behind the enemy line alone, so they were disturbed by the missing person and immediately moved in to support the five remaining.

Actually, saying "Mayumi and the others" might have been imprecise as well, since Mayumi was firing support spells from the aircraft.

Hailstones rained down on the enemy troops. Not drops of ice but bullets of dry ice—reaching inorganic supersonic speeds—that pierced their defensive clothing.

It was a spell called Magic Bullet.

The enemy troops were caught in a crossfire, with bullets firing at them from above, behind, to the side, and various other angles. One after another went down, unable to locate where the spell was coming from.

An attack from air to ground, aided by the advantage of her invisibility: Like that, Mayumi's spell took control of the area in less than five minutes.

"Sorry for the wait, Mari. I'll lower some ropes, so come on up."

"Great, thanks!"

Feeling unsatisfied by Mayumi's easy domination of the enemy troops with overwhelming firepower—though she hesitated to call it that—Mari cheerfully called out to her underclassmen.

They walked up in pairs, Isori with Kanon and Kirihara with Sayaka. It would be difficult to blame them for letting their guards down. Until a moment ago, they'd been right in the heat of battle, and now the overhead defense of the helicopter, no longer camouflaged, gave them relief. But the true value of guerilla fighters was surprise attacks in situations like these.

"Watch out!"

Mari was the one who gave the shout.

The first to move was Kirihara. He flung Sayaka to the side and swung his katana. He instantly activated High-Frequency Blade and repelled a bullet headed for his chest, but he could only cover his upper body.

A shot pierced through his right leg.

It tore the leg right from his body.

"Kirihara!" cried Sayaka.

"Kei!"

In another spot, Isori had pushed Kanon to the ground and was now covering her with his body.

Blood flowed from his entire back.

Stab wounds from a frag grenade—and likely fatal.

"Kei! Kei!!"

"Kirihara! Talk to me!!"

The two girls clung to them and cried out.

Mari tried to cast a spell against the ambushing guerillas, but it misfired due to an overwhelming force of influence covering the area.

Hastily, she looked to the side—to where it was coming from.

There, she saw Miyuki, smoothly floating down from the helicopter as though unrestrained by gravity. With a fearsome expression, she landed and lifted her right hand in front of her.

Miyuki had blown a fuse.

To her, Isori and Kirihara were no more than acquaintances. But just the fact that a cowardly ambush had hurt her acquaintances was enough for her to snap.

Even in that state, though, her mind was cool as ice.

It looked like she'd jumped out on reflex, but she had a perfect grasp on the gravity on her body.

She didn't need a CAD.

The magic area she unleashed completed her special, singular magic.

Miyuki hadn't only sealed Tatsuya's power.

She was constantly using half of her magical control to seal his strength.

Her magic's tendency to run amok was a side effect of having to suppress her brother's magic.

In releasing Tatsuya's abilities now, she also released her own.

The Yotsuba, as a family, had no nickname.

Each individual in the family had unique strengths, so you couldn't place it in one category. However, they were no more exempt to the genetic rules of magic than other families.

Miyuki's mother had possessed peerless outer magic that could interfere with people's mental structure. It wouldn't be strange if the power to inhibit the brain had been passed down to her daughter.

And because she possessed such magic, she could carry out her role of suppressing Tatsuya's mental strength.

Yes—her freezing magic was a derivative of the magic she'd been born with, changed in form to interfere with the physical world instead.

She held out her right hand.

And then the world froze.

It looked like the world had come to a stop with Miyuki at the middle.

The roads, the building walls—none of it was covered in ice.

The world of awareness was what she'd frozen.

Mari, Kanon, and Sayaka, as well as the wounded Kirihara and Isori, who had come into contact with its waves, were unchanged.

But the enemy soldiers pointing guns and about to toss hand grenades were stiff, unmoving.

And not frozen, but stilled.

It wasn't their bodies that had been frozen, but their minds.

The outer magic mental interference spell, Cocytus.

Once frozen, the mind would not return.

Once frozen, the mind would not perceive death. Nor would it order the flesh to die.

Once frozen, the bound body could not die, instead transformed into a statue of the last position the mind had willed.

Nobody here could explain what Miyuki had done.

But all of them saw an illusion of the world freezing.

All of them felt in their gut what she had done.

Even without words, they felt the terror of losing their minds.

Miyuki looked to her side, then up, then back down, giving a lonely smile.

But soon her head came back up, and she shouted and waved her arms:

"Tatsuya!"

Everyone present, aside from Kirihara and Isori, looked that way.

They saw a soldier all in black about to make a landing. He came down right next to Miyuki, lifted his visor, and lowered his mask.

Tatsuya's face was stern as he dashed to Isori's side.

"Tatsuya, please!" Coming up next to him, Miyuki clung to his hand.

Tatsuya nodded, then took the CAD from his left hip.

"What are you doing?!"

He pointed his silver CAD at Isori.

There was no time to stop him.

All Kanon could do was shout.

The trigger was pulled.

Kanon reflexively shut her eyes.

[Beginning eidos change history trace…]

Tatsuya's expression didn't change.

[Reconstruction point confirmed.]

This magic truly needed only a split second.

But Miyuki knew that at that moment, her brother was experiencing a pain that defied imagination.

Miyuki's eyes keenly picked up on the sweat forming on Tatsuya's brow.

Unconsciously, she looked away.

But Tatsuya's eyes, now merely part of a biological robot for using magic, only saw the information he needed.

[Beginning reconstruction...]

The other spell Tatsuya could use freely, Regenerate, triggered.

It traced eidos change history, reconstructed their state before injury, and copied them.

It attached the copied information bodies as a magic program to the eidos, then it overwrote the information recording the injured state with information from before the injury.

Information accompanied events...

...and information altered events.

In accordance with the basic principles of magic, a status alteration on the wounded flesh began. Soon, it was restored to a state in which it wasn't damaged.

It wasn't repairing the wounds, but canceling the fact that wounds had been sustained.

The world's corrective force sprang into action, trying to make the alteration applied to Isori's flesh make sense.

The grenade fragments were determined not to have struck Isori's body.

The fragments disappeared from Isori's body.
Not dismantled, but suddenly scattered about him.

Brrz. Isori's body appeared to haze over.
And then, a moment later, no wounds were left on his body.
In fact, even the blood staining his clothing had vanished.

[Reconstruction complete.]

* * *

Isori's flesh anchored to the world in which the grenade never wounded him.

Begrudging confirmation of Regeneration's effect on Isori, Tatsuya pointed his CAD at Kirihara and pulled the trigger.

Visually, one could call his wounds more dramatic.

No sooner than his torn-off leg was dragged back to his thigh and fully connected had Kirihara's body hazed over with a similar *brrz*.

A moment later, a boy with all his limbs lay there.

Tatsuya returned his CAD to his left hip, then embraced Miyuki without a word.

"Ah…!"

Miyuki's eyes widened as Tatsuya brought his hand around her and whispered something in her ear before pulling away.

He took a step back, pulled his mask back on, and lowered his visor.

Tatsuya, now back in his black-clothed form, hit his belt buckle and danced up into the sky.

Mizuki watched him leave in a daze.

In her ears, her brother's words—*You did well*—played again and again.

Face dubious, Isori looked down at his own body.

Kanon, who had been staring at him blankly, suddenly embraced him and started crying.

On the other side, Kirihara, seeming confused, jumped a couple of times and stood on one leg while Sayaka watched him with a tearful smile.

Upon hearing the tapping of a light footstep behind her, Miyuki turned around. Erika was there, having jumped off the copter, her taller-than-she-was sword in hand.

"Nice work. That was some crazy magic, huh?"

Miyuki answered Erika, who started talking as usual, with a reserved smile—one that also looked scared. "…Even the Angel of Death would yield the way to my brother," she said. "But that spell, it was…"

"Hmm? Oh, sure, Tatsuya's spell was great, too, but I was talking about what you did. That was amazing, taking down the bad guys like that. Guess I should have expected it from you!"

Erika's expression was neither an act nor a bold front. It just showed pure praise for Miyuki's skill.

There was no fear in it.

So…

"…Thank you."

…Miyuki found herself able to answer in her usual tone.

◇ ◇ ◇

North of the hill the Magic Association branch stood on, the invading army's offensive had been pushed back, and now its troops had rounded the southern side to attempt one final attack.

They'd already given up on securing hostages.

They didn't have enough troops to hold territory for long, either.

At this rate, they would have to retreat empty-handed. They resolved to, at the very least, steal some of the modern magic–related data stored at the association and kill as many magicians as possible to whittle away at Japan's magical military strength.

Getting the retreat timing right would be incredibly difficult, though. Deciding when to pull out when you were at an advantage was hard, too, but without dealing a decisive defeat to the enemy or acquiring anything from the battle, they couldn't easily get over their regret and leave.

They would hold the enemy's offensive in place, then strike at the rear. At a glance, it was a very dynamic tactic; the commander leading the diverted unit thought this as well, and felt uplifted by it.

Their detached unit of only armored cars and upright tanks hadn't encountered the enemy yet. This strategy depended on the prediction that the defenders had no mobile forces, and from one of the armored cars, the commander saw that seemed to be correct.

It was just then that it happened. With his upper body out of the car's rear hatch, the soldier assigned to keep watch looked up at a black shadow passing overhead.

The soldier wasn't able to identify it.

And then a bullet, fired from above, pierced through his head.

The invading army's vehicles frantically started communicating and pointed their machine guns upward.

As if to mock their reaction, the unit in black—the Independent Magic Battalion's flight corps—descended quickly from the sky. They landed on top of buildings along the road and showered them in a rain of concentrated fire from above.

Their rifle bullets, with strengthened penetration, rained down like a deluge, saturating the invaders' magical defenses and piercing the upright tanks' cockpits. Grenades with high explosive power blew away the armored cars' wheels, and sprayed heated metal powder that lit fire to their fuel.

The invading army wasn't helpless, either, though. They fired high-explosive shells at one building, turning it into rubble, and then they shaved away at another's wall with their heavy machine guns. They blasted flying soldiers staring down their barrels.

But the black unit's firepower didn't wane in the slightest. In fact, from within the torrential fire in the wreckage, from atop the building with the damaged wall, came an even fiercer salvo.

The invading troops were gripped by fear—fear that their enemies were immortal monsters.

They immediately got an opportunity to see with their own eyes how it happened.

One flying soldier lost his footing and fell on the road.

An upright tank's machine gun bored a hole into his body.

Thanks to the bulletproof jet-black combat suit, he didn't die immediately, but it was a fatal wound without a doubt.

However, a demon in black with a silver CAD in either hand descended next to him, and the moment he pointed his left at the soldier, the soldier's wounds vanished.

Then that man's right hand aimed at the upright tank targeting him. Noise shot through the armor-protected upright tank, and the twelve-foot machine turned to dust and disappeared.

"...*Maheśvara!*"

A scream spread over the radio waves.

Some spurred by terror to flee and others spurred by terror to charge collided with one another in waves, throwing the invading army's battle line into chaos.

This panic ended with their annihilation.

◇ ◇ ◇

On the camouflaged landing ship's bridge—in other words, its command center—a grave, tragic air had descended upon them.

"The detached unit is gone...?"

Even as his staff officer cringed with fear under his captain's— also the invading army's commander's—glare, he did his duty: "Estimating from our reports, they appear to have encountered an aerial unit using flight magic and were destroyed without any successes."

"..."

"...Also—and this is unconfirmed intel, but..."

"What?"

"We heard the word *Maheśvara* in their radio chatter."

"*Maheśvara?!*"

Half of the people on the bridge peeled their eyes wide open.

"Someone who was in the battle three years ago was present in our detached unit."

"…What does it mean?" asked an adjutant, who was among the other half, to the staff officer who had brought the report.

"…Foul nonsense!"

However, the one to answer him was the commander in chief himself.

Three years ago—that unknown demon who had defeated them at Okinawa.

That awful nickname that had begun to be whispered among the soldiers who had returned after the exchange of captives.

The Great Asian Alliance Army's higher echelons denied his existence, and their soldiers were forbidden from saying that name aloud.

It was a nightmare they thought they'd buried.

But however much they tried to cry out and deny it, the nightmare was real, and it was baring its fangs at them once more.

◇ ◇ ◇

Using their mobility, the IMB's flight corps fell upon the enemies fighting the Magic Association's volunteer army from the rear.

Forty of their soldiers had been sent to the front lines—no more than a single platoon. The speed of their mobility, however, was contrary to normal battlefield sense, raising their strength by two to three times that number.

And they didn't have to worry about troop attrition.

The jet-black combat uniforms they wore—MOVAL suits—were completely bulletproof. Every member possessed high-level magic capabilities for combat as well, so their defense against magical interference was just as firm.

Still, that didn't mean the enemy couldn't deal them any damage. Anything worn by a person has a limit on weight; failing to match up to tank and warship armor is unavoidable.

Thus, bullets still hit them.

Explosions still wounded them.

Sometimes they even ended up with holes in their chests or guts.

But as long as they didn't die instantly, they didn't stop. Soldiers fell, bleeding from gunshot wounds—and a moment later, they stood as though nothing had happened. They had no scars, no traces of blood on their suits. In fact, there weren't even any holes in those suits.

Every time a tall soldier with a silver CAD in both hands held out his left one, a wounded soldier was revived.

And the soldier, released from death, would fight on even more fiercely.

The invading army's troops couldn't believe what was happening before their eyes.

They knew they'd dealt fatal wounds, but it was like none of their attacks ever happened.

They'd had to have stumbled into a daydream.

A dream of the worst kind—a night terror.

Even as it eroded their sense of reality, they realized the causal relationship in what they were seeing.

The silver gun in the left hand was reviving the black-clad soldiers—they didn't know how it was doing that, but they understood that one fact instinctively, and they pointed their guns at the soldier.

But their bombardment would never reach.

Both bullets and grenades dissipated in midair.

Everything that right hand pointed at vanished into dust.

—— The Divine Left ——

* * *

Those to whom his left hand extended would return from the jaws of death…

—— The Demon Right ——

…and all his right hand pointed to, both man and machine, disappeared.

The two English phrases one soldier from Hong Kong had used three years ago to circumvent the army's gag order rippled through the ranks of the invaders…

—— Maheśvara! ——

…and turned into a huge wave that swallowed up their will to fight until nothing was left.

◇ ◇ ◇

The enemy's offensive stopped with unnatural timing. By Katsuto's intuitive prediction, it should have taken a bit longer for the enemy to turn and flee. Sooner than anticipated though it was, he wasn't about to let this chance escape.

"The enemy is afraid!"

In the volunteer army, assembled around the Magic Association, he belonged to the youngest echelon. Regardless, he'd taken the reins of command. Not that some with a keen eye didn't see through his age to his experience. But nobody objected to his innate ability to lead them.

Of course, the fact that his magic power was overwhelming, higher than anyone else's, helped a lot. Almost nobody misunderstood that—if he hadn't joined the fight, it would have been them getting pushed back and eventually being forced to retreat.

But it wasn't only his strength. That was actually a secondary factor. The volunteer troops had acknowledged Katsuto as their general because his commands had driven away their cowardice.

It was true that to win battles, supply was important. Training troops to a higher level was vital as well. Tactics that efficiently used troops, methods of transport, and means of communication were irreplaceable support mechanisms.

But after everything was spent, morale had the final word. A troop's combative spirit sometimes overcomes every disadvantage to achieve victory. In ground combat, at least, morale continues to be a factor in victory that nobody could ignore.

And it took a rare talent to draw out one's troops' spirits—the makings of a general.

"Push them back!"

At Katsuto's enjoinment, a barrage of magic fired.

A magical salvo made up entirely of weighting-type spells came at them, all attuned to match so that they wouldn't cancel one another out.

For the invaders, who were already about to flee, it was a decisive blow. Most of the soldiers and magical troops not inside mechanized weapons were mowed down. Half of what few upright tanks still remained fell over. Their remaining forces that had endured the assault—the armored cars, upright tanks, and a handful of soldiers and magical troops—began their defeated retreat.

Smashing his Phalanx into the fallen upright tanks one after the other, Katsuto swung his hand down in a wide arc.

"Forward!"

An order to pursue, to not give them time to regroup—that was how the volunteer soldiers' morale reached its peak.

◇ ◇ ◇

Masaki was just as ignorant as Katsuto of the enemy's back line collapsing from the IMB's attack. He did, however, simultaneously realize the winds had changed.

Like him, Masaki had fallen into a leader-like position among the volunteer troops, but rather than aggressively issue them orders, his stance was to go to the front line and protect them.

Right now, he stood alone before Genbu-Mon Gate, Yokohama Chinatown's northern gate. Postwar redevelopment had seen the buildings become walls, preventing entry and exit via all but the four gates at the cardinal directions. Most believed this was planned rather than a spontaneous development feature.

Was it to close themselves in, or close others out?

It was, most likely, the latter.

Right now, the four gates, which were thrown wide open at normal times to handle tourists, were shut tight.

Masaki had no intent of complaining about the fact that they were closed. Personally, he didn't like the idea of clustering together with one's own countrymen while living in another country and making that community into a veritable fortress. But right now, he wasn't standing at the closed northern gate in order to make a fuss about it.

"Open the gate! If you don't, you will be treated as holding secret communication with the invaders!"

As his words described, he was standing here ready for combat because enemies had fled into said fortress.

He didn't know when bullets would start flying from the other side.

Maybe what came flying would be grenades, or magic.

There was no assurance that explosives, or spells with enough force to penetrate his own defenses, wouldn't rain down on him.

Therefore, he had mustered his nerve and stepped up to the gate, ready to cast a spell at the drop of a hat.

Behind his words, Masaki was resolved to break through using force. He'd demanded they open up, but if they'd been willing to let everyone in so easily, then the enemies wouldn't have fled into town in the first place.

Even if the people in town weren't secretly communicating with the enemy forces, the first thing the enemy would have done was take control of the gates' opening and closing. Unarmed townspeople didn't seem fit to resist that.

And so, when he saw the gate creak open not a moment after his shout, he had to sidestep it, startled and dumbstruck.

A group came out, led by a young man about five or six years Masaki's elder, and he had a noble air about him.

They had soldiers from the invading army bound up with them.

"I am Gongjin Zhou," said the man.

"…Gongjin Zhou?"

"It is my real name," replied the man, appearing used to the reaction. He smiled to himself at Masaki's confusion.

"I apologize. I'm Masaki Ichijou."

Considering it would obviously be bad to forego a self-introduction to this older man, Masaki hastily—but evenly—named himself.

The man Zhou gave a bow, purposely lowering himself, then stepped to the side and offered the prisoners behind him (strictly speaking, captives) to Masaki. "We are not connected to the invaders. In fact, we're victims as well. We've taken the liberty of cooperating with you so that you understand that fact."

With a face that was the very definition of sincere, the young man appealed to his innocence. There wasn't a single tuft of a cloud in it—at least, not on the surface.

But Masaki found himself unable to believe the charade. For no reason he could name, he knew that's what this was.

Obviously, the man would insist they'd allowed the invading forces to enter; as a result, the aggressors would drop their guard and be captured more easily. It was a persuasive insistence, and one that made sense.

But how had they captured the armed soldiers to begin with?

He had to be wary.

* * *

That was the impression Masaki got from this man Zhou.

But that wasn't enough to give Masaki the right to investigate a civilian.

In addition, on the surface, one could say their cooperation had put an end to this front of the battle.

Masaki thanked Zhou. Then, aided by other volunteer soldiers, received the captive enemies.

He didn't realize the process had removed him from the front lines.

◇ ◇ ◇

Silence filled the helicopter escaping inland from the coast.

For some reason, there was an awkward air inside it, where everybody hesitated to speak.

Enduring the unnatural silence, though, was also something they couldn't do.

"…It happened to my own body, and yet…I still can't believe it."

Isori was the first one to say something.

"…What in the world happened? How and why is this even possible?" Kirihara, the other related party, was the next to offer a confused question to nobody in particular. "If you told me it was all an illusion, maybe I could believe it then…?"

"But it wasn't," replied Isori. "I almost died, and your leg came off—that's the absolute truth."

Another silence descended on them. The air got even heavier than before, presented with the altogether grave reality.

"…Shiba, just answer me this."

And, perhaps, at last:

Mari asked the question of the only one here who knew the truth—Miyuki.

"What is it?"

Her response was utterly calm, but she couldn't entirely hide the stiffness in her face.

Or perhaps she simply wasn't trying to hide it at all. Maybe she was purposely wearing this hard, crystalline expression to ward them off.

"How long will Tatsuya's spell's effect last?"

Magic-based healing was temporary. That was an underlying principle of healing magic. While the effects were active, a medic would reapply it several times, tricking the world several times, until finally the false healing took root in the real world. The shorter the time of the effect, the sooner the medic would need to apply a new healing spell.

"It's permanent."

But they didn't expect the answer they got.

"Continuous treatment will not be necessary, the way it is for normal healing magic."

Miyuki's response was based on a 100 percent understanding of Mari's intent, and made in regards to Isori and Kirihara listening as well.

"There are also no restrictions on exercise. You are able to go about your life exactly as before."

"...Is that even possible?"

Mari didn't seem convinced by her answer.

"Do you not believe me?"

"It's not whether we believe you or not," said Kanon—Mari wasn't the only one unconvinced. "I'm grateful he saved Kei...but I've never heard of healing magic you can use once to fully heal someone. It goes against the foundation of healing magic. Are they really cured? Then was what he did *not* healing magic? What the hell did Shiba do?!"

"Kanon, calm down." After Kanon burst into a heated barrage of questions, Mayumi calmed her down. "Miyuki, please don't be offended, okay? Kanon is just worried about Isori."

"I'm aware of that. It doesn't bother me." Miyuki answered Mayumi's follow-up with a reserved smile.

"But I am interested in what he did. If it wasn't healing magic, then what on earth—?"

"Mari! It's not courteous to ask about other people's spells!"

Just as the mood started to soften a bit, Mari destroyed it with her remark, earning a harsh reproof from Mayumi.

"Thank you, Saegusa. But I don't mind." Miyuki returned her own gentle rebuke. "I believe it is only natural you would wonder about it. I'm sure my brother would allow me to reveal it, if it was to you."

That meant they couldn't tell anyone else. And if they wouldn't protect the secret, the conversation was over.

"I won't tell anyone."

"I'll keep it to myself."

Mari and Kanon answered in very quick succession.

The other members also gave their own oaths in turn.

"We'll keep everything we hear now a secret. That goes for Nakura and the others as well."

And at the end, Mayumi said that.

"Well, it isn't actually all that important, but…"

Miyuki gave an unusual dry grin.

Whatever Mayumi promised, it would end up in the other Saegusa's ears. Miyuki decided that was all right, though. They knew what he could do now, so there wasn't much point keeping how he did it a secret.

After all, nobody could imitate it anyway.

"The spell my brother used isn't healing magic."

Assuming a proper posture, Miyuki began to quietly speak. Everyone listening, without realizing it, straightened up as well.

"The spell's name is Regenerate. It travels back twenty-four hours through eidos change history, makes a full copy of the eidos before receiving wounds from an external source, then makes them into a magic program with which to overwrite the current eidos. The overwritten target will, in accordance with the information that overwrote it, revert to a state before having received those wounds."

She paused there a moment, then looked around at everyone's face in turn.

"Do you all know why magic's effects don't last forever?" she asked, then continued without waiting for an answer. "The reason spell effects aren't perpetual is because of the restorative force of eidos. This restorative force is eidos trying to return to a previous state, before they were overwritten. However, the eidos copied by Regenerate are also none other than eidos, which express the past in and of themselves. A target overwritten with its own information will not revert back to a state of having been wounded, but instead take root in the world in a state where that time passed without those wounds happening. It makes everything like it never happened."

Mari and Kanon exchanged glances.

Mayumi blinked several times.

Isori froze completely, and Kirihara made a face like he'd been bewitched by a fox.

Though their expressions were different, everyone felt the same thing.

"Then Tatsuya can heal any wound in one go? I can't believe it. Even for Tatsuya, that's…"

Mikihiko was the one to actually give voice to that feeling.

"Not in one go, Yoshida," Miyuki denied with a smile. "In one instant. And the object doesn't have to be a living creature. Whether it's a human or a machine, my brother can instantly restore it."

Mikihiko froze, his jaw on the floor, and Miyuki smiled again, both amused and a little lonely. "This spell is the reason my brother can't use other magic freely. His magic region is completely taken up by this godlike magic, which doesn't allow any room for other spells."

Not a person here doubted the adjective *godlike* as anything but literal.

Because it wasn't a boast—it was a *miracle*.

"...So that's why Tatsuya is so unbalanced," murmured Mayumi.

"Yeah..." muttered Mari. "With a high-level spell like that on standby, it's no wonder he has trouble with other magic..."

Miyuki had only told them half the truth. She had no intent of revealing the other half. But her upperclassmen misunderstood, conveniently for her, so all she did was wear her lonely smile.

"But that's amazing, isn't it? He could cure any wound as long as it happened within twenty-four hours, right?" blurted out Kanon, as if to sweep the depressed air away.

"Yeah. The demand for someone like that during a disaster or in a field hospital would be immeasurable. He could save thousands of lives." Isori agreed, having understood the full meaning behind it, his voice passionate.

"That's right! Compared to that, who cares if he can't use other magic? Why did he keep such an amazing power secret? He could save so many lives with it. He'd be a real hero—not famous for taking lives but for saving them!"

"You're right... He can make any and all wounds go away like they never happened. Do you think he can use a spell like that without giving anything in exchange?"

In contrast to the excited Kanon, Miyuki was extremely calm, and her face wasn't very expressive. And then her cold, sharp gaze pierced Kanon.

When they saw it, Kanon, as well as Mari and Mayumi, came to the realization that she was forcing herself to remain calm by freezing her violently raging emotions in ice.

She was weeping, lamenting.

She was berserk with anger.

"He traces eidos change history and makes a full copy of them. To do that, he needs to read in *all* the information they store."

Miyuki's voice was still calm, even businesslike. But Mayumi, and Mari, and Kanon, and Isori, and everyone else listening to it felt a chill run down their spines.

"That, of course, includes the pain the wounded person experienced."

They heard someone gasp.

"He doesn't merely retrieve the pain as information. The sensation of pain, the signals created by the nerves of the person's wounded flesh—it flows into him as direct information. He doesn't perceive it through the brain, but rather directly through his mind."

Somebody began to cough. It wasn't someone trying to clear their throat but rather a biological reaction due to their inability to breathe.

"In addition, it comes to him compressed into a moment. For example…after you were injured, Isori, about thirty seconds passed before my brother used the spell. Compare that to the approximately zero point two seconds he took to read the eidos change history. In that moment of time, my brother's mind experienced the pain you did, compressed, and one hundred fifty times worse."

"A hundred and fifty…" moaned Isori. To be honest, he couldn't imagine what that would be like. But if he'd been exposed to that kind of pain, he wasn't sure he'd even stay sane.

"The longer the duration of the injury, the more pain is compressed. In order to erase wounds an hour old, he would be required to endure pain of at least ten thousand times the injured."

Miyuki subtly looked away from Kanon—so that she wouldn't release her anger on her, on anyone but herself.

"Every time my brother heals someone's wounds, that's the kind of price he pays, all right? Are you still going to say he should be using that power for others just because they want it?"

She was quietly raging.

Above all, at herself.

For her selfishness, for desiring her brother not to use Regenerate.

◇ ◇ ◇

"Captain, our forces have begun retreating!"

"Good."

Colonel Xiangshan Chen of the GA3's Special Convert Forces nodded upon hearing his subordinate's report, no surprise, nor frustration, nor shock to his voice. He hadn't exactly predicted their forces would have a high chance of successfully retreating, but he'd considered the possibility as part of achieving their strategic objectives. If they did, the tactical victory didn't matter. That was how he'd built up the position he now held.

"We will now execute plan number two."

Twenty soldiers followed him. He couldn't call it very much, but they were all veterans of back-line destruction missions. They had much higher levels of training than the infiltration operatives he'd brought with him at the beginning.

"Captain Lu."

And though they'd gotten the better of him once, Chen said the name of the subordinate he trusted as combat strength above all the rest.

"You may have personal feelings on the matter, but put revenge out of your mind. Obsessing over a Relic of dubious value was a mistake to begin with."

"I understand."

Whatever he may have been thinking, Ganghu Lu answered his superior officer in a perfectly controlled tone. He was clad in his rightful equipment—a suit of spell armor called Baifujia.

"Let's head out."

On Chen's command, his force quietly began to move.

Their destination—Bay Hills Tower, the Magic Association of Japan's Kanto branch.

◇ ◇ ◇

The heavy air hanging in the copter with Mayumi and the others suddenly broke when Mizuki blurted out, "Ah?!"

"What's wrong, Mizuki?" asked the Shiba sister—the cause of the silence weighing down on them—in a gentle voice. She probably thought they couldn't go on like this, so she'd inquired directly.

"Umm, near the Bay Hills Tower, I thought I saw an aura like a wild beast…"

Even after getting on the helicopter, Mizuki had been taking off her glasses every now and then and looking down at the ground. She'd set about keeping watch spontaneously, saying that it was all she could do, but now it seemed to have borne fruit.

"Like a wild beast? You mean, aggressive and violent?"

Mikihiko, even as he was asking, took out a paper talisman without waiting for an answer. He triggered its spell, then held it out in front of him, looking through it at the Bay Hills Tower, already small in the distance.

"An enemy attack?!" he cried in surprise.

"Are you sure?"

"But the volunteer army should have pushed them back…"

Erika and Kanon expressed their doubts in turn.

Mikihiko gave an affirmative nod to Erika's question, then shook his head at Kanon. "It's a surprise attack—a small group from the rear. I sense a terrible magical power. We should go back—the association is in danger."

The last sentence was directed at Mayumi.

Uncertainty came into her eyes, and she and Mari exchanged glances.

"My lady Mayumi."

And then came the voice of Nakura, from the copilot seat.

"We've received an emergency transmission from the Magic Association over the shared Ten Master Clans line."

"Give it to me!"

Mayumi snatched the communicator from Nakura's hands.

What she heard from the receiver was the exact emergency Mikihiko had announced. The enemy was few, but so were the magicians left at the association. They doubted they'd be able to hold out for long.

Mayumi made up her mind so quickly it was like she'd never been unsure at all. "Nakura, bring the helicopter to the association!"

Without waiting for an answer, she connected to someone else on the communicator. She got through right away.

"What's wrong, Saegusa?"

What came back was Katsuto's tension-filled voice. Mayumi picked up on his slight impatience and doubt, and knew the association had requested his help as well.

"Juumonji, this group will go to the association offices," said Mayumi, doing away with any preface. "We're turning the helicopter back there now, so we won't be long. You concentrate on eliminating the enemy forces."

Katsuto didn't know Mayumi was currently fleeing in a helicopter, and she didn't know he had taken command on the front lines.

But Mayumi was sure that Katsuto would never be watching the situation unfold from a safe place. And if he had joined the battle at some point, she knew he'd be something their line couldn't do without.

Even Katsuto couldn't be in two places at once. He couldn't take out enemies coming from two different directions at the same time.

"Thanks."

"No problem."

When Mayumi ended the call, the helicopter had already wheeled around.

Chen's unit's surprise attack caught the Japanese completely off guard. Not with the attack itself, which had only a few people, but by the fact that the invaders had kept such elites in reserve.

Having invaded from the sea, the army of the GAA—or so it was surmised—was now at a devastating disadvantage. Their Yamate unit had fled from the volunteer army under Katsuto's command, while the Kannai team had been captured thanks to a *betrayal* in Chinatown. They'd been completely destroyed in Yamashita Town by a flight corps all in black. The invaders shouldn't have had any room to conserve military strength.

But in reality, a small, elite unit had launched a raid. Though they were less than a platoon, every individual had incredibly high combat power. One soldier especially, wearing a white, Chinese-style suit of armor, was easily climbing the hill—treating armored-car machine-gun fire like it was nothing and breaking through the many barricades one after another.

Mayumi's group, after landing at the heliport, saw it happening.

"Is that—?!" cried Mari in shock at seeing the white-armored soldier—or, more accurately, sensing him.

"He's from before…" said Mayumi, also identifying the man's face with perception magic. She narrowed her eyes. "Ganghu Lu, was it? He escaped."

"Ganghu Lu?!"

"Erika, you know him?"

Erika nodded excitedly to Leo's question. "He's real strong."

"Truly."

But neither Erika's short reply nor Leo's grunt had any sign of cowardice. In fact, their eyes were glittering. The sight gave their oldest pair of seniors a headache rather than worry.

Looking down at the enemy unit pressing closer, Miyuki took out her CAD.

"Whoa there, Miyuki!" called Mayumi hastily. She'd been preoccupied with Erika, but she'd noticed just before things got dangerous. "Are you trying to override the association's magic, too?!"

Miyuki specialized in magic that affected areas. As soon as she cast one spell, any others with a weaker influence would be erased. If she'd been close enough to identify all her allies, she could have defined her spell's target more precisely to avoid getting in their way, but Mayumi didn't think she could do something that delicate from this far away—all the people looked like ants.

"It will be fine. I'll end this with one attack." Sure enough, Miyuki's answer was a violent one—she'd quiet both enemy and ally in a single stroke.

The suggestion was an ill fit to her graceful appearance. Mayumi wanted to hold her head in her hands, at the end of her wit. "You can't. If the worst happens and you miss one, it'll be your responsibility."

The Shiba girl thought, *I'd never miss any*, but she knew Mayumi was saying that out of worry for her, so she obediently put her CAD back in her inside pocket.

"You protect the branch office floor, Miyuki. I know this seems like I'm pushing responsibility on you, but you're the only one we can leave the final bastion to."

"Certainly."

Miyuki saw through Mayumi's plan of flattery but withdrew without further question.

"Kirihara and Mibu, can I get you to escort Miyuki, and Shibata as well?"

The setup was clearly one made in consideration for Kirihara's previous wound. Kirihara, though, accepted it anyway, without acting obstinately.

"Isori, Kanon, Yoshida, would you mind putting down the enemy soldiers aside from that white-armored one?"

After saying that, Mayumi looked to Mari. "Mari?"

"Right." Mari nodded. "We'll take that man down. Erika, Saijou, you two will help out." She looked straight at Erika.

"Don't have to tell me twice," she said.

Leo said nothing. He simply nodded firmly next to Erika as she gave an aggressive reply.

The Baifujia armor Lu wore was a Chinese magic/Taoist spell armor that amplified his Gang Qigong. It was when he was clad in this light armor, with its surface area not much different from off-road motorcycle protection, that he could display his true abilities as Ganghu Lu, the world's greatest close-combat magician.

Machine guns from armored cars lined up like a barricade, aimed at Lu, and fired. Their guns had power equal to or surpassing that of high-powered rifles. Lu easily repelled them. Not only with his armored surfaces but also with his uncovered ones. That was what was meant by amplifying Gang Qigong. Furthermore, the element symbolizing Byakko, the white tiger, was metal. This white suit of armor further strengthened the rampart-like defensive spell laid over his body. In the lead, he broke through one barricade after another, and the surprise attack force closed in on the association offices.

Then, in front of the final barricade, Ganghu Lu came to a truly detestable girl. He reveled at the unexpected chance at revenge. He'd agreed to Chen's commands, but in his chest smoldered a desire for vengeance. Neither his side wound nor his back wound hampered him when he was wearing this armor. He charged at the girl who had humiliated him over two opportunities—Mari.

Mari readied the tri-sectional sword the association had supplied her with—an armament device based on her hidden weapon. Her left hand held it while her right hand hovered above the CAD on her wrist. At her waist were two small-hilted blades, along with various drugs and cylindrical containers packed onto her belt. Her clothing, a woman's combat suit, was also borrowed from the association. Mari was fully decked out, but how far could she really go against Ganghu Lu bearing his full powers? Mari herself knew the answer better than anyone.

Then, from the side, Erika charged at Ganghu Lu, who had been looking only at Mari.

Mountain Tsunami ensued.

Even for Ganghu Lu, it was moving too fast to avoid. If he'd been watching Erika from the start, he might have been able to, but with his tunnel vision now, he couldn't dodge.

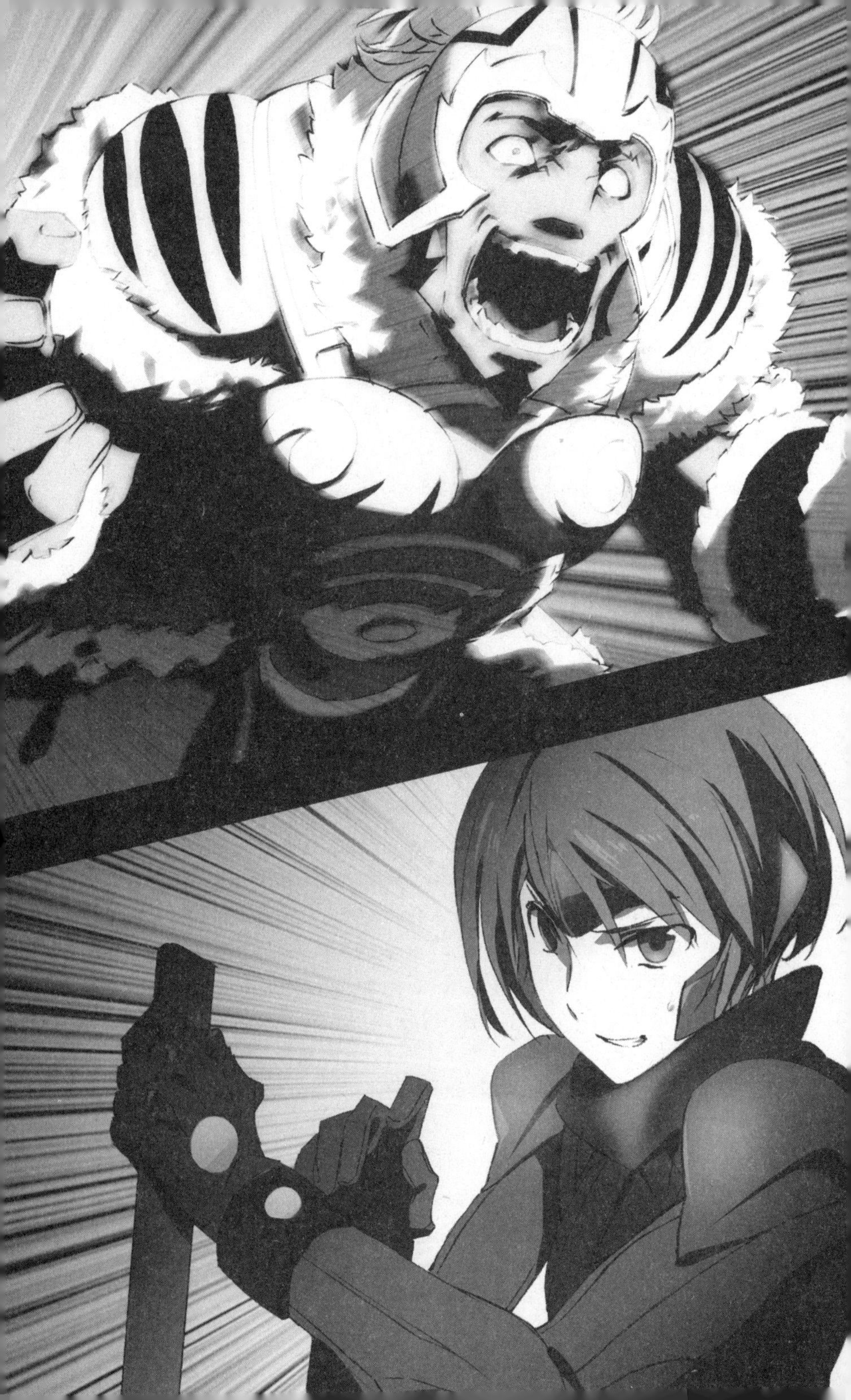

Lu turned to face the diagonally slashing long sword, then raised both arms to block the Orochi-Maru. The pavement at Lu's feet peeled up. He'd been driven down by Mountain Tsunami's force, but Lu's Gang Qigong had stopped the blade's deadly pressure.

"Seyyy-yah!"

A roar came from behind Lu.

With a shout, Leo swung the *Usuba Kagerou*. He aimed for the lower body—a slashing attack to cut down the legs.

If it had been a straight downward swing from in front of the man, he might not have been able to see the virtually zero-thickness blade. But the swing was horizontal, so Lu's eyes caught the dark shadow of the carbon nanotube band.

The man's body shot up into the air and sent a cannonball-like flying kick at Leo. Leo switched his horizontal slash to an upward one to follow the man, but he didn't make it.

"Guoh?!"

A short grunt came from Lu in midair.

In the middle of his flight path toward Leo, Mayumi's magic had caught him. Each of her individual shots had only a tiny bit of weight, but hundreds of them hitting him at once were enough to send a human body flying. Lu's kick missed its mark and passed by Leo's side. The moment after landing, a perfect opportunity to strike came—but not this time.

"Panzer!"

Just after Leo intoned his voice command, Lu thrust both hands into Leo's chest. It was a tiger fist, unleashed with blinding speed after Lu had gotten up.

Leo's body flew and crashed into one of the vehicles in the barricade.

"Why, you!" Erika swung down her Orochi-Maru.

This time, Lu brilliantly avoided the head-on downward slash.

The sword was about to slam into the road but didn't—instead, it bounded up toward Lu's side. Erika had swung down without restoring the inertia, then restored it right when she made the quick turn. A Mountain Tsunami variation: Mountain Tsunami Tsubame-Gaeshi.

But despite her upswing's weight, it wasn't fast enough to cut through Lu's Gang Qigong. Lu let the blade slide across his side and closed in on Erika.

She took her left hand from the Orochi-Maru and received his palm thrust with her arm.

Erika and her weapon both went flying.

A momentary suspicion flashed through Lu's face.

For an instant before his strike, he'd felt too little resistance. Had Erika used the Orochi-Maru's functions to cast an inertia-canceling spell?

But, like Leo, Erika crashed into the barricade, fell to the ground, and stopped moving. If she'd completely nullified inertia, she wouldn't have been damaged from her collision with it, but it seemed her instantaneous response had been incomplete.

Lu immediately returned his attention to Mari. But that iota of time was a precious one.

When he turned back, Mari's right hand had already followed through. Between her fingers were three slender cylinders.

Lu stopped breathing. He hadn't forgotten about the spell that led to his bitter defeat. In a hypoxic situation, simply stopping his breath wasn't enough; if the air, with its low oxygen concentration, reached his lungs, it would eat away at his body. So Lu controlled the back of his tongue and closed off his respiratory tract, physically stopping his breath.

But Mari didn't use the same trick this time. Her strengths lay neither in having powerful, unrivaled magic, nor in being able to swiftly cast her spells. Combining a plethora of spells and activating them at the same time to slip through an opponent's defenses was the combat tactic that defined her. At First High, Hattori had a similar quality, but in terms of pure hand-to-hand combat, Mari had far more variations than he did. In particular, she specialized in magic that used an opponent's sensory organs already open to the outside world—for example, their hearing or their smell—to diminish their fighting strength. With her technique, she was named one of the "three giants," a magician good enough to rival the two direct Ten Master Clans descendants, Katsuto and Mayumi.

Lu's Baifujia was a traditional Chinese suit of armor, so there was no airtight mask on it. This couldn't be helped, as it was an old-style magic spell armor, and normally he'd never find himself suffering a gas-based attack when already mingled with the enemy, so given the Baifujia's applications, he didn't mind.

But what if there was a magician who *could* launch a gas-based attack, in an abnormal way, from a sword's range?

Mari's air-current control sent the three containers' volatile chemicals scattering and mixing, creating a scent that would induce a feeling of intoxication, and it directly reached the inside of Lu's nose, where his olfactory organs were.

Lu's body had been trained to resist poisons, so he quickly overcame the aroma's effects. But by the time his physical functions were restored, her three-sectioned blade was already at his throat. He saw it trace a black line—the edge of a Pressure Cut—and decided to get out of the way instead of blocking it.

At the same time that he pulled his head back, he did a front kick. It wasn't a technique, just a brute force attack, but he still had an easy time knocking Mari into the air.

Following up on his evasion of the repulsive blade and his peeling back, he opened his air passage.

Now looking up, he perceived a white mass descending.

As the small, fist-sized clump of dry ice fell *slowly enough to be seen*, Ganghu Lu struck it with his right palm.

A moment before the dry ice made contact, it reverted to carbon dioxide. The vapor expansion–induced shock wave assailed Lu, and now that his air passage was open, the high concentration of CO_2 in the air made it to his lungs.

Mayumi's trump card for personal combat—Dry Meteor. A four-process spell that converged, condensed, accelerated, and sublimated carbon dioxide. In the end, it was magic that rendered an enemy disabled with a shock wave and CO_2 poisoning.

The greatest close-combat magician in the world had been finished off by a teenage girl lauded as the greatest user of long-range precision magic in the world.

"Mari, are you all right?!"

"Erika?! Leo?! Are you okay?!"

Kanon and Mikihiko went running to them. Behind Kanon, one could see Isori's face, exhaustion starting to show through. He must have been cleaning up other enemy soldiers aside from Ganghu Lu.

"I'm fine," Mari answered immediately. "Thanks to all this protection."

"You two don't look hurt yourselves," said Mayumi, peeking over the barricade, referring to Kanon and Isori.

"Nothing to see here," said Leo as well, awkwardly getting to his feet, appealing his healthy condition to Mikihiko. His hardening magic–based armor seemed to have been enough.

"...Same here, somehow."

And the last one, Erika, responded with an irritated voice, still lying on the ground.

"Erika?!" Mikihiko quickly ran to her side. A look of worry came to Leo's face as well.

However, as soon as Mari looked in her direction, Erika abruptly rose.

"Erika, should you be up?" asked Isori, who wasn't speechless at her surprising move like Mikihiko and Leo were.

"I'll be fine. Minor concussion. I was conscious, anyway," said Erika, ending with a deep sigh. "Guess I lost."

Rather than being happy about the defeated enemy, she grumbled about *herself* having lost. It was so like her that Mikihiko and Leo couldn't help trading tired grins.

◇ ◇ ◇

Xiangshan Chen proceeded down the hallway to the Magic Association branch office by himself. He wasn't moving particularly fast, nor especially quietly. He was walking normally. He eschewed the elevator from the first floor in favor of ascending the stairs, but nobody had challenged him yet.

All their caution would be on his subordinates, who had climbed up from the base of the hill, purposely revealing themselves. He knew that, and he didn't doubt it. After all, he'd planned it that way. Ganghu Lu, wearing his flashy white suit of armor, would be serving as a suitable decoy.

Qimen Dunjia. A method of telling fortune by direction. Just as *ninjutsu* was advanced but wore the mask of simple martial arts, the old-style magic Qimen Dunjia had another side.

Magic to *control* direction. A secret art that guided others' awareness in a direction of the caster's wishes.

Anyone whose sense of direction had been muddled couldn't reach their destination. For example, someone would try to go perfectly straight yet end up circling the same location. To them, their carriage, proceeding at a walk, would appear to be moving at a strange speed, and they would never catch up, no matter how much time passed. So the other face of Qimen Dunjia was a mental interference spell that specialized in directions.

It didn't have to be a geographical direction based on longitude or latitude, either. One of Qimen Dunjia's fundamentals was to twist the destination of one's attention. *Thanks to his subordinates' work*, Chen had easily arrived at the Magic Association of Japan's Kanto branch.

He placed his hand on the door, but it was locked. This was something he'd expected, and without panicking, he removed a terminal from his inside pocket and held it to the door's key-card panel. The physical contact made the Electron Goldworm, set up to undo locks, take hold over the key system. An alarm rang out that the lock had broken, but Chen didn't heed it. It would take long enough for staff to return. He set foot into the association's branch office—and was suddenly arrested by a strange chill.

"Is this Qimen Dunjia? Thank you for the opportunity to learn from it."

A beautiful voice like a ringing bell sank into Chen's ears. *He wasn't frozen*, and yet he had to work hard to move his body and look at where the voice had come from.

There was a person—one who didn't seem real, one who was so fleetingly beautiful as to seem like a dream of Shangri-la, a girl *he knew well from pictures*, staring at him with a cold smile.

"Miyuki Shiba…"

"If you know who I am, then you must have been the one following my brother about like a fly."

For some reason, there was a hint of relief in Miyuki's voice.

That made him suspicious, too, but a different question came from Chen's mouth, a more pressing one. "Why are you here? Did my spell not work…?"

The temperature of Miyuki's smile rose slightly. That simple action forced Chen to rally all his strength to hold back his own mind. "I received a warning," she answered. "To take care of my direction."

Chen's eyes went wide. That meant they'd predicted this plan.

"To be honest, that wasn't enough for me to understand, but I figured that if I had to keep an eye on directions, I would get by if I kept my guard up in three hundred sixty degrees—in every direction at once."

That's absurd, thought Chen. If that was all it took to break the spell, Qimen Dunjia would have died out long ago. But he changed his mind. The fact was that she *had* broken it. He felt a different chill than the one from the outside holding his body in check.

"Fortunately, we have a magician who can see the invisible, which is how we spotted you, as you were using a spell *in an effort not to be seen*."

Chen wanted to point out, *That has nothing to do with keeping your guard up in all directions!* but his tongue was unable to get the words out.

"In any case, if you were our little voyeur, then having you leave the picture will be a relief for a while."

Miyuki gave a happy, and even more beautiful, smile.

That smile made Chen realize what his fate was.

It had taken this long to figure it out—that his body temperature had dropped abnormally low.

"Please, take a nice rest. I've improved in many ways myself, so you shouldn't be asleep forever."

That was the last thing Chen heard before his mind was shut away into the darkness.

◇ ◇ ◇

Meanwhile, as Miyuki captured Xiangshan Chen, Tatsuya had neared the enemy's throat with Yanagi's team.

Katsuto had fiercely expelled the invading army with the volunteer soldiers he had taken control of, but they generally moved on foot, while Tatsuya's group had more mobility. They used the revolutionary troop application brought about by their flight devices—which let each individual soldier fly—to its fullest as the Independent Magic Battalion drove through the enemy's rear and flank.

Originally, the IMB had been an experimental force that applied brand-new magic technology for military affairs.

Their high-mobility combat, made possible by their MOVAL suits, could be called their true ability on display.

The trend of offensive weaponry eclipsing defensive weaponry had continued into the modern day. Under a technological system involving portable infantry missile launchers for breaking through heavy tank armor, ground forces had to take up extended formations. And if the situation was such that their opponents were spread out, they could use their mobility and striking power to effectively *eliminate whole groups at a time.*

Not eliminating an entire unit at once, but eliminating the spread-out groups of soldiers within that unit, individually.

Their MOVAL suits' mobility and armament devices' striking power made this tactic possible, and the Independent Magic Battalion destroyed the enemy army.

Rifles with upgraded piercing ability.

Portable fuel-vaporizing, explosive-loaded missiles with restricted-combustion gas-diffusion direction.

Powder rail guns that fired high-heat metal powder using electromagnetic force.

All the weapons with material-based and construction-based problems, weapons impossible to use with only non-magic technology—the battalion was wielding them to their full extent.

They made ample use of magic itself, too, of course. The most stand-out ones included Captain Yanagi's Floor Flip and Tatsuya's Mist Dispersion.

The sight of steel hunks weighing several tons rolling across the road was a thrilling sight indeed. But no matter how flashy it may have been, Yanagi's Floor Flip was a support spell; on its own, it wouldn't finish the enemies off.

In contrast, Mist Dispersion could be called a plain, quiet magic. It had no sound or light. And, since he upped its dismantling level to avoid getting caught in gunpowder or fuel explosions, no flammable materials combusted or produced flame.

They just disappeared.

They turned into dust, then into vapor, then dispersed—and then it was over.

With only that, enemy vehicles and enemy soldiers both stopped existing.

The sight of such a cruel spell, which wouldn't even let them leave a corpse behind, uprooted any last semblance of fighting spirit among the enemies.

Fifteen minutes after contact.

That was the enemy's limit.

Unable to overcome troop attrition—and, more importantly, the loss of morale—the invading army broke rank and began to flee.

YOKOHAMA INCIDENT OUTLINE
5

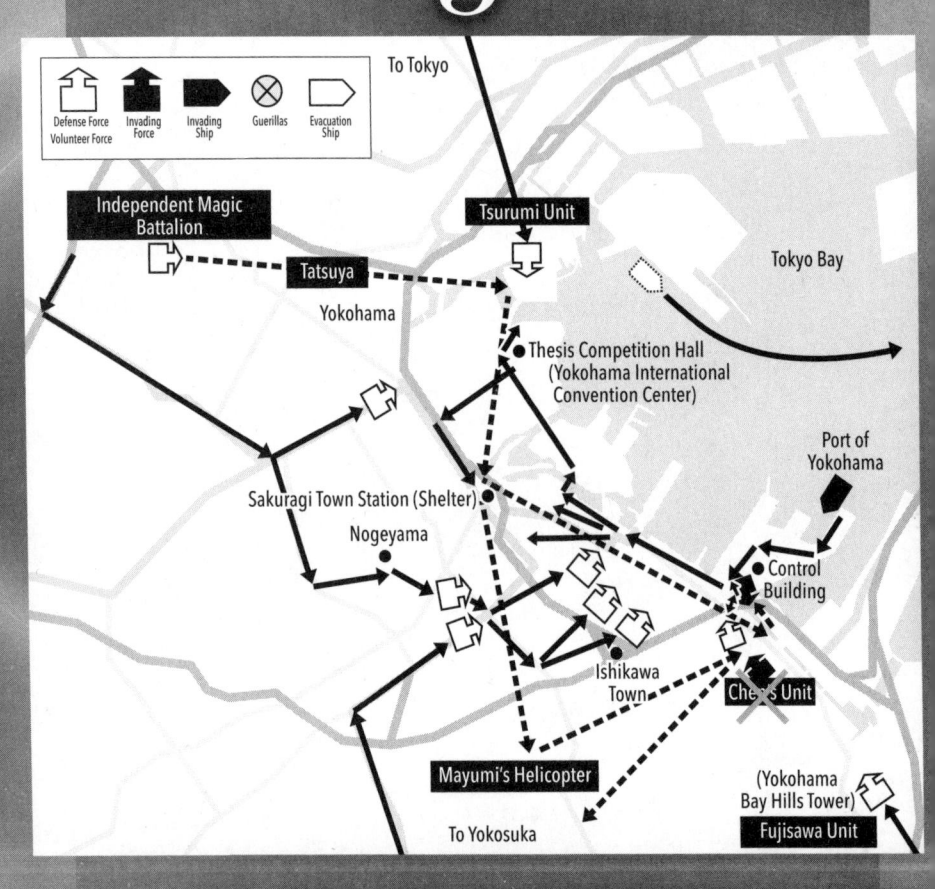

Legend: Defense Force Volunteer Force | Invading Force | Invading Ship | Guerillas | Evacuation Ship

To Tokyo

Independent Magic Battalion

Tsurumi Unit

Tatsuya

Yokohama

Tokyo Bay

Thesis Competition Hall (Yokohama International Convention Center)

Port of Yokohama

Sakuragi Town Station (Shelter)

Nogeyama

Control Building

Ishikawa Town

Chen's Unit

Mayumi's Helicopter

(Yokohama Bay Hills Tower)

To Yokosuka

Fujisawa Unit

OCTOBER 30, AD 2095
5:30 PM, PRESENT TIME

[13]

The Independent Magic Battalion finally had the enemy's headquarters, the disguised landing ship, in their sights.

The deployed enemy forces had consisted of twenty large, wheeled vehicles, sixty upright tanks, and eight hundred combatants. That included numerous magicians.

It wasn't enough to hold an occupation, but it was enough striking power for a single situation. Now, its armored cars and upright tanks numbered zero, and their troops had been annihilated, sustaining a 70 percent loss.

Standing at the forefront of those who had driven them into a disorganized escape was a flight unit of only forty people.

The Yokohama Incident had entered its final stage.

◇ ◇ ◇

Katsuto, who had completely taken up the mantle of volunteer army commander, received a report from the Magic Association's branch office.

"Sir, the enemy warship appears to have left the coast!"

Katsuto raised his eyebrows slightly in surprise. "I didn't think the enemy troops had finished retreating."

There were no longer any enemies in sight who were engaged in combat. Of the ones they'd been crossing blades with a few moments ago, some had stayed as a way to buy time, then fled. But all the survivors of that remaining group had surrendered by now, too.

However, this was too early for them to have gotten all their remaining soldiers onto the ship. There should have been more of them around the coastal areas.

"The enemy appears to have given up on collecting their remaining forces. Shall we begin the mop-up operation, sir?" the messenger asked, eyes sparkling. He was still young, probably around Katsuto's age. They'd just come out of a difficult fight where many of his allies had died. It was only natural that revenge would be burning in his heart.

That, though, was exactly why Katsuto shook his head. "That isn't our job. It would be an unnecessary risk. We should leave the rest to the JDF."

"…Understood, sir!"

He probably wasn't fully convinced, but he also didn't seem willing to go against the Ten Master Clans' magician who had brought them victory.

The young man spread the word to the entire volunteer army to cease hostilities.

◊ ◊ ◊

From the north, the Tsurumi battalion; from the south, the finally-arrived Fujisawa force; and from the west, the Hodogaya garrison and a Fujisawa detachment that had joined them. Unable to endure the three-pronged pressure, the enemy stopped collecting its ground forces midway through and made for a retreat.

Yanagi never intended to let the enemy ship, hastily leaving port, out of his sight. "We'll leave the stranded troops for later units and attack the enemy's ship directly. Take out its navigation!"

If they used the MOVAL suits' aerial mobility, they could soar over the remaining soldiers' heads, board the ship, and take it over from the inside, but Yanagi wasn't planning on risking it or burdening themselves with the work.

They formed ranks, placing soldiers with directional bomb-vaporization missiles in the center and those carrying super-penetrative rifles as their escort.

But the very moment before they took off, a voice told them to stop.

"Captain, please refrain from any direct attacks on the enemy ship."

"Fujibayashi? What's the problem?"

The one who had cut into their comm had been Fujibayashi. *"The ship is using a hydrazine fuel cell. The effects on aquatic life in the Tokyo Bay would be too great if you destroyed it there."*

Yanagi quietly clicked his tongue in frustration.

He didn't ask her how she knew that.

One of the spells in Fujibayashi's repertoire could scan a target by detecting electron ray emission and reflection. For her, who could tell the difference between a normal magician and a Generator based on subtle brainwave-pattern differences from over a mile away, it wasn't difficult to identify the molecular composition of large amounts of fuel stored in a container without even any radiation barriers.

"Then what do we do?" he asked.

"Pull out, Yanagi."

"Major?" asked Yanagi dubiously as the person on the other end of the comm changed suddenly. Not at the change specifically, but at the order.

"Make no mistake—this doesn't mean the operation is over. Leave it to the units from Tsurumi and Fujisawa to clean up the remnants, and return to base for now."

"Roger that, sir."

This time, his answer was swift and without hesitation, as though he'd organized his thoughts while listening.

Soldiers given flight by the MOVAL suits were great for assaulting the enemy's headquarters or launching surprise attacks from the flank, but they weren't suited to operations like mop-ups that called for numbers and time.

And besides, however elite their troops and optimized their systems, they would always accumulate exhaustion when using magic for long periods of time.

Yanagi gave the order to his subordinates to go back to their mobile base.

◇ ◇ ◇

Leaving the returned Yanagi in command, Major Kazama took Captain Sanada, Second Lieutenant Fujibayashi, and Tatsuya to the Bay Hills Tower rooftop.

The mop-up operation (the battle to clear away the remaining enemy troops and restore the region to a non-combat state) was almost complete. There were sporadic flashes of light and gunshot noises here and there, but they, too, would calm during this evening. They also planned to open up a temporary tunnel tomorrow to the shelter, which had been buried underground when the passage collapsed. The people who had evacuated there were actually in a more pleasant environment than the temporary shelters constructed aboveground.

The current time was 6:00 PM.

Twilight—the hour of monsters.

"Enemy ship traveling south through Sagami Sea at thirty knots," reported Lieutenant Fujibayashi to Kazama, watching a small, portable monitor. "It's about halfway between the Bousou Peninsula and Ooshima. I don't believe sinking it now would cause problems."

Kazama nodded and turned to Sanada. "Unseal the Third Eye."

"Yes, sir."

After receiving a key card from Kazama, Sanada, face almost imprudently happy, unlocked a large case sitting next to him. They'd gotten this case delivered posthaste from their Kasumigaura headquarters. It was locked with a compound key, which needed a key card, a vein-authentication key, a password, and voiceprint recognition.

"Form is emptiness and emptiness is form."

"*Password accepted.*"

The voice response was an unnecessary thing, a hobby of Sanada's, but this strict seal was no game.

Inside was a large rifle-shaped CAD.

Sanada took the CAD—the Third Eye—and handed it over to Tatsuya, who was still in his MOVAL suit and helmet.

Tatsuya pulled a cord out of the stock and plugged it into the suit's right wrist joint. The cable extending from the joint went through the suit, connecting to the helmet.

"Specialist Ooguro," said Kazama, calling Tatsuya by his code name. "Use Material Burst and sink the enemy ship."

"Yes, sir."

Tatsuya's voice was tense.

He hadn't used the spell in real battle in three years, but he had no fear he'd succeed at Material Burst itself. The tension made him excited as he gave a warrior-like tremble.

Tatsuya faced south and placed the stock on his shoulder.

"Stratospheric surveillance camera link established," Fujibayashi, looking at the laptop monitor next to them, reported to Kazama.

It wasn't something Tatsuya needed to be told. The linked infrared image of the enemy ship was now displaying in his visor.

The border surveillance cameras, loaded onto stratospheric platforms floating in the sky in a loop around the Japanese island, had sent their images to the Third Eye through its antenna.

Tatsuya, identifying the target and data from the same screen Fujibayashi was monitoring, probed the current status of the ship's side view.

Countless water droplets stuck to the ship's hull. From those, he selected droplets stuck to the deck exactly above the hydrazine fuel tank.

Then, on a single drop of seawater the surveillance cameras' analytical functions could never pick out, aided by the Third Eye's long-distance precision aiming assistance system, he used his ability to see eidos and took aim.

"Activating Material Burst," he said, pulling the trigger.

A sense of relief had washed over the Great Asian Alliance's disguised landing ship as they traveled south through the Sagami Sea.

"Japan didn't attack us after all."

"Hmph…as if they'd have the gall."

"They could have been cautious of hydrazine leakage, sir."

"Same thing. They're still obsessed with their hypocritical environmental concerns, which let the enemy retreat before their eyes."

The state of mind, no matter what nation the soldiers were from, would seem the same in that nobody used the word *flee*.

They'd realized they were being monitored somehow, whether it was from satellites or the stratospheric platforms, but they didn't think any further attack would come.

One couldn't call that a misstep, either. Basic theory stated that if Japan had wanted to, they'd have attacked long ago. They'd at least be trailing them with a ship or an aircraft.

"…Remember this. We'll pay you back double for this humiliation."

Their return home was already a predetermined fact for them, and more than a couple of officers were quick to swear vengeance.

And then, when they were about to pass east of Ooshima—

An alarm went off, indicating a psi-wave fluctuation. It alerted them to a CAD aiming-assistance system locking on to them.

"What is—?"

Going on, was probably what the captain wanted to say.

That, too, was only natural, for there was no trace of an enemy in at least a six-mile radius.

But the ship's captain couldn't finish his short line.

A burning-hot orb of light sprang to life on the deck.

It heated the air until a shock wave occurred, melted the deck, and caused a jet stream of vaporized metal, completely burning all flammable materials to a crisp—including the hydrazine—and then, turning into a giant ball of flame, it engulfed the ship.

The scorching hellfires created by Material Burst could be seen from the Bay Hills Tower and through stratospheric surveillance cameras as well.

The ultimate dismantling magic, Material Burst: a spell that dismantled matter into energy.

It was not a pair annihilation reaction. Tatsuya had broken matter down directly into energy, so the energy loss from neutrino emission that occurred during a matter-antimatter reaction didn't happen. As Einstein's theory predicted, the matter converted to energy at a factor of the speed of light squared.

The amount of heat created by the breakdown of a single drop of water, fifty milligrams of mass, was equivalent to one ton of TNT.

All that heat had been instantaneously created in the space of a water droplet.

"...Explosion confirmed at the enemy ship's coordinates. We can't make out the situation due to the water vapor explosion, but I estimate it has sunk," reported Fujibayashi, looking at the monitor.

"I did sink it, ma'am," corrected Tatsuya, then asked, "Any danger of a tsunami?"

"Everything's fine; we don't need to worry about that."

"Pinpointing a water droplet fifty millimeters square at a distance of fifty miles or so… We've demonstrated the Third Eye's full capabilities, sir," reported Sanada to Kazama, elated.

Kazama nodded silently to him, then said to Tatsuya, "Excellent work."

"Yes, sir." Tatsuya saluted.

Kazama nodded, then declared the operation over.

◇ ◇ ◇

Gongjin Zhou learned of the Yokohama invasion ship's *disappearance* while at a banquet by himself. His master, who had the power to know all the information being exchanged in the world, had notified him by encrypted mail.

Gongjin Zhou gave a thin smile. No part of his heart mourned their deaths. They were all simply people who happened to live in the same country as his ancestors. Zhou had never received any protection from *their country*, not even once. For all that, it was now natural for them to ask him for aid or demand money from him. He had no reason whatsoever to feel goodwill for them. In the same way, he had no reason to have goodwill toward this country's *government*, either.

Nations were better off weak. That's what Zhou thought. The weaker a nation, the stronger the money. If every nation was weaker, state controls would loosen, too. Then they'd be able to do their work freely.

His current objective—to catch many magicians in battle and let them die, thereby weakening national military force of magic—had, in the case of this nation, failed. But *that* country would have sustained more than few losses. Plus, that country seemed like it was planning on mobilizing their tactical magician, their trump card, momentarily. Zhou's master had made sure of it. When that happened, this nation's tactical magician would likely take the field.

Which would survive? Or would it end with both of them dead?

Gongjin Zhou lifted his glass of wine, an evil smile coming onto his face.

◇ ◇ ◇

Miyuki returned home and spent the night by herself.

Being alone wasn't unusual. Tatsuya would, at times, be absent for Independent Magic Battalion drills and training. But he would always faithfully contact her, and he'd called her today as well.

Besides, even if the two of them were far apart, they were always connected. Not in an abstract or theoretical sense—his power was always keeping watch over her surroundings, always protecting her from threats.

It was the same now. Even if she cut off her influence over her brother, her brother almost never cut off his protection of her. Tatsuya was always unconsciously watching over her.

It made her feel incredibly guilty, but she was still happy for it.

All of a sudden, the phone's incoming-call melody began to play.

It was a tune that almost never played.

——And thus, destiny knocked on the door——

As that phrase suggested, this melody was always one that changed the girl's fate.

She quickly rose, took a moment to groom her appearance, then went in front of the camera and opened the call channel. "Hello, Aunt Maya. It's been a long time since I last heard from you."

"I'm sorry for calling so late, Miyuki."

"Please, don't mention it." Miyuki came up from her deep bow and saw in the screen an elegant woman smiling, wearing a long dress all in a color close to black.

Her real age was over forty, but she looked no older than thirty—and that applied not only when seen through a screen but also in real life.

Unlike Miyuki, who gave the impression of being unapproachable due to being too beautiful, this woman had a mature prettiness that the opposite sex wouldn't be able to help feeling attracted to.

She was the younger twin sister of Miyuki and Tatsuya's mother, and the current head of the Yotsuba family.

The strongest magician in the world.

It was Maya Yotsuba, in the flesh.

"Well, all right... Still, you must have been through a lot today."

"I apologize for causing you worry," answered Miyuki shortly, sitting down gracefully in front of the camera.

Maya nodded gently at her niece. *"I'm relieved to see you safe and sound. Well, Tatsuya is with you, so I knew there was nothing to worry about, but… By the way, where might Tatsuya be at the moment?"* asked Maya, as though she'd just remembered.

But Miyuki wasn't fooled. This question was clearly the reason for her aunt's call. "Unfortunately, my brother still has work left to do, and hasn't returned."

"Oh! I'm sure Tatsuya is goofing off somewhere, leaving his cute little sister behind at home, isn't he?" Maya put a hand to her cheek as if to say, *What a handful.*

"I truly apologize for troubling you so. I myself don't know the full details of what my brother is doing…" In contrast, Miyuki carried through with her courtesy, never letting her respectful attitude diminish. "However, Aunt Maya, it is no cause for worry. My brother's strength is always protecting me."

"Oh, yes, that's right. Miyuki, even if you can break his chains, he can't cancel his own restrictions, can he?" Maya smiled sweetly. Behind her smile was an indication that she knew Miyuki had undone his shackles without her permission.

"Yes, that's correct, Aunt Maya. Wherever my brother might be, he would never in his life abandon his duty as my Guardian." Nevertheless, Miyuki's civil attitude remained intact.

"That's a relief to hear. Oh, yes. Why don't the two of you visit the mansion, say, this Sunday? I'd very much like to see you in person. It's been a long time."

"I'm much obliged. When my brother returns, I will tell him as well."

"I'll be looking forward to it. Good night, Miyuki."

"Good night, Aunt Maya."

The screen blacked out, and seeing that the call had completely ended, Miyuki let out a heavy breath and collapsed down onto the sofa.

Talking to her aunt always put immense pressure on her. And for some reason, she only called when Tatsuya was away—likely with the knowledge that he was.

That was how her aunt was. She doubtlessly knew more than even Miyuki did about him.

Nevertheless, Miyuki could never let anything careless slip in front of Maya. If she made any unprepared remarks, it would only put more limitations on her brother.

She opened the curtains and looked into the western sky where her brother was.

In order to bring the incident to a complete close, her brother had accompanied Kazama to Tsushima. That was, at the very least, what he'd told Miyuki when he contacted her, and he would never lie to her.

She knew it needed to be done.

Tatsuya being treated as necessary was an even happier occasion for Miyuki than it was for him.

Still, today,

tonight,

in her heart,

she wanted Tatsuya at her side.

She was the only one in the house right now.

Enduring the weight of reaped lives was painful and lonely on her own.

Tatsuya... she thought, softly wrapping her arms around herself.

She thought of the warmth of her brother's arms gently cradling her, and her grip on herself tightened.

◇ ◇ ◇

October 31, AD 2095.

Today was Halloween, but Tatsuya, who was not Christian, had no special attachment to the day. He had come, instead, to the Tsushima Stronghold.

Thirty-five years earlier, near the end of World War III, or the Twenty Years' Global War Outbreak, this island had been attacked by the Great Asian Alliance's Goryeo Autonomous District's army, which had killed 70 percent of the island's inhabitants. The attack had been the result of Japan placing a cursory defense force on the island, despite it not being within their border, though the real reason was to needlessly stimulate other nations.

The Goryeo Army had its own justification. And those were the times.

But it didn't change the fact that 70 percent of the islanders had died, 20 percent of those who escaped had suffered minor to major wounds of some sort, the remaining 10 percent had been kidnapped, and the island occupied.

After they'd retaken Tsushima, the Japanese government had turned the island into a fortress. A frontline base with a giant military port, steadfast ramparts, and top-of-the-line anti-air, anti-ship armaments. The Tsushima Stronghold.

"Specialist, come to the operations room" came an order through the comm in his left ear after the call noise.

Tatsuya left the roof and went back into the fortress.

The Korean Peninsula was visible as a shadow across the sea he'd been staring at.

"Good, you're here" came an offhanded response to Tatsuya, who, still in his MOVAL suit, helmet, and mask, entered the room and saluted. Kazama instructed him to take a seat.

The strange sight of him, hidden behind an all-black one-piece suit and a full-face helmet, drew stares from the stronghold's staff, but Tatsuya ignored them and sat on a chair in the corner of the operations room.

A few moments later, Yanagi and Yamanaka showed up.

As soon as he saw everyone had gotten there, Kazama got right down to business. "As we expected…" he said, "the enemy navy is preparing to sortie. Take a look at this image."

On the large display using an entire wall was a photograph that appeared to have been taken by a satellite. It showed a fleet with almost ten large ships and twice as many destroyers and torpedo boats getting ready to leave a port.

"This photo is from five minutes ago. Judging from this, the enemy will leave port in no less than two hours. Considering the scope of this mobilization, this isn't a tentative attack—we can assume they want to occupy either northern Kyushu, San'in, or Hokuriku."

"Do they mean to start an actual war, sir?" came the question from a young second lieutenant. Kazama looked at him—judging by his age, he must have been assigned to the fortress recently.

"I'm sure they think they've been at war ever since three years ago," answered Yanagi sarcastically, rather than Kazama.

The lieutenant who asked the question went red with embarrassment and withdrew.

"Sorry about that. Seems like our unit is unacquainted with courtesy," said Kazama, first saving face, then driving the point home again. "But in the end, Captain Yanagi is correct. There is no peace treaty between Japan and the Great Asian Alliance—not even a truce. If they're mobilizing their fleet without so much as a notification, they probably decided they don't care if we interpret it as a preparation to attack."

Customarily, if for a noncombat purpose, large-scale naval mobilizations came with notifications to nearby countries or international announcements, even if communications would be confined to that country's waters.

Moving a fleet without making their objective public during a ceasefire or a cessation of hostilities was generally interpreted as an expression of intent to reopen warfare against another country.

The mood in the conference room tensed all at once.

"In response to the enemy fleet that has already finished mobilizing, our navy has, unfortunately, just started mobilizing yesterday. At present, we can only combat the enemy's naval forces using ground or air strength."

The air increased in weight.

"A difficult battle would be unavoidable."

Nobody requested permission to speak.

"So, in order to solve this situation, the Independent Magic Battalion will be deploying its strategic magic weapon. Permission for this operation has already been received from a joint staff conference."

The fortress's staff looked at Kazama with eyes that were a mix of anticipation and doubt.

"For this, we'd like to borrow observation room one. Also, if this attack succeeds, then at the same time…"

Kazama continued his explanation.

However, Tatsuya didn't feel the need to listen to any more. His job was only to attack with the strategic magic weapon, and he would have nothing to do after that.

He'd looked over the stronghold-related documents on his way to Tsushima.

Observation room one was one of the facilities that kept watch on enemy shorelines using low-altitude satellites.

That was the only piece of information Tatsuya needed to know: what they'd be doing there, and what they'd be making him do.

Tatsuya, still in his MOVAL suit, Third Eye in hand, stood in the center of the full sky screen.

This screen was made to process satellite imagery in three dimensions and observe an enemy camp from a desired angle. Right now, at Tatsuya's request, it was showing an image looking down from a hundred feet above sea level, and at a horizontal distance of three hundred thirty feet.

"Specialist Ooguro, are you ready?" asked Sanada.

"Preparations complete, sir. Link with the satellite is good," answered Tatsuya, standby complete, his voice altered by his helmet.

"Prepare to activate Material Burst."

At Kazama's voice, Tatsuya raised the Third Eye.

The Chinhae Naval Port.

The Great Asian Alliance fleet assembled on the other side of Geojedo Fortress.

The battle flag of the center battleship, likely the flagship.

He aimed at its waving colors.

Using the 3-D image as a handhold, he accessed its eidos.

The battle flag weighed approximately two pounds.

"Preparation complete," he whispered.

But a whisper was enough in the deathly silent room.

"Activate Material Burst."

"Activating Material Burst."

Tatsuya repeated Kazama's order and pulled the Third Eye's trigger.

From inside Tsushima Stronghold, across open sea, to the Chinhae Naval Port—

Tatsuya's spell converted approximately two pounds of mass into energy.

The heat released, based on Einstein's theory, was equivalent to twenty-two megatons of TNT.

The screen blacked out.

The immense heat had caused the satellite's safeties to kick in.

So the only thing they could see of the hell created there was the scar it left behind.

Suddenly, on the flagship stopped in the back of Chinhae Naval Port, a sun was born.

There was no other way to describe the heat, but nobody there would be able to tell future generations about it.

The immeasurable incandescence vaporized the metal on the ship, tossing heavy-metal steam all about.

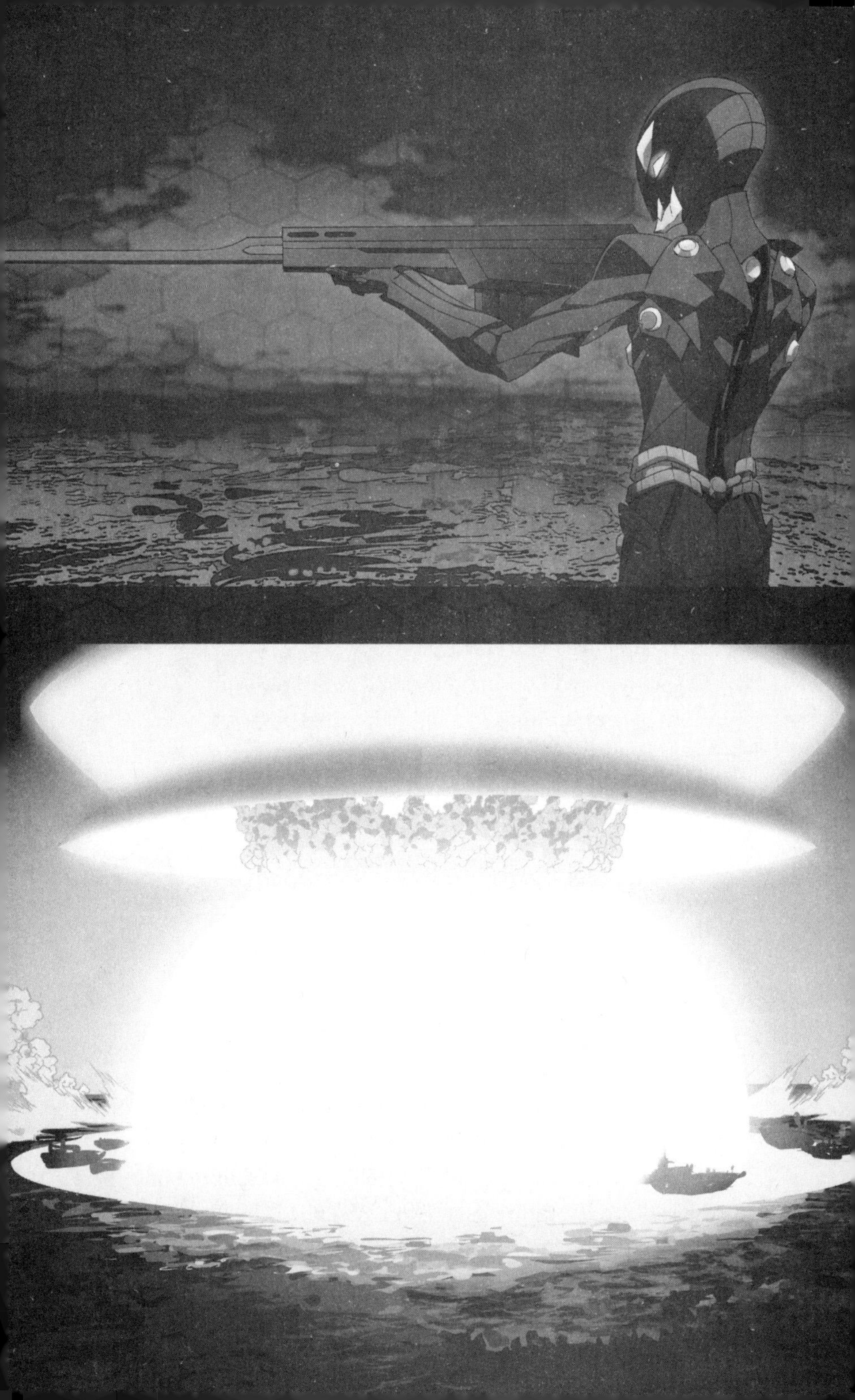

The air rapidly expanded, crossing the speed of sound.

In that jet stream of heat rays, shock waves, and metallic vapor, both the fleet and the Chinhae Naval Port were annihilated.

Things nearby, man and object alike, were vaporized.

Those men and objects a little farther away exploded and were reduced to ashes.

The inferno scorched the surface of the sea, causing a water vapor explosion.

Whirlwinds and tsunamis sprang forth, swallowing up the Geojedo Fortress on the opposite shore. If the island of Geojedo hadn't served its purpose as a levee, then Tsushima and the northern Kyushu coast wouldn't have avoided damage themselves.

The destruction didn't stop with the Chinhae Naval Port.

The shock wave spread to nearby military installations. The only good part about it was that there was no civilian city near the naval base.

When the flaming atrocity settled, there was nothing left.

When the satellite image restored, every single one of the Tsushima Stronghold staff, without exception, gasped.

One of the younger officers had to run to the bathroom to regurgitate the contents of his stomach.

Nobody could laugh at his behavior or call it unsightly.

Because even the members of the IMB couldn't hide their pale faces.

They had, for the first time, seen what strategic magic truly was.

"Enemy status?" asked Kazama.

Fujibayashi hastily checked the monitor. "Enemy fleet destroyed… No, they've disappeared. Shall we go on the offensive, sir?"

As she said, it would be easy to occupy the place now.

But Kazama didn't nod his head. "We don't need to. We're omitting our later plans and ending the operation."

"Everyone prepare to return home!"

After Kazama's command, Yanagi ordered the withdrawal.
Tatsuya placed the Third Eye on the floor.
Behind his helmet, in his eyes, was not a single trace of unrest.

◇ ◇ ◇

The Scorching Halloween.

That was the name historians in later generations would give to this day.

It was a turning point in military history—even seen by some to be a turning point in history at large.

It was the incident that proved the superiority of magic over mechanical weapons as well as atomic, biological, and chemical.

It was the event that made it clear that magic was the force that separated victory from defeat.

And it was the true first day of the history of glory and suffering that would come to the race called magicians.

Afterword

Thank you for purchasing another volume of *The Irregular at Magic High School*. For those new to the series, I'd like to take this chance to ask for your continued support in the future.

Volume 7 was probably an adventure as far as light novels go. What did you all think? Did you enjoy reading it? Although it wasn't quite up to the level of extremity that was rather commonplace in the Showa era, I do worry a bit whether this book, as outdated a form of entertainment as it is, hasn't fallen out of favor with current trends.

The one thing I struggled with the most in this volume were the diagrams showing the battle's progress (the maps and sketches). I don't know the official way to make these, and those more knowledgeable will probably look at them and ask themselves, *What on earth is this?* Please forgive me on this point.

Ms. Ishida, the illustrator for this novel, put in a lot of hard work as well. I asked her to change the protagonists' combat gear designs several times purely out of an uncouth obsession. As the author, I think they look cool... They look cool, right?

Also, I believe the main characteristic of Volume 7 were all those special movers showing up. If you enjoyed the extreme plot, then as a writer, I couldn't possibly be happier.

Now, allow me to make some announcements as to future plans.

To begin with, Volume 8 is scheduled for release this winter. I believe its subtitle will be unchanged as "Reminiscence Arc." Past episodes will be the focus. The plan is to have more reveals than the Web novel did.

Next, and this announcement was on the advertisement on the book as well, but I've been allowed to write a voice drama. Its release is planned for the same time as Volume 8. It might actually come out earlier. It will be a drama version of the main story in the Reminiscence Arc. It will come with a newly written short-form booklet.

Also, as announced on the ad wrapped around Volume 6, the first volume of *The Irregular at Magic High School*'s manga, serialized in *GFantasy*, was released at the same time as this book. The first volume of *Dengeki Daioh*'s serialization, *The Honor Student at Magic High School*, is planned for release on October 27, 2012. Please show both of them your support.

Finally, as I'm sure many of you are aware, starting next month in *Dengeki Bunko Magazine*, I'll be serializing a story. It will be the first episode of the Second-Year Arc—a version based on having read up to Volume 7 without any spoilers. Therefore, when the serialization is made into a book, there will be extra episodes, but I'll be writing the whole main story for it.

Between the *Dengeki Bunko Magazine* serialization, the voice drama, and the main Dengeki Bunko book, I'll be working at full capacity from this autumn to winter, so please continue all your support for *The Irregular at Magic High School* in the future.

(Tsutomu Sato)

I'm Hayashi, and I do the composition for the manga version of *The Irregular at Magic High School*. Congratulations on the release of Volume 7, Mr. Sato! As a reader myself, I was awaiting it with anticipation! With all the different mind-sets of those around Tatsuya drawn forth into battle, the youthfully dramatic scenes, and the mysteries of your detailed world setting slowly but surely coming into view, every part of it drew me in. I was so deeply engrossed in reading *The Irregular at Magic High School* that I forgot to sleep and eat. I hope I can depict this feeling in the manga as well, so I'll keep working my hardest on the *GFantasy* comic version along with Mr. Kitaumi!

Tsuna Kitaumi

I'm Yu Mori, and I do the spin-off comic, *The Honor Student at Magic High School*. Congratulations on the release of Volume 7! I consider it an honor to be able to contribute to an extremely important scene here. When I had the opportunity to read it, I was first surprised by the detailed settings and world. Then I was surprised again after reading to a certain point, and I thought, *Oh, so that's why they're like that!* After that, I reread it and discovered new things I didn't notice the first time through, taking a pleasing sort of KO. It was a happy job for me to be absorbed in the worldview, in which both the world itself and the relationships were set up in a very detailed way. Magic is a special power, but it isn't omnipotent by any means, and in this world, it's not enough to solve everything. There is a charm to them as they worry over this or that while trying to do the best they can, and it makes me want to work hard to convey that as well. And personally, there are a lot of cute girls, so I want to put effort into drawing them as well. As a fan, I'll be looking forward to the continuation.